A HEART FULL OF MEMORIES

HEART OF THE HILLS: BOOK TWO

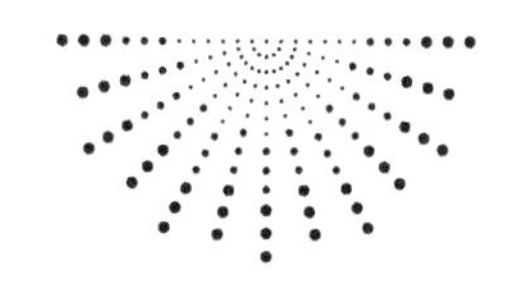

POPPY PENNINGTON-SMITH

First published 2021 by Bewick Press Ltd.

BEWICK PRESS LTD, MAY 2021

www.bewickpress.com
www.poppypennington.com

CHAPTER ONE

CAT

Cat Goodwin was standing in the kitchen of her parents' large Italian ranch house. Outside, lazy raindrops were sliding down the French doors which, in summer, opened onto a fragrant garden of herbs and flowers.

As the rain clouds began to clear, Cat tucked her dark brown hair behind her ear and fiddled with one of her yellow earrings; she always chose a yellow pair when the weather was gloomy.

It was late January. Christmas was over, and Tuscany's usual heat was being dampened by a short, cloud-kissed winter. A winter that was making the ranch house feel uncustomarily chilly.

Turning to switch on the kettle, Cat avoided making eye contact with the envelope on the counter. It had arrived a few days ago, but she'd wanted to wait until her parents were gone before opening it.

"Cat?" Amelie's voice bounced into the room and Cat turned to see her sister nudging the door open with her foot while holding a large cardboard box.

"What on earth?" Cat abandoned the kettle and helped carry the box to the kitchen table. As they set it down on the weathered oak, it made a soft thudding noise. Both sisters stood back and looked at it. "It's from London," Amelie said, frowning.

Cat slipped her arm around Amelie's waist and gave her a squeeze. "From Jed?"

"I guess so."

"I thought you told him not to worry about sending your things?" Cat had returned to the kettle and was taking Amelie's favourite mug from the shelf above the sink – the one with poppies and a curved handle.

"I did. But it looks like he didn't want them cluttering up his apartment any more." Amelie sat down and flicked the box with her index finger.

"Are you going to open it?" Cat handed her the mug then set a small jar of honey down beside the box and slid into the chair opposite.

Amelie wrinkled her face. Without the glow of the summer, the splash of freckles on the bridge of her nose looked more pronounced. Cat smiled as she remembered trying to recreate them on her own nose with an eyebrow pencil when they were teenagers.

"I'll make you a deal…" Cat crossed one leg over the other. "If you open your box, I'll open my letter."

"You haven't read it yet?"

Cat shook her head. "I didn't want to do it with Mum and Dad around. Just in case–"

"In case it upsets you?"

Cat met her sister's eyes and shrugged. "If I'd ended up in floods of tears, they wouldn't have wanted to go away."

Amelie made an *I get it* face, went to fetch the envelope, and put it purposefully down in front of Cat. "But you can't leave it much longer."

Spooning honey into her tea and stirring it a little too energetically, Cat looked up at Amelie. "So, I guess I'll go first then?"

"Looks like it…"

Cat picked up the envelope. Five months ago, she had finally opened the first letter that her birth mother sent her. This was the second.

The first letter had arrived, via the adoption agency, just after Cat's thirtieth birthday but she'd refused to read it. Instead, she had left it lingering in the bottom of a suitcase for three years until, finally, she had given in to temptation.

Its contents had been disappointingly brief.

Dear Catherine,
Happy 30th Birthday
There are too many words and not enough pages, so I will keep this short.
I would very much like to meet you and to get to know you. I

think of you often, and I am sure you must have questions for me too. Perhaps you could write to me?
Aida Borrelli, your mother.

During the long months of not opening that first letter, Cat had imagined that it would change everything. That it might finally answer the questions she'd held in her heart for so long: Why did you give me away? Who are you? Who am *I*? When it didn't answer any of those things, she felt… nothing. Just numb, empty, and completely underwhelmed.

She had replied, similarly briefly:

Dear Aida,
Thank you for your letter. I have many questions and would like the opportunity to talk to you. Perhaps you could send me your phone number or an email address and we'll take it from there?
Best wishes, Cat

Afterwards, as she'd shown Aida's letter to her parents and her siblings, the boys had suggested looking for a social media profile that might shed some light on the situation.

"What was the surname again?" Ethan had asked, flipping open his laptop.

"Borrelli." Ben, the younger of the twins, had picked up the letter and waved it at Ethan. But midway through Ben telling Ethan how to spell *Borrelli*, Cat had closed the lid.

"No," she'd said, folding her arms in front of her. "I don't want to know what she's like. I want to talk to her first, listen to what she has to say… I don't want an image in my head that I can't shake if she doesn't reply."

"Of course she'll reply," Mum had said, putting her hand on Cat's arm. "She reached out to you, love."

Now, facing a brand new envelope with a brand new letter, Cat closed her eyes as she remembered her parents' faces; they had tried so hard to look like they were perfectly happy about the situation, even though their insides had probably been in turmoil.

"Cat, your hands are shaking. Do you want me to…?" Amelie reached for the envelope and Cat let her take it. This one was just like the first – plain, indistinct, normal. Not a single thing about its appearance betrayed the fact that whatever was inside could change Cat's life forever.

"Yes. Tell me what it says."

Amelie moistened her lips and pressed them together. Her hands were steady but Cat wondered if she was thinking about her own birth mother as she peeled back the sealed flap.

From different families, Amelie and Cat had both been adopted into the Goodwin household as children. Cat, when she was six years old. Amelie, a few years later, at the age of four-and-a-half.

Growing up, it was something that had drawn the two of them closer together – a shared understanding that Ben and Ethan, their twin younger brothers, would never fully appreciate. As they'd reached their early teens, however, Cat had noticed one kernel of difference in the way she and Amelie felt about being adopted; they both adored their parents, Rose and Thomas Goodwin, and firmly believed they were the parents they'd been destined to have. But while Amelie was perfectly content with knowing very little about her early years, Cat secretly longed for a fuller picture.

She remembered her foster parents very clearly – Gianni and Lucia. An elderly couple who had lived in a small townhouse near *Pisa.* When Cat was taken into care at two-and-a-half years old, she was placed directly into their home and that was where she'd remained, for four years, until Rose and Thomas finally completed the adoption process and brought her home to the ranch

Gianni and Lucia were not unkind, but they were perfunctory in their attitude towards her. They fed her, clothed her, and took her to school. They provided her with a small pink bedroom and a modest selection of teddies and dolls to play with. But they didn't *love* her, and perhaps that was the difference; Amelie's foster parents, although she was only with them for eighteen months, were the opposite of Gianni and Lucia. They were younger, warmer, and they adored her.

Cat studied her sister's face. Amelie's eyes were scanning the letter but her expression was painfully unreadable.

"Well…?" Cat tried to loosen the tightness in her shoulders and pulled her long cream cardigan a little closer around her waist.

Slowly, Amelie slid the letter over to her and smiled. "It's a bit like the first one. Short, but…" she pointed to the bottom of the letter, "there's a phone number."

Cat had been pacing up and down for at least five minutes. "I'd love to talk to you," she read in Italian. "Perhaps you could call me when you feel ready? Here is my number." Cat waved the letter in the air.

Amelie blinked patiently but didn't interrupt, just sipped her tea and watched.

Above the ranch, the sun had broken through a hole in the clouds and was shining directly onto the French doors making the room feel far too warm. Dramatically, Cat flung them open and stepped onto the damp paving stones outside. The smell of mint wafted beneath her nose from the raised bed in front of her. Cat breathed in deeply.

After counting to ten and watching the chickens tentatively step out of their coop one by one, Cat turned back to Amelie and – through the open doors – said, "So, now what do I do?"

"Call her?" Amelie offered. "Isn't that what you wanted?"

"No. I wanted… information. I wanted to know something about her. I wanted her to say something."

"Something?"

"Anything."

"She's probably nervous, Cat. Scared of saying the wrong thing."

Cat sighed and scrunched the letter between her fingers. "But now I have to pluck up the courage to *speak* to her, Am, and I'm not sure I'm ready for that. I wanted to write for a while. Or email. Get to know each other a little. I didn't want to go straight to phone calls. It feels… too much."

"So, tell her that." Amelie gestured for Cat to come back inside and sit down.

Amelie was being uncharacteristically pragmatic, and Cat was fighting the urge to take her whirlpool of emotions out on her sister.

Tucking the letter back into its envelope, Cat shook her head. Her shoulder length hair bounced with the movement and she wished it was still long enough to tie out of the way when it became irritating. "I'll decide what to do later." She looked at the box which still sat between them. "It's your turn."

Amelie bit her lower lip and tugged the end of her pony-tail. "What if it's booby-trapped?"

Cat laughed, pushing her chair back so she could fetch a knife from the wooden block on the kitchen counter. "You think something awful is going to jump out at you? Like what?"

"I don't know." Amelie took the knife and began to slice through the thick parcel tape that was holding the box lid together. "An ugly clown holding a sign that says, *You left your fiancé on your wedding day, how can you live with yourself?*"

Cat folded her arms and raised her right eyebrow at her sister. "Come on, Am. You can't keep beating yourself up. Jed wasn't right for you. You didn't love him."

"I know." Amelie chewed her lower lip. "I just still can't believe I'm *that* girl. The one who breaks someone's heart because she was too cowardly to speak up sooner."

"Stop procrastinating." Cat knocked on the side of the box with her knuckles. "And stop feeling sorry for yourself. No one thinks badly of you... except *you.*"

"And Jed... he thinks badly of me."

Cat opened her mouth to contradict her sister, then closed it again. Amelie was right, of course; Jed did think badly of her. But everyone *apart* from Jed had been more than a little bit relieved when, in August last year, Amelie had backed out of their extravagant wedding and declared – finally – that she just didn't love him enough to become his wife.

"Okay." Amelie breathed in sharply. "Here we go..." Wincing, she opened the lid and stuck her hand inside.

Cat peered into the box.

"It's just books." Amelie was frowning. "And a note that says: *clothes to follow.*"

Cat had sat back down and was leafing through a signed copy of Anna Parks' latest novel. "Well, that's two anticli-mactic openings. A letter with nothing but a phone number, and a box with nothing but books."

Amelie sat down too and sighed as if she'd been holding

a balloon full of air in her chest all morning and had only just allowed it to deflate. "You know," she said, "I think he's already got a girlfriend."

"Jed?"

"Mmm."

Cat put the book down and put her hand purposefully on top of Amelie's. "Then what are you feeling bad about? Jed is your past. Your future is back here, in Italy, with us..." she smiled and a let a twinkle of mischief dance across her face, "and Skye."

Amelie met Cat's eyes. She was trying not to smile but, as always, at the mention of Skye Anderson, she'd begun to blush. "Yes," she said. "And Skye..."

CHAPTER TWO

SKYE

Skye Anderson had been lingering outside the ranch house ever since he saw Amelie struggle up the steps holding a large cardboard box. Unless she'd been indulging in some serious online shopping, it had to contain her things from London, which brought an instant smile to his lips; she was staying in Italy. She was definitely staying.

Leaning on the bonnet of the truck he'd purchased just before Christmas, as the rain finally stopped, Skye shrugged out of his jacket and looked across the damp fields and dewy trees of *Heart of the Hills* ranch. Every day for five months, he'd woken up to this view and been forced to remind himself that he and his father now owned most of it. *Heart of the Hills* was no longer a Goodwin family business. It was a Goodwin-Anderson partnership, and the difference between all of this and his previous life in America was almost too much to comprehend.

A few years ago, Skye had been serving in the Veterinary Corps of the U.S. Armed Forces, leading and taking care of a canine unit that had since been disbanded. Now, he was resident vet on a Tuscan ranch and had nothing but horses and guests to worry about.

Horses, guests... and his love life.

For at least the fiftieth time in the past twenty minutes, Skye looked at the house and pushed his dark curly hair from his forehead. Ever since that balmy day in August – when Amelie finally admitted she wasn't in love with her British investment banker fiancé and called off their wedding – Skye had been faltering. She knew that he liked her. He knew she liked him back. But how soon was *too* soon to take things to the next level?

"You haven't asked her on a date yet?" Amelie's brother Ben had said to him as they shovelled fresh forkfuls of hay into the stables that morning. "What are you waiting for?"

"I don't want to push her. She went through a lot."

"It's been five months, Skye."

"I know, but I've had a crush on her since we were kids. When we start dating properly, I want it to be perfect timing."

"At this rate, perfect timing will be your ninetieth birthdays," Ben had laughed. "Just ask her out, Skye. She called off the wedding because she fell for you. I think five months is enough of a cooling off period for you to take her to dinner."

But as Skye watched the house and waited for Amelie to appear from inside, he knew that *dinner* wouldn't be enough.

Their first date needed to be magical. Memorable. Different. Not just dinner.

Ben was right though; five months was too long and the longer he left it, the more difficult it became. Taking his phone from his pocket, he Googled – in shaky Italian – ideas for romantic dates in the *Sant' Anna* area. He was midway through a blog post that described a remote, tumbledown church that could only be reached through the woods to the North of *Sant' Anna* when his phone began to ring.

Skye frowned at it. It was a U.S. number. Since leaving the States, he'd had little contact with his friends from the Corps or from his time at university, and it wasn't a number he recognised as belonging to any of his American relatives.

He contemplated ending the call; he'd yet to buy an Italian cell phone with an Italian number, so it could easily just be someone trying to sell him health insurance. But, perhaps to try and make himself look busy in case Amelie came outside and wondered why he was hanging around, he pressed the green button instead of the red.

"Skye Anderson." He spoke casually into the phone.

Silence greeted him.

"Buddy, I'm in Europe. This will cost you a fortune if you don't speak up," he laughed.

The caller cleared their throat. "Skye?"

Skye's fingers tightened around the phone. He turned away from the ranch house and lowered his voice. "Molly?" Instinctively, he lifted his index finger to the scar on his forehead.

"I wasn't sure you'd still have this number." Molly's bright, Texan accent made him close his eyes.

"Yeah. Still the same."

"Have you got a minute to talk?"

Skye swallowed hard. His scar had begun to throb. Behind him, the ranch gates clattered as they swung open to allow Jean the stable manager onto the property. Skye's muscles tensed at the noise. "No," he said. "I haven't."

And then he hung up.

CHAPTER THREE

AMELIE

The room Amelie had always known as the 'library' was one of the most peaceful in the entire ranch house. With a bench that her father had built into the nook of the bay window, floor-to-ceiling shelves, and two large comfy sofas, it had always been her favourite place.

With her cardboard box of books sitting on the coffee table in front of her, Amelie looked around the room trying to spot a spare shelf. Most were full but over Christmas her mother had cleared out some old children's books to donate to charity. So, there was a small section beneath the window seat itself that was empty.

Amelie heaved the box down onto the floor and sat cross-legged next to it. The books Jed had returned to her were mostly hardbacks – signed editions that she'd been personally gifted by the authors she took care of when she worked in London.

Sifting through the heavy volumes, memories danced across their covers. As Commissioning Editor at Orchid Books, the biggest women's fiction imprint in the U.K, Amelie had spent her life surrounded by words and the people who created them. If it hadn't been for Jed, she never would have given it all up; after their whirlwind engagement, he'd suggested that she quit so they could start a family as soon as they were married. She'd gone along with it because she liked the idea of being a full-time mum but, as the wedding had drawn closer, she'd realised that she didn't much like the idea of being Jed's wife. The future she thought she wanted for herself had shifted to something entirely different.

No matter how much she missed her job, however, it was hard to feel regretful when everything that happened had led to her being back home in Italy. Back at the ranch. Back with her family. For good, this time.

Amelie smiled as she began slotting the books onto the shelf below the window seat. Being home at *Heart of the Hills* felt so good that she could barely remember why she'd decided to leave in the first place.

"Need a hand?" Skye Anderson's delectable American voice filtered into the room and instantly made her skin feel warmer.

"I'm almost done, actually." She turned to look at him then gestured to the small stack of books beside her.

Skye sat down and casually picked up the book closest to

him. “Funny,” he said, examining the shelf, “I imagined you having *way* more books than this.”

“I think Jed picked out the signed copies and left the rest.” Amelie twitched as Jed’s name left her lips; it still felt odd for Skye to be in the room when she thought about her ex-fiancé, even though nothing had really happened yet between her and Skye. There had been a lot of *almost* somethings, but they hadn’t so much as kissed while Amelie was still engaged to Jed. In fact, they still hadn’t kissed. For five long months, she’d been waiting for him to finally ask her out. And she was starting to worry that he never would.

Skye handed her the book he’d been holding and, together, they made quick work of organising the rest of the pile.

“You’re quiet this morning,” she said as he helped her to her feet.

“I am?”

Amelie nodded. “Usually, I can’t shut you up. Everything okay?”

Skye brushed his fingers through his hair and met her eyes. For a moment, she thought he was going to tell her something but he blinked whatever it was away and shrugged. “Just tired, I guess.”

“Well in that case, why don’t we grab some coffee and head down to the barn?”

Skye agreed, and followed her into the kitchen. As Amelie filled two takeout flasks with fresh coffee, she noticed him take his phone out of his pocket and squint at it. He was reading a text, his lips pressed together into a tight thoughtful line. His jaw twitched, but when he realised she was watching him, he shoved the phone back into his jeans pocket and smiled at her.

"Just Dad," he said, "reminding me that the roof guys should be coming today."

"Well, that's exciting." Amelie led the way out of the kitchen and down the front steps. "If the roof's going on, that must mean we're nearly finished."

Skye tilted his head from side to side. "Nearly. Still a way to go. I hope it'll be done by the middle of February."

They were heading down the long winding track that led from the ranch house to the stables. It was damp under foot and Amelie wished she'd put a jacket on top of her thick grey sweater. She'd looped a light blue scarf around her neck, but it was more decorative than functional and wasn't doing a very good job of protecting her from the chill in the air.

As they walked, Amelie considered asking Skye what was really the matter. But she'd learned by now that sometimes he just wasn't in the mood for talking. Usually, it was if he'd been haunted by bad dreams the night before. It seemed to be happening less often lately but, while she'd tried several times to help him talk about them, he still hadn't told her any real details. All she knew was that something awful had happened overseas. Something which had led to him leaving the Veterinary Corps, and which had resulted in the scar on his head – as well as others he hadn't allowed her to see.

When they were younger, and Skye's family had visited

the ranch each summer, Amelie had never imagined he'd end up in the army. He had always loved animals, though, so that part fitted. Most days, since he and his father had become owners and co-managers of *Heart of the Hills*, she'd marvelled at how happy and at home Skye seemed. Today, however, there was a greyness to his mood. For the first time, she found herself wishing that he would open up to her a little more.

"Looking good, huh?" They had stopped in front of the barn. Skye was smiling up at it.

Since a fire had ripped through the yard last August, not long before Amelie's wedding, they had been using the old stables on the far side of the ranch, but the new stables were finally finished and the barn wouldn't be far behind.

"Should be ready just before your parents get back from their vacation." Skye leaned on the gate that separated the yard from the path.

Amelie smiled and hugged her arms around her waist. Her parents had been through so much in the last few years. Selling *Heart of the Hills* to Alec Anderson hadn't been an easy decision. Amelie knew that her father especially had been very worried about how things would work once Alec and Skye owned the business. But, right from the beginning, Alec had made it clear that Rose and Thomas Goodwin were still the managers of *Heart of the Hills*. "I'm here to learn from you and to back you up," he'd said when the two families got together to sign all the paperwork. "Me and Skye? We'll do what you tell us to do. We'll speak up if we have ideas but any changes will be made *together*. Okay?"

Amelie smiled as she remembered her dad shaking Alec's hand and fighting back tears. There was no doubt about it, Skye's father saved the ranch and, in a way, he saved the family too.

"It's amazing, Skye." She looped her arm through his and leaned her head onto his shoulder. "Mum and Dad will be blown away when it's finished."

Skye hesitated for a moment then put his arm around Amelie's shoulders and hugged her. The scent of his cologne made her want to nuzzle into his neck and, as always happened when she was close to Skye, her skin had begun to prickle nervously.

"Skye?" She stood up and looked at him.

He met her eyes, but then his phone began to ring. Taking it from his pocket, he scowled. Amelie was almost certain that his cheeks were flushed. "Sorry, Am." He waved it at her and began to walk away. "I have to get this."

CHAPTER FOUR

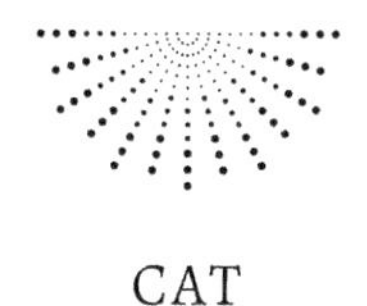

CAT

TWO DAYS LATER

CAT WAS ALONE in the ranch house. Amelie had gone riding with Skye. Ben was helping Jean exercise the horses, and Cat was sitting at the reception desk which stood proudly in the middle of the entrance hall. She had spent the morning absentmindedly preparing the paperwork for a group of English riders who'd be arriving in late March – when the ranch reopened after its winter hiatus.

But now she was finished, she had a much more important job to do.

With shaking fingers, Cat dialled the number that she'd scrawled on her palm and waited. It rang, and rang, and rang. Then finally, just as she was about to hang up...

"*Pronto*." The voice on the other end of the line was

short, sharp, and female. "*Pronto*," the woman repeated, sounding irritated.

"*Aida Borrelli*?"

"*Si*."

"*Salve, mi chiamo Cat...*"

There was a long pause, and a change in background noise which indicated that Aida had moved into a different room. "*Catherine*?"

"*Si*."

Another pause. Then, "Oh, thank you. Thank you for calling."

Cat swallowed hard. Her tongue felt too big for her mouth and her clammy fingers were struggling to hold on to the phone. "You speak English?" For some reason, this surprised her.

"A little." Aida laughed. The softness of it sent a tingle down Cat's spine. "Not very well, I'm afraid. But I tried to keep it up. In case we ever—"

"No, you speak it *very* well." Cat bit her lower lip and rolled her eyes at herself. *Think, Cat. Say something. Anything.* "I'm sorry it took me so long to reply to the letter you sent... the first one, I mean."

"Please, don't apologise." The Italian lilt in Aida's voice was almost exactly how Cat had imagined it. She closed her eyes and tried to absorb it – imprint it onto her memory. "You should never apologise to me for anything," Aida added quietly.

Cat was tapping her fingers on the desk in front of her.

She had so many questions to ask and they were clambering over one another, becoming muddled in her mind.

"Are you well?" Aida asked the question purposefully – as though she truly needed to know whether Cat was all right.

"Yes," she smiled. "I am. I'm–"

"Excuse me?" Cat looked up to see a tall, slim stranger standing in front of the reception desk. "Do you work here?" he asked pointedly.

Cat faltered. Her fingers gripped the phone a little tighter and she blinked at him.

"I asked if you work here?" The man repeated his question in an accent Cat couldn't place.

"I'm sorry, Sir." Finally, she recovered her voice. "If you could just give me one moment." She held her index finger up at him and tried to turn back to the phone. Already, her heart was thudding against her rib cage as she pictured Aida becoming frustrated and hanging up.

"Actually, no. I can't. I've had a terrible journey and I would like to check into my cabin now please."

"Cabin?" Cat frowned and shook her head; no guests were arriving for at least another month. Turning away from him, she spoke hurriedly into the phone. "Aida? I'm sorry. May I call you back? I'm at work and–"

"Of course," Aida said quickly. "I'm at work too. My boss will be very grumpy if I don't return soon."

Cat tucked her hair behind her ear and smiled. "Okay. But I'll call again? Or text?"

"Yes. That would be lovely."

"Okay."

"Okay," Aida repeated. "Goodbye, Catherine. I will talk to you soon."

As Aida's voice disappeared, Cat held the phone to her ear for a moment longer. She wanted to savour it; sit and dissect how it had sounded, whether it was similar to her own. She wanted to call Amelie and Ben and get them up to the ranch house straight away so they could go through every last second of the conversation in minute detail.

Behind her, the stranger who shouldn't have been there loudly dinged the silver bell on the front of the desk. When Cat looked at him, he was scowling at her from beneath heavy eyebrows. "Stefan Hurst," he said, shoving a handful of printed booking details toward her. "I reserved a cabin."

Before saying anything, Cat leafed slowly through the paperwork. It was in German, which explained the accent. Although Cat's German wasn't nearly as good as her Italian or her French, when she reached the final page, she nodded. Clearing her throat, she straightened the print outs and passed them back to him. "I'm terribly sorry, Mr Hurst. You're at the wrong ranch."

Stefan Hurst narrowed his steely blue eyes at her and folded his arms in front of his chest. He was wearing a thick cardigan with patches on the elbows and Cat was finding it extremely difficult to decide how old he was. "That cannot be correct."

"Your booking is for *Sunset Ranch*. We are *Heart of the*

Hills." Cat paused, then added, "You didn't see the sign on the gate?"

"I was asleep," Stefan blustered.

Before Cat could say any more, he turned and stormed out.

She stood up and peered out of the window, unsure whether she should be outraged at his behaviour or amused at the ridiculousness of it. At first, she thought he was trying to leave but then she realised that Stefan was, in actual fact, marching up to the front gate to examine the sign on it – as if Cat was the one who'd made a mistake instead of him.

When he returned, at a much slower pace than the one he'd left with, he scraped his fingers through his slightly floppy hair and shook his head. "How?" he said forlornly. "I told the driver to take me to the ranch in *Legrezzia.* Is there more than one?"

Cat turned her computer screen towards him – because, clearly, he was the kind of person who needed visual confirmation of the facts before he believed them – and carefully typed *Legrezzia.*

"See this?" she asked, pointing to the spot on the map that depicted *Heart of the Hills*' nearest village. "This is *Legrezzia.* And this is us." She indicated the ranch itself some five miles from the village.

"Yes."

"*Sunset Ranch,* the ranch you made your booking with, is in ***La****gr****a****zzia.*" Cat emphasised the 'ah' sounds and studied

Stefan's face carefully as she spoke. "We are in *Legrezzia.* For *Lagrazzia*, you'd need to head back to *Pisa* airport then travel another three hours in pretty much the opposite direction.*"*

Stefan swallowed hard. He looked grey around the edges, and Cat was trying not to enjoy it too much.

With a grimace, he looked at the clock. It was mid-afternoon – far too late to start a return journey to *Pisa*. Cat was about to suggest he call one of the B&Bs in the slightly larger nearby town of *Sant' Anna* when she heard a car pull up outside. A few moments later, as Stefan furiously tapped out a text message on his phone – ignoring her completely – the door opened and Alec Anderson strode in.

As usual, he was smiling. He was about the same age as Cat's father but – with silver hair, a bright white smile, and a tanned complexion – he looked unmistakably Californian. To most, he came across as a savvy, confident, and probably slightly ruthless businessman. He'd amassed a small fortune in his lifetime, and any other person in his position could very well have behaved like an utter monster because of it. But Alec was different. He and Skye were two of the most down-to-earth people Cat had ever known, and she was not-so-secretly thrilled that in the end Amelie had chosen Skye over that dreadful dullard Jed.

Alec stopped inside the doorway when he saw Stefan. "We have a visitor?" he asked, eyeing up Stefan's black duffel bag.

"Alec, this is Stefan but I'm afraid he's not actually *our* visitor."

Alec leaned casually on the front of the desk, moving closer so Cat could lower her voice.

"He booked into a place called *Sunset Ranch* in *Lagrazzia.* But the taxi driver misunderstood and brought him here from *Pisa.*" Cat gestured to the map that was still up on her computer screen. Alec let out a low whistle.

Trying to catch Stefan's attention, he said, "Well that's some journey you've got to make, my friend."

Stefan looked up and slipped his phone into his jacket pocket. "I cannot travel today. There are no trains nearby."

"The nearest station is *Sant' Anna.* There'll be a train to *Pisa...*" Cat quickly checked the date on her calendar, "the day after tomorrow. From *Pisa*, you can–"

Stefan waved his hand at her. "Thank you. I will see to it."

Cat pursed her lips; it was taking all of her willpower to resist being snippy.

As if he'd sensed she was about to lose her patience, cool as a cucumber, Alec patted Stefan firmly on the shoulder. "Listen, why don't we get you set up in one of our cabins for the night? We're closed to guests right now but we can make an exception while we figure out how to get you to where you're supposed to be. How does that sound?"

Stefan held Alec's gaze for a moment then nodded curtly. "Thank you. I will accept."

Prompting herself to be helpful, Cat added, "If you give me your paperwork, I'll call *Sunset Ranch* and explain what happened. Perhaps they can send a driver to *Pisa* to collect you?"

Cat held out her hand and Stefan thrust his booking forms into it. "I appreciate that," he said, without meeting her eyes.

"Right then." Alec pointed to the row of keys on the wall behind Cat. "Cabin Five is a good one."

"The beds won't be made up," Cat said, "but I'll bring down some sheets and pillows in a while."

"Great, and ask Nonna to rustle up some refreshments?"

"Sure."

Cat watched as Stefan followed Alec wearily out of the door and down the path that led from the house to the guests' cabins. He was one of the strangest people she'd ever met; incredibly grumpy, slim and oddly dressed, with a ridiculously thick beard. But his eyes were different; his eyes were kind, blue, and – for the few seconds that he'd met her gaze – something about them had made her not completely detest him.

Shaking her head, she turned back to Stefan's paperwork. There was a phone number at the bottom of the confirmation email. She was about to dial it when her mobile vibrated. Picking it up, her breath caught in her chest. It was a text message from Aida.

Cat, it was lovely to speak to you. I hope you didn't get into trouble at your work. I have a free day tomorrow if you would like to talk again. I very much hope that you do. Aida x

Cat traced her finger over the words. When she reached the kiss at the end, she let it linger. Before she could sink back into remembering her and Aida's brief conversation, she shook herself out of her thoughts; she'd deal with the grumpy German first, and save Aida for later.

Not long before sunset, Cat made her way from Nonna's kitchen to Cabin Five holding a tray of antipasti, some sugar, and a pot of fresh coffee.

After knocking awkwardly on the door with her elbow, it took several long minutes for Stefan to answer. When he did, he looked like he'd been midway through a nap – crumpled and a little confused.

"I brought you some snacks." Cat smiled and handed him the tray. "Nonna will prepare something for your dinner too. Do you have any allergies? I should have asked before–"

"Nonna?" Stefan was sniffing the coffee.

"Our chef. Everyone calls her *Nonna* – she's been here almost as long as the ranch itself."

"I see." Stefan looked up. "No allergies. But I don't like to eat late." He cast a glance at the darkening sky as if it was already approaching 'late'.

Cat nodded. "Understood."

"Did you call the *Sunset Ranch*?"

Cat pulled her cardigan closer around her waist. With the sun fading, the air was becoming cooler and she wished that Stefan would open the door and invite her inside for a moment. "I did. I'm afraid there was no answer but I left a voicemail and I emailed them too. I'll keep trying."

Stefan was studying her face. Cat wasn't sure whether he was trying to understand her English or if he thought she was lying to him. He nodded and stepped back into the cabin, still holding Nonna's tray, then nudged the door with his foot so that it began to close. "Please inform me if you hear from them."

"Of course–" Cat was about to ask if he needed anything else, but the door clunked shut before she had the chance.

Turning away from the cabin, she let out a loud *pfft* and shook her head. "What an idiot."

Back at the house, she took her phone from her pocket and checked the time. She'd asked Ben and Amelie to join her for dinner at seven. Now that the three of them were back at the ranch full-time, they ate together most evenings anyway, but tonight she had made it a formal invitation; she needed to tell them about Aida. She needed to go through every last detail of the conversation they'd had, and she needed her siblings there to listen to her.

Cat was in the garden picking basil that she intended to whizz up and turn into pesto when she heard Nonna's door open.

Their long-serving chef was like a grandmother to everyone. She had her own spacious living quarters next to the Goodwins' kitchen that opened onto the garden, and her own kitchen, which she used to prepare meals for the guests.

"Catherine..." Nonna bustled outside with a broad excited

smile on her face. She always found the winter months difficult; she lived for the times when the ranch was full of guests and when she could spend all day cooking up luscious meals for them. This year was especially hard because they were running at zero capacity while they refurbished the guest cabins and rebuilt the barn.

Of course, Mum and Dad had suggested that Nonna take the time to go and visit family or simply enjoy a well-earned rest but she had refused. Instead, she had spent the last few months experimenting with new recipes and practicality force feeding Alec and Skye. Having a guest onsite who had requested dinner was clearly very exciting.

"What does this young man like to eat?"

"I'm not sure, Nonna. He's quite skinny, so probably not a lot." Cat smiled and perched on the smooth stone wall that separated the patio from the herb garden.

Nonna put her hands on her hips. "He's not a vegetarian is he?" She did *not* agree with vegetarians.

Cat laughed. "I don't think so. He seemed to like the antipasti you sent, but he doesn't like to eat late. So, I think it should be something that's quite quick to rustle up."

Nonna's expression dropped a little; she'd clearly been envisaging cooking up a storm for at least a couple of hours. "I see." She wiped her hands on her apron then crossed her arms in front of her chest. "No matter, I will think of something." She turned to go, then looked back at Cat's freshly picked bunch of basil. "You are cooking tonight?"

"Pesto." Cat stood up and walked over to the door that

led into the family kitchen. “It won’t be as good as yours but I promised to cook for Amelie and Ben.”

“Pesto with...?” Nonna was looking at her with wide eyes.

“Gnocchi.” Before Nonna could say anything, Cat added, “Homemade. Not shop bought. In fact,” she said, “I’m using your recipe.”

Nonna paused for a moment but then her lips parted into a proud smile. “Good. Save some for me to try, and don’t forget...”

“Make the dough when the potatoes are still warm?”

“Yes. Warm potatoes.” Nonna nodded approvingly. “Good girl.”

CHAPTER FIVE

AMELIE

As Cat served up a huge pile of fresh gnocchi, accompanied by a luscious green pesto that she'd made from scratch, Amelie and Ben watched her carefully. They were sitting at the large wooden table in their parents' kitchen, each nursing a glass of wine, waiting for Cat to sit down and finally tell them how her conversation with Aida Borrelli had gone. But Cat seemed unable to settle; three times now, she'd gotten back up from the table to fetch something and every time Ben or Amelie tried to instigate the conversation, she interrupted them.

At ten past seven, as Cat grated parmesan into a bowl, Ben's iPad lit up and began to ring. It was positioned at the fourth – empty – place around the table, facing inwards as it always did when they were trying to make it feel like their brother was with them instead of hundreds of miles away in New York.

"Wow, he's on time for once." Ben answered the call and waved at his twin brother.

On screen, Ethan stifled a yawn. He looked tired. "Are you on lates this week?" Amelie asked, leaning closer to examine the shadows beneath her brother's eyes.

"Sure am. In the E.R." Ethan fought another yawn and reached for a mug of coffee. In the background, his New York apartment looked surprisingly tidy. "It's good, though. I think I like emergency medicine."

"Really?" Ben looked surprised, perhaps because he – like the rest of them – had pictured Ethan ending up as a plastic surgeon or a pharmaceutical rep when he reached the end of his medical degree.

Ethan took a large drink of coffee. He was wearing crumpled pyjamas and had set up his iPad on his kitchen counter so that he could perch on a stool in front of it. "Yeah. I mean, sure, it's stressful. But good." Ethan looked past Ben as if he'd only just remembered the reason for their scheduled video call. Grinning at Cat, he said, "Don't tell me you cooked? Times really are changing."

Cat narrowed her eyes at Ethan's sarcasm then lifted her bowl of gnocchi and pretended to waft its heavenly smell in his direction. "Just because you're fed up of eating bad takeout and giant hamburgers, don't take it out on me."

Ethan reached for something off screen then grinned at the camera. "Actually," he said, "look what I found..."

Amelie, Ben, and Cat all leaned closer to the iPad. Ethan

was holding a cream-coloured cardboard box. When he opened it, Amelie laughed. "Is that a box of *struffoli*?"

"Sure is." Ethan took one out and popped it into his mouth. "There's an Italian bakery not far from the hospital."

"Better watch out, Eth," Ben patted his stomach with an exaggerated gesture. "You won't fit on the plane next time you visit."

"Speaking of which..." Cat interrupted. "When will that be? Your next visit? It already feels like an age since we last saw you."

"It has been an age," Bed added. "He didn't make it back for Christmas because he was meeting Elena's parents." Ben wiggled his eyebrows at Ethan.

Amelie's mouth dropped open a little. "Is that what you were doing? Meeting Elena's parents? How did it go?!"

Ethan opened his mouth to reply then stopped. "Hang on a minute, aren't we supposed to be talking about Cat?" He had widened his eyes and was looking pointedly at Cat. "How was your conversation with Aida?"

Cat blinked at him for a moment. Ethan was never one to be subtle but he could have at least eased into the subject – let them rib him for a few minutes about his newly serious relationship before diving right in.

Amelie was about to tell Cat she didn't have to talk about it just yet when Cat cleared her throat and said, while moving a forkful of gnocchi around her plate, "It was good. I think."

Ben pushed Cat's wine glass towards her and nodded for her to drink some. "Good?"

After a couple of sips, clearly trying to formulate the right words, she began to fiddle with the bright blue earring in her right ear. "She knew it was me right away – as soon as I said my name. She seemed pleased to hear from me. She sounded nice, warm… friendly, I suppose. And I think her laugh sounded a little like mine."

Amelie and Ben were listening closely. For once, Ethan was too.

"It wasn't a long conversation." Cat nodded toward the front of the house. "I was on reception and this German guy arrived out of the blue. He told his driver to bring him to *Legrezzia* instead of *Lagrazzia*."

On screen, Ethan winced. "Ouch. That'll cost him in taxis."

Cat nodded then straightened up in her seat and said, "So, yeah. It was short, but she texted me afterwards and said she's free tomorrow if I want to talk again."

"And do you?" Ben asked. "Want to talk to her again?"

"I don't know." Cat shrugged. "I suppose... yes. I suppose I do." Her lips curved into a smile and she rubbed the back of her neck. "I liked her. I know it sounds silly but there was definitely something about her. Some kind of chemistry between us, I think."

Up to now, Amelie had been slowly eating her gnocchi and absorbing Cat's words, allowing the twins to ask most of the questions. As she noticed the slightly giddy look on Cat's face, before she could stop herself, she said, "It was only one conversation, Cat. Don't get too carried away."

Almost as soon as the words left her mouth, she wished they hadn't.

"I'm not getting *carried away*," Cat replied tightly. "I'm not a silly teenager, Amelie. I know I need to be careful. I'm just saying that I got a good feeling, that's all."

Amelie nodded. "I know. I just–"

Cat pursed her lips and gave a reedy sigh. "I know you don't approve, Amelie, but let's not fight over this. Okay?"

Amelie met Cat's gaze. A thousand thoughts were racing through her head but she didn't dare say any of them out loud. It was her place to be supportive, not critical. She'd learned last August that – between her and her sister – there was such a thing as a little *too* much honesty. "I'm sorry. I'm being overly protective." She reached for Cat's hand and squeezed it. "I'm really glad she seems nice."

"She does." Cat topped up her wine glass, her features softening a little. "She really does."

After dinner, Amelie offered to clear up the kitchen so Ben could go down to the stables while Cat went upstairs to call their parents. They had all agreed that, while it had been prudent not to tell Mum and Dad about Aida's second letter before they went away on holiday, they deserved to know Cat had made contact with her birth mother.

Their parents would, of course, smile and tell Cat they thought it was great news – any other reaction might come across as them trying to stop Cat from getting to know Aida – but Amelie couldn't imagine how news like that would feel to them. In fact, it made her stomach churn just thinking about it.

She had just finished putting away the wine glasses when she heard familiar footsteps in the doorway. Looking up, she smiled.

"Evening." Skye was leaning against the door frame. Pushing his dark curly hair from his face, he smiled back at her.

"You missed Cat's famous pesto." Amelie dried her hands and turned away from the sink.

"No one invited me."

"You're always invited, you know that."

Skye stopped in front of Amelie and put his hands into his pockets. Not for the first time, she wished he would stop being so courteous around her. They'd been side-stepping around one another for five long months. In the beginning, as she rode the aftershocks of her broken engagement and Jed's broken heart, she had appreciated it. She'd been grateful to Skye for giving her space, for being there but not being over-bearing or pushy. Now, though, it had been so long she was beginning to wonder whether he'd changed his mind.

"Listen," she said, breaking away from his gaze, "do you fancy a coffee? I know it's getting late but I don't think I could sleep yet."

"Sure. Dad's on a video date with your Aunt Katie. Not sure I want to interrupt that one."

"A date?" Amelie's eyes brightened. She knew her aunt and Skye's dad had hit it off, but she didn't know it had progressed beyond a few phone calls.

Skye laughed a little. "Well, he says it's not a date but he put on his good shirt. So, yeah, it's a date."

As Amelie turned on the coffee machine and chose a decaf capsule, she folded her arms in front of her stomach and said gently, "How do you feel about that? Are you okay with it?"

For a fraction of a second, Skye's smile faltered. His mother, Della, passed away just three years ago and he wasn't yet able to talk about her without looking as though he was about to cry. Sincerely, he said, "Yeah. I am. I want him to be happy." He swallowed hard and forced his smile a little wider. "Mom would want him to be happy."

Amelie wanted to reach out and touch Skye's arm, or stroke his shoulder, or slip her arms around his waist and hug him tight. Instead, she cleared her throat and said, "Speaking of mums... Cat called her birth mother today."

As the two of them headed from the kitchen to the library, each holding a mug of coffee, Skye looked at Amelie. "Did it go okay? Their talk?"

Amelie pushed open the library door and settled herself on one of the sofas. "She seemed really happy about it."

"Ok*ay*..." Sitting down beside her, Skye dipped his head to meet Amelie's eyes. "But *you* don't sound too happy?"

For a long moment, Amelie stared into her coffee mug and tapped her fingernails on the delicate floral pattern. She had tucked her feet up beneath her and was resting her mug in her lap. "I'm happy for her. Of course, I am. I'm just..." She sighed. "I'm worried, that's all."

"Worried Cat will get hurt?"

Amelie nodded. "Mmm. Right now, Aida seems too good to be true. She reached out, wants to get to know her, seems apologetic and genuine."

"But–"

"But Cat was taken away from her when she was only two years old, Skye. So, whatever's lurking in her past, I'm not sure it's going to be a big warm happy ending like Cat's hoping for."

"People change." Skye was resting his arm on the back of the sofa, his fingers tantalisingly close to Amelie's shoulder. "Perhaps Aida turned her life around?"

"Perhaps." Amelie pressed her lips together then tried to smile. "Perhaps."

"You've never wanted to find your birth parents?" The question rolled easily off Skye's lips and, somehow, Amelie didn't mind him asking it.

"No. Never." She paused as she tried to find a way to explain. "Sometimes I think Cat believes I'm in denial over it. Repressing my feelings or refusing to acknowledge them but, genuinely, I'm not interested in knowing anything about them."

Skye was watching her closely in a way that always made her feel like she was the most interesting person in the world.

"Rose and Thomas Goodwin are my parents. They raised

me. They kissed me better when I scraped my knees, they grounded me when I behaved like a brat... they gave me a family." Amelie picked at a loose thread in the hem of her grey sweater. "Cat says she needs to know where she came from as if knowing will make her whole. But I know who I am." She looked at Skye and waved her hands at herself. "For twenty-five years, I've been Amelie Goodwin. What happened when I was Amelie Russo doesn't shape my idea of myself. Not one bit."

Skye smiled at her. It was the kind of smile that made her stomach do somersaults. The kind that made her feel beautiful, and brave, and *impressive*. His fingertips brushed her shoulder. "No one's saying you and Cat need to feel the same way about this, right? You're different. That's okay. You've just got to let her figure it out *her* way." He smiled again and bit the corner of his lip as if he was trying not to laugh. "So, you might need to bite your tongue a little. Keep your thoughts to yourself?"

Amelie wrinkled her nose at him. "What if it ends badly?" She rested her fingers on top of Skye's and stroked his knuckles. "I don't want her to get hurt. She knows nothing about this woman–"

"Ah–" Skye pressed his index finger to Amelie's lips to stop her from talking. "Let her figure it out… remember?"

As he smiled at her, Amelie's heart fluttered. A fizz of nervousness trickled down her arms. Skye took his finger from her lips and brushed his hair back from his face. They were close, so close she could feel the air turning to static between them, but then he picked up his coffee cup and leaned away from her into the plump cushions behind him.

For maybe the hundredth time in five months, Skye Anderson did *not* kiss her. And Amelie was beginning to wonder if he ever would.

CHAPTER SIX

SKYE

BEFORE HE LEFT AMERICA, Skye had found it almost impossible to get out of bed in the morning. Most nights, he would wake not long past midnight, drenched in sweat with his heart thundering against his rib cage. Dreams – nightmares – of his last few weeks in the Veterinary Corps had haunted him. They had come in flashes. Nothing concrete. More of a feeling than a retelling of events; a feeling of complete and utter terror. Afterwards, he'd find himself unable to go back to sleep. He'd think of his unit, the decisions he made which led them into danger, and the dogs. His beloved dogs. He would toss and turn, and eventually slump in front of the T.V. Sometime before five a.m., he would lose consciousness. He would only wake again, around mid-morning, when his father decided it was finally time to disturb him.

In Tuscany, though, almost every morning, he woke naturally just before sunrise. Rested. Excited for the day ahead. Sure, he had bad nights. But only a couple of times a week. In fact, recently, they'd been as infrequent as a couple of times a *month*.

His therapist – the one his father had insisted on him continuing to see via video call – said it was because he was finally processing what had happened and that the fresh environment was helping him to move past his trauma. However, she was also adamant that if he started talking about his time in the army with those closest to him – Amelie and his father – he would see even more progress.

Deep down, Skye knew she was right; Dr. Melissa Cooper was the only person he'd spoken to *properly* about what happened, but she was a professional. When he spoke, she looked at him with a completely steady, unflinching expression. His father would not look at him that way and neither would Amelie. They'd want to wrap him up and hold him close, they might even cry for him, and he wasn't sure he could hold it together if that happened.

So, for now, Skye was content with being better than he used to be. Not *better* but in a better place.

Walking over to the window, he opened the shutters of the cabin he'd been staying in since he arrived at *Heart of the Hills* and yawned. He could hear his father snoring in the room next door and, not for the first time, reminded himself that they really needed to sort out their living situation. When they took over as owners of the ranch, they had agreed that Rose and Thomas

Goodwin – and their children – should stay on to help manage the place and that they should remain in the ranch house because it had been their family home for over three decades. Which meant that Skye and his dad were, technically, homeless.

Padding into the kitchen to make coffee, Skye knocked on his father's door on the way past it. He was standing by the large glass doors in the open plan living area when his dad appeared, surprisingly bright-eyed, and fully dressed.

"Morning, kiddo," he said enthusiastically. "Coffee?"

"In the pot." Skye nodded towards the countertop. "You're up early."

Dad rubbed his hands together. "I have to head to the city for a few days. Need an early start."

Sitting down in one of the large armchairs near the window, Skye sipped his coffee. "The city?"

"Deal's nearly done, which means we can start looking at places to live." Dad sat down opposite him and casually crossed his right ankle over his left knee. He had been in the process of selling his remaining businesses in the States since they'd purchased *Heart of the Hills* last August. It looked like – finally – he'd managed it.

Skye raised his eyebrows and looked around at their cabin. "As much as I love the cabins here, I can't say I'll be sad to have a little more space." He smiled and tilted his head. "Preferably somewhere where the bedrooms are *very* far apart, so I don't have to hear you snoring in the early hours."

His father let out a deep, throaty laugh and shook his head. "Ha. Yes. We need to talk about that don't we?"

"About?" Skye stood up and refilled his coffee cup.

"Whether we live together or apart and *where* we live. Ideally, we need to be onsite, but building here would take up valuable land and I'm not sure that's a good idea." His father was thinking out loud, and now Skye was too. An idea had come to him a few days ago but he'd been sitting on it, unsure whether it was feasible.

"What if we didn't take up land?" He sat back down and leaned forward onto his knees. When his father narrowed his eyes at him, Skye continued. "What if we convert the old stables? When the new ones are done, the old ones will become obsolete. Before the fire, they were just sitting there empty."

"Go on…"

"There'd be room to create two houses. One each. Maybe conjoined with a courtyard? It wouldn't eat into the value of the land. If anything, it'd add to it."

A smile flitted across Dad's lips. It contained a whisper of pride, which made him blush.

"It's probably not feasible." He rubbed the back of his neck and shrugged. "Just an idea."

"No," his father said, leaning forward to pat Skye's knee. "It's a great idea, son. A *great* idea. I'm just a little annoyed I didn't think of it myself." He grinned then looked at his watch and abruptly stood up. "I have to get going. We'll talk more when I'm back."

Skye stood up, and his father wrapped him in a firm hug.

Patting Skye's shoulder, he said, "You've given me something to mull over on the train ride to *Florence*. Well done, son."

"See you, Dad." Skye leaned back against the arm of the chair as his father headed for the door. When it closed, he smiled to himself. Thinking about living somewhere close to *Heart of the Hills*, but not on the ranch itself, hadn't felt right. The possibility of living on site, waking up every day to the horses and the hills and the Cyprus trees... that felt very right indeed. He couldn't wait to tell Amelie.

It was a bright but cold morning. Ben was already down at the stables when Skye arrived, his breath blooming in thin white clouds in front of him as he shovelled muck into a wheelbarrow. Tall with thick dark hair, he was almost identical in appearance to his brother Ethan – even though the two of them were not technically identical twins – but Skye had always secretly preferred Ben for company.

Skye had known the Goodwins since they were all kids. Each summer when he'd visited the ranch with his mum and dad, he'd become a fifth member of their pack, but it was Amelie and Ben he'd gravitated towards the most; they were the softer of the four siblings. Cat was cool, but somewhat spikier than Amelie, and Ethan had an air of bravado about him that made Skye bristle. He was pretty sure it was all for show but, with Ethan now living in New York, Skye hadn't gotten as close with him as he had with Ben.

"You know what?" As Skye approached, Ben leaned onto the top of the fork he was using. "The sooner we move the horses up to the new stables, the better."

"Not keen on carting manure up the hill for much longer?" Skye looked back in the direction from which he'd come – up a slope that led back to the upper paddocks and the yard.

"Are you?" Ben had started shovelling again.

Skye joined him. "Keeps me in shape," he said, rolling up his sleeves. "And helps burn off some of the food Nonna keeps feeding me."

Ben laughed. "Yeah, she's figured out you're a foodie. You'll never escape now. She'll be testing new recipes on you ten times a week."

"Fine by me." Skye was thinking of the *arancini* Nonna had made him last week. He'd eaten the whole tray and hadn't even felt bad about it. In fact, he'd contemplated asking her to make another batch so he could wrap them up and present them to Amelie. But the more he'd thought about it, the more it had seemed a little silly.

"What is it?" Ben was now brushing down Rupert, Amelie's favourite horse, but had stopped to narrow his eyes at Skye. "You've got that faraway look again."

Skye gave a dismissive *pfft* and turned towards the stables. When he returned with Shadow – a large black horse with deep soulful eyes – he gave a groan and pinched the bridge of his nose. "It's Amelie."

Ben rolled his eyes. "Not sure I want to hear this," he said, either not keen on talking about his sister's love life or just utterly fed up of listening to Skye say the same thing over and over again.

"That's just it, though, there's nothing to hear." Skye gave a futile wave of his hand. "I just can't pluck up the courage to ask her out. And the longer I leave it, the worse it gets."

Ben, who had heard all of this before, multiple times, breathed in slowly as if he was summoning the will power to be sympathetic. "Stop putting it off and just *ask* her. What are you waiting for? You fought in the Middle East, you trained dogs with huge pointy teeth, and you're frightened of asking my sister out on a date? If it was Cat, I'd get it. But Amelie..." Ben laughed. "She's not scary. A little loopy sometimes. But not scary."

Skye tilted his head to the side; he wasn't so sure about that. When Amelie was feeling enraged or impassioned about something, she could be plenty scary, but that wasn't the reason he hadn't asked her out. Feeling his cheeks start to flush, Skye cleared his throat and concentrated on Shadow's mane. Without lifting his eyes to meet Ben's he said, "What if she's changed her mind? What if she doesn't feel the same way any more?"

Ben shrugged. "There's only one way to find out..."

CHAPTER SEVEN

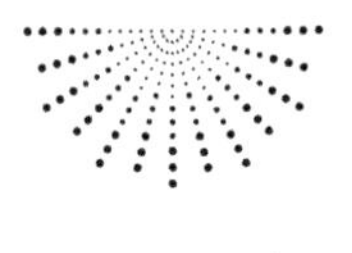

AMELIE

Amelie had been staring at her laptop all morning. She'd positioned it on the desk in her mother's office so that when she looked up, she saw rolling hills, blue skies, and horses in the paddocks. However, even the view that she normally loved wasn't inspiring her.

A few weeks after backing out of the wedding and sending Jed back to England alone, after crying too many tears and eating too much ice cream, Amelie realised one day that she seemed to have accidentally relocated to Italy. If she'd returned to London, she'd have had no job and nowhere to live. Even if she could have rectified those things, she found that she didn't actually want to.

It was as if London was a very definite chapter of her life, and she was ready now to start a new one. Back home in Tuscany where she belonged. The only problem was, as

Christmas approached and rolled into a new year, she had begun to feel a bit like a spare part.

Ben had been working at the ranch for over a year and was now irreplaceable. Cat took to her new receptionist role as if she'd been born to do it. Her parents did what they always did, and Skye slotted straight in as their resident vet and Ben's sidekick. Even Alec seemed to know intuitively what to do and when to do it, but Amelie didn't. She floated between family members offering assistance, but none of them really needed her.

In the end, she'd decided to do the one thing she'd always wanted to do – write a novel. After all, what better opportunity? She had her old bedroom in the ranch house, enough savings from her job at Orchid Books to pay her parents a small amount of rent, and endless days of peace and quiet.

The only problem was… she didn't actually know what to write about.

When a knock on the door made her jump and gave her an excuse to turn away from her computer, she found herself sighing with relief.

"What are you up to?" Ben looked flushed and smelled of horses.

"Trying to start my novel," Amelie replied, wincing at how pretentious she sounded.

"Any luck?"

"Not so far." She stood up and pointed towards the kitchen. "Do you need lunch?"

"It's Friday. I'm going to head into *Legrezzia* and grab some food from the market."

Amelie looked at her laptop then defiantly shut the lid. "I'll come with you. I need a break."

A knowing smile flitted across Ben's lips but he didn't pull her up for wanting to procrastinate. Instead, he told her he'd change and meet her back downstairs in a few minutes.

As she waited for him, Amelie looked toward the library; last night, she'd been so certain that Skye was going to kiss her. *Finally* kiss her. But he hadn't. Perhaps she should have kissed him? Perhaps he was waiting for *her* to make the first move?

She was twisting a loose strand of hair between her thumb and index finger when Ben clattered back down the stairs. He stopped on the bottom step. "Not you as well," he said.

Amelie blinked at him.

"You're thinking about Skye?" He walked over and stood in front of her.

"How did you–?"

"Let me guess... he hasn't asked you out yet and you're worried that he never will?"

Amelie opened her mouth to speak but Ben cut her off by grabbing hold of her arm and practically dragging her out of the house. As he jogged down the steps, pulling Amelie along with him, he took out his phone.

"Skye? Can you meet me up at the house for a minute? It's important. Thanks." After hanging up, Ben put both hands on Amelie's upper arms and very sternly said, "Don't say anything. Just wait."

Although part of her wanted to giggle, Amelie also felt suddenly nervous; what was Ben playing at?

A few minutes later, as she was contemplating insisting that they got into the truck and started for *Legrezzia*, Skye appeared. She'd recognise his frame anywhere; excessively tall, like his father, and with the most luscious dark curly hair she'd ever seen. When he saw her, he waved. He was wearing jeans and a petrol blue sweater that made the sea-green of his eyes sparkle even more than usual.

Amelie felt herself starting to blush.

"Everything okay?" Skye looked from Ben to Amelie and back to Ben.

"No," her brother said abruptly. "Everything is *not* okay." Ben turned to Amelie but pointed at Skye. "Amelie, Skye is crazy about you. He's been haranguing me for weeks about how he's supposed to pluck up the guts to ask you on a date. It's been so long he's worried you don't like him any more." Ben ignored Skye's cheeks, which were almost flame-red with embarrassment, and now pointed to Amelie. "Skye, Amelie is freaking out because you promised *five months ago* that you'd kiss her one day and now she thinks the day will never come."

Ben had almost visibly shuddered when he said the word 'kiss' in reference to his big sister, and now Amelie's cheeks were burning too.

"Sort it out, you two, *please*." Ben took the truck's keys

from his back pocket and began to weigh them up and down in his palm. "I spent three years listening to Cat complain about her ex, and I'm not going to spend another three being a sounding board for the two of you. I've got my own life to worry about."

Amelie wasn't sure whether Ben was smiling or grimacing as he turned away from them. "Sort. It. Out!" he said, marching towards the truck. "Amelie, I'm leaving in five minutes."

As Ben slammed the driver's side door shut and turned up the radio, Amelie looked down at her boots and willed the beetroot tinge in her cheeks to subside. She only looked up when she realised that Skye had stepped closer and was reaching for her hands.

"Amelie," he said, sucking in his breath as if he was preparing to make a speech, "I absolutely, one hundred percent, still intend to kiss you."

Amelie blinked at the boldness of his statement. After months of tip-toeing around one another, he'd said it. Out loud. Her lips parted into a smile. "You do?"

"Heck, yeah." Skye brushed a strand of hair from her face, then shook his head. "But first," he said formally, "Amelie Goodwin, could I please take you out on a date tonight?"

"Tonight?" Amelie's heart skipped a beat; she was grinning like an idiot now.

"We've already waited too long. I've no idea where we'll go or what we'll do, but it'll be a date. A *real* date." He lowered his voice and rested his forehead against hers. "Just the two of us."

Amelie began to giggle. She couldn't help it; nerves and excitement were bubbling up inside her. She felt more like a teenager than a thirty-year-old woman. "I'm going into the village, I'll ask Bea for a table at *Signiorelli's*," she said softly, feeling as if she should take at least some role in the proceedings.

Skye was grinning at her and when Ben loudly beeped the horn, he said quickly, "Okay. *Signiorelli's*. I'll drive us."

As Amelie reluctantly turned away and jogged to the truck, she rested her palm against her chest. She was going on a date with Skye Anderson. Finally. A date.

CHAPTER EIGHT

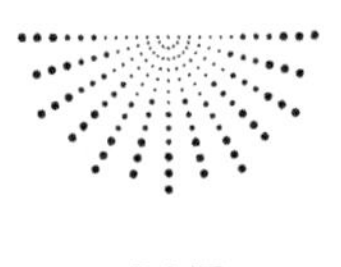

CAT

CAT WAS SITTING on Amelie's bed, watching her take clothes out of her wardrobe, examine them, and put them back in. She'd been trying to pick an appropriate outfit for her date with Skye for over half an hour and looked like she was starting to panic.

"Jed hasn't sent any of my good dresses yet." Amelie turned away from the wardrobe and reached for the glass of wine Cat had poured her. She twirled the stem of the glass between her fingers as if she didn't really want to drink it then put it back down.

"It's *Signiorelli's* not *The Ritz*." Cat laughed but then saw the slightly alarmed look on Amelie's face and stopped.

"You think I should go casual? Jeans? Should I wear jeans?" Amelie flopped down on the chair next to her dressing table and buried her head in her hands. Peeping out from between them, she said, "I'm a grown woman. I used to have an executive office, and now I'm behaving like a teenager. What's happening to me?"

Cat smiled, fiddling with her own wine glass. "Did you feel this way when you went out with Jed?"

Amelie took her hands away from her face and sat up a little straighter. "No, I don't suppose I did."

"Then it's a good sign. It means this is something real. It's exciting!"

A smile fluttered across Amelie's lips. "Yes," she said. "A good thing. Okay, I'm going to shower. Pick something for me to wear, would you? I'm clearly incapable of making the decision myself."

"Yes, ma'am." Cat offered a stiff salute, but as soon as Amelie was out of the room, she picked up her phone and typed a message.

Skye – Amelie is freaking out. Are you going smart-casual, tuxedo, or flip-flops and shorts?

A few seconds later, Skye replied: *Ha. I'm kinda freaking out here too. Decided jeans and lucky shirt.*

Quickly, she replied: *Got it. Have a good night :-)*

When Amelie returned, Cat was standing at the foot of the bed and had laid out a pair of light blue, skinny jeans, a navy shirt with little gold bees on it, and high-heeled navy court shoes.

"Really?" Amelie was wrapped in a towel and frowned at the outfit. "You think that's fancy enough?"

"The navy brings out your eyes and the jeans make your

legs look amazing." Cat kissed her sister firmly on the cheek. "Trust me."

"Wait, where are you going?" As Cat walked towards the door, Amelie put her hands on her hips.

"I have to go check on the angry German." Cat rolled her eyes. "He's supposed to be taking a train to *Pisa* tomorrow but he hasn't told me what time to book the taxi for."

"You should let him sort it out on his own. He sounds awful."

"Exactly. He's awful. Precisely the sort of person who'd write us a one-star review even when he's not a paying guest." Cat realised she'd left her wine on Amelie's bedside table, so quickly drank down the last few mouthfuls and grinned. "That should make him a little more tolerable."

"Good luck," Amelie called as Cat reached the doorway.

"You too. Find me when you get back. I want to know *everything*!"

Stefan Hurst hadn't ventured outside of Cabin Five since his arrival. He'd eaten his meals in his room and hadn't once asked if he could explore the ranch. As Cat stood outside his door, she shivered. It was dark and, without the sun, there was a chill in the air.

This time, when Stefan answered, Cat smiled and breezed past him into the cabin as if he'd welcomed her inside.

Closing the door behind him, Stefan folded his arms and tapped his foot uncomfortably.

Cat glanced around the room. Not a single thing was out of place. No coffee cups in the sink. No signs of life except for a blank open notebook sitting on the coffee table.

"How are you, Stefan?"

"Well, thank you."

Cat nodded. "Are you enjoying your stay?"

"It has been fine, thank you."

She paused – clearly, he still wasn't much of a conversationalist, despite the fact he had perfectly good English. "Okay, well, I just came to ask what time your train's booked for tomorrow? So I can organise a taxi to take you to *Pisa*."

Stefan looked like he wanted to sit down but didn't. Cat found herself examining his face, wondering what he'd look like if he didn't have an enormous beard that obscured half of his features. "Actually, I have been thinking that perhaps I could stay here?" He spoke so quickly that Cat barely had time to absorb what he'd said.

"Stay here?"

"Yes."

Cat laughed and tried to arrange her features into something polite and friendly; the last thing they needed right now was an unwanted and *unpaying* guest on the ranch. "The thing is, Mr. Hurst, we'd love to have you but we're not running any treks or lessons at the moment. We're renovating ready for the spring, so we have no tutors onsite and–"

Stefan finally sat down and gestured for Cat to do the

same. When he looked at her, he smiled and it caught her off guard. "To be honest," he said, "I'm not very good at riding."

"But you booked a holiday on a ranch?"

"My sister booked it for me. We grew up on a farm in Germany. She thought it would be good for me. I've been a little stressed lately."

"Oh, I see." Cat had no idea what to say; Stefan's sudden display of human emotion was completely unexpected.

"I have looked at the website for *Sunset Ranch* and it seems very much… *busier* than here." Stefan waved his arms around the cabin. "Here, it is quiet. Peaceful."

"Won't your sister be a little annoyed if you don't turn up at the place she's booked?"

"She only booked it. I am paying for it," Stefan said bluntly, meeting Cat's eyes. "If it is agreeable for me to stay here, I will call *Sunset Ranch* and tell them I won't be arriving."

Cat's mouth was hanging open. It wasn't often she was speechless.

"I will pay whatever you ask for the cabin," Stefan offered, staring at her.

Unable to think of a single good reason to say no, and aware Stefan had just offered to pay 'whatever they asked' for the cabin, Cat nodded. "All right." She extended her hand to shake his. "Welcome to *Heart of the Hills*, Mr. Hurst. We're thrilled to have you."

Instead of heading straight back to the house, Cat wandered from the cabins down to the pool. Usually, when they had guests on the ranch, it was uncovered, reflecting the sparkling stars from the sky above. Now, it was hidden by a winter tarpaulin, but it was still one of Cat's favourite places to sit.

Perching on the end of a cushion-less sun lounger, Cat took out her phone. Just as she'd promised, she had called Aida Borrelli that morning. She had wanted to do it as soon as she woke up, but she'd busied herself until just after eleven before allowing herself to. In a way, it felt a little like dating; judging the appropriate time to call, worrying whether feelings were mutual, scared to get in too deep too fast.

Cat had called Aida twice. Both times, there had been no answer.

Since then, all day, she'd been trying to persuade herself that Aida was simply busy, perhaps called into work unexpectedly, or that she'd had an appointment she'd forgotten about. But a voice in the back of her head whispered, *What if she changed her mind? She said she'd be free to talk. What if she's decided she doesn't want to?*

Cat scrolled to Aida's number. There it was – in her phone – her mother's number. How many years had she dreamed of this? How many times had she longed to hear Aida's voice, to know where she was and what she was doing?

Taking a deep breath, and trying not to think of Amelie's concerned face when she'd first excitedly told her about their first phone conversation, she tapped the call button and waited.

This time, it had barely rung twice when Aida picked up.

"Catherine," she said, sounding a little breathless. "I'm so sorry I missed your call this morning."

Cat released the air from her lungs and scraped her fingers through her hair. She felt the tension dropping from her shoulders and smiled. "It's no problem. Really."

"What must you have thought?" Aida asked, although she didn't offer an explanation for why she hadn't been able to answer. "How are you?"

"I'm well. And you? You said you had the day off work… what is it that you do?"

Aida chuckled and Cat heard her repositioning the phone on her ear. "I am a waitress. Nothing special. What about you? What are you doing? Are you married?"

Cat bit her lower lip. She wanted to have this conversation but having it over the phone, without seeing Aida's face, felt a little too strange.

"I'm sorry. Too many questions," Aida said when Cat didn't reply.

"No, not at all. It's just… maybe we could meet and talk in person?" Cat swallowed hard. Her skin was fizzing and her mouth was dry.

She expected a long pause, an awkwardness, for Aida to tell her it was too soon. Instead, quickly, she replied, "Yes, I would like that. I live on the coast near *Pisa. Cecina.* Do you know it?"

"Near *Pisa*? We must be close..."

Aida cleared her throat. Tentatively, she said, "You are nearby?"

Cat nodded. "It sounds like it. I'm in a village near *Sant' Anna*." On the other end of the phone, Aida had gone quiet. "I'll look up *Cecina* on the map. We could find somewhere between us to meet? For coffee?"

There was a pause, then Aida said firmly, "Yes. That would be wonderful."

CHAPTER NINE

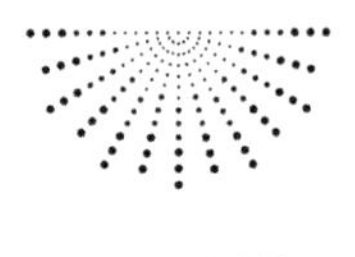

AMELIE

As soon as she saw Skye, the butterflies in Amelie's stomach relaxed. He smiled at her, opened the passenger door of his new truck, then closed it once she'd climbed inside.

"You look great," he said as he started the engine. "Really great."

Amelie allowed herself to breathe out. She was right to have trusted Cat's choice; Skye was wearing jeans too, and a pale blue shirt that brought out the Californian tan of his skin. "You too," she said, then laughed. "I can't figure out whether I should be acting the same as normal or differently… now that we're on a date."

Skye started the truck and drove through the gates. It was dark and the moon was bright. "Me neither," he said. "I mean, I want it to be different. I don't want you to feel like we're just hanging out."

"What if we hold hands?" Amelie asked the question before she had time to think about whether or not it was a good idea but didn't look away from Skye's face.

Slowly, a smile spread across his lips. It dimpled his cheek. "That – Miss Goodwin – is an excellent idea." He reached over and took her hand in his, squeezing it tightly then stroking her palm with his thumb.

Amelie settled back into her seat. Tonight, she was going to get her kiss. She was sure of it.

They arrived at *Signiorelli's,* a café-come-restaurant owned by one of Amelie's mother's oldest friends, just after seven. At this time of year, the chairs and tables which usually sat outside in the piazza were accompanied by patio heaters and thick blankets. As if she'd sensed their arrival, Bea Romano bustled out of the door and waved at them.

"Amelie! There you are." She walked over and offered both Amelie and Skye a kiss on the cheek. "Now, would you like to sit inside or outside?"

Amelie glanced at Skye, "Outside?"

He nodded in agreement.

"*Perfecto*. I will bring you the menu and some candles. Sit… sit." Bea gestured to a nearby table then hurried back inside.

As Skye pulled out Amelie's chair for her, she giggled. "Wow, you really are turning on the charm this evening, aren't you?"

Skye made a show of straightening his collar and cleared

his throat. "But, of course." When he sat down opposite her, he reached out and clasped her hands between his. "Seriously, though, Am. I'm sorry it took us so long to do this."

"Don't be sorry. We're here now."

Several hours later, Bea sidled up to their table and stood with her hands behind her back. "I'm sorry to interrupt…"

Amelie had been laughing at Skye's exaggerated impression of the American twang Ethan had developed since he'd begun studying in New York, but stopped and looked up. Wiping happy-tears from her eyes, she shook her head. "No, no, you're not. Is everything okay?"

Bea looked from Amelie to Skye and smiled at them. Stepping aside, so they could see the front of *Signiorelli's* and the other tables, she said, "Of course, it's just that… we're closing."

Amelie was genuinely shocked. A little while ago, almost every table in front of the café had been full. Now, they were empty. Inside, she could see that Bea had begun stacking chairs on top of the tables so she could mop the floors. Amelie looked at the clock which hung in the centre of the piazza and squinted at it. "Ten p.m.?"

Opposite her, Skye was checking his watch. "Time flies," he said, smiling.

"Gosh, Bea, I'm so sorry." Amelie tucked her hair behind

her ear and felt herself blush; she'd been so lost in Skye that she'd genuinely lost all conception of what was going on around her.

"Don't apologise, it's lovely to see you *finally* spending some proper time together." Bea grinned then then waved her hand at the air. "Usually, I'd let you stay a little longer but I lost one of my part-time girls yesterday, so I have no extra hands to help clear up." She glanced back at the restaurant and hid a small quiet sigh.

"We can give you a hand," Skye said, already standing up, but Bea shook her head so vigorously her curls fell in front of her face.

"Absolutely not." She waggled her finger at him. "No. I won't hear of it."

Skye put his hands on his hips, but Bea was already heading back inside.

"I will bring the bill and then you can take a romantic stroll," she called. "The river is beautiful at night."

They had paid and were tucking their chairs back under the table, preparing to leave, when Amelie said, "Skye, can you give me a moment? I want to have a word with Bea about something."

He smiled at her and gestured to the fountain. "Sure. I'll wait over there."

Amelie nodded, then trotted quickly inside. Bea was cashing up the till but stopped when Amelie entered.

"Amelie, did you forget something?"

Amelie walked over to the counter and rested her forearms on it. "I just wanted to ask you something."

Bea widened her eyes, waiting for Amelie to continue.

"The part-time girl who left – are you thinking of replacing her?"

"Yes, I'll need to…" Bea trailed off then tilted her head. "Why? Do you know someone who needs work?"

Amelie felt her nose twitch, the way it always did when she was considering something. "Actually, *I* do."

"You?" Bea laughed. "My darling, I think you're a little over qualified."

"Perhaps," Amelie replied. "But I'm bored, Bea. I'm no use to man or beast on the ranch. I'm just hanging around getting in the way."

Bea looked at Amelie as if she was thinking very hard about whether to agree. Finally, she said, "Okay. Come tomorrow and we'll see how you get on. If you like it, the job's yours."

When Amelie returned to Skye, she was practically bouncing on the balls of her feet. He looked at her quizzically and she grinned at him.

"What are you so happy about?"

"Oh, nothing," she replied. "I just think I might have finally found a way to keep myself busy."

Skye studied her for a moment then, as if he'd been working up to saying it, blurted out, "I have a surprise for you. Back at the ranch. Will you come with me?"

Amelie looked down as he lightly brushed his fingers against hers. She wanted to reply, *I'd go anywhere with you, Skye Anderson.* Instead she simply said, "Of course. Lead the way."

CHAPTER TEN

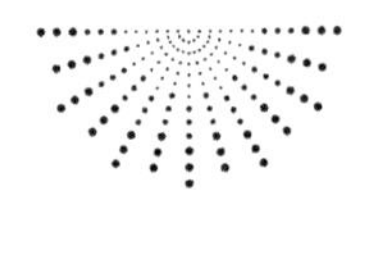

CAT

"*CECINA* IS ONLY AN HOUR AWAY, so I could suggest we meet in *Sant' Anna*? Or is that a little selfish? Making her come here?" Cat had one of her father's old road maps out on the kitchen table and Ben was next to her, examining it.

"Of course, it's not selfish. It's good to be somewhere *you're* comfortable. And…" he nudged her and grinned, "if you meet in *Sant' Anna* I can put on a disguise and go with you. Sit nearby. Keep an ear out–"

"I'm not sure you'd need a disguise, seeing as she hasn't ever met you," Cat laughed. "But thanks for the offer."

Sitting back and sipping his tea, Ben looked at her. His eyes, as always, were full of warmth and they made Cat feel a little tearful. "Hey," he said, wrapping his arm around her, "it's okay to be an emotional wreck. This is a big deal."

Sniffing, Cat wiped her eyes with the back of her hand and leaned into her brother's shoulder. Although he was younger, he was far taller than she was, and quite often behaved like the most grown up of all the Goodwin siblings. "Do you think Amelie's right?" Cat asked. "About being careful?"

Ben let her go and stood up to fetch a packet of biscuits from the cupboard. When he handed it to her, he said, "Yes, but that doesn't mean you can't enjoy it at the same time. Right?"

Cat dunked a biscuit into her tea and ignored the look of disgust on her brother's face; he'd never been the biscuit-dunking type. "Right," she said. "I'll text Aida and ask her to meet me in *Sant'Anna* when she next has a day off?"

"Sounds like a plan."

"Do you think Mum and Dad will mind?"

"They didn't mind you replying to her letter or calling her."

"Yes, but meeting her is a little different." Cat reached for another biscuit. "I don't want to hurt them, Ben. I want to get to know Aida but I don't want them to think–"

Ben shook his head. "They won't. They know you love them." He was about to say something else when he looked toward the entrance hall. "Did you hear something?"

"It sounded like the bell?" Cat frowned as the pair of them stood up. "Not another unexpected guest, surely? Stefan staying is one thing, but–"

"Stefan's staying?" Ben asked as they crossed the kitchen.

"Seems like it." Cat pushed the door open and stepped

into the hall. She stopped abruptly, causing Ben to bump into her but then he whispered, “Who the heck is that?”

Cat looked at Ben, then at the tall blonde woman standing by the reception desk. “I have no idea.”

CHAPTER ELEVEN

AMELIE

OUTSIDE THE OLD barn and stables, Skye stopped and pointed at them. "Well," he said, "what do you think?"

"I think it's the old barn and stables?" Amelie was beginning to feel the evening chill and shivered, despite the fact Skye had given her his jacket when they returned to the truck.

"It is."

"I'm sorry, I don't get it…"

"You remember Dad and I have been trying to think about where we'll live long-term?"

Amelie nodded; she'd been trying not to pay too much attention to the idea that Skye might move somewhere off-ranch, and that she might not see him around the place every day.

"Well…" Skye waved at the barn.

For a moment, Amelie just stared at him, then her eyes widened. "The barn?"

"When the horses are moved back up to the yard, Dad and I could convert this and the stables into two separate dwellings," he said, stepping forward and gesturing for Amelie to follow him as he walked through the barn's open door. "It'll add value to the ranch without taking away land, we can create a separate access road, and it's far enough away that your mom and dad won't feel like we're living on top of them."

Amelie looked up at the old wooden eaves above them. Through a hole in the roof, she could see a sliver of stars. "It'll be a lot of work, Skye."

"But you like the idea?"

"I do," she said, allowing herself to move a little closer to him. She was still looking at the stars. When she looked back, she said, "Skye? Thank you, for tonight. It was lovely."

Skye took hold of her hand and laced their fingers together. "I'm sorry it took me so long to ask you out properly."

"Well," she said, smiling, "I could have asked you, couldn't I? I guess I was just worried that you'd..."

"What?" Skye searched her face.

"That you'd changed your mind."

Starting to stroke the spot just below her ear, Skye said, "I will never change my mind about you, Amelie Goodwin."

Smiling, Amelie slipped her hand around his waist. "I

was also worried because of what you told me on my *un*wedding day. Do you remember?"

Skye began to blush. "Yeah," he said. "I remember."

"You told me that the day you kiss me will be the day you tell me that you're falling for me." Amelie laughed. "And that's a lot of pressure you put on yourself."

Skye's fingers had moved to the back of Amelie's neck. He smiled at her and shook his head. "Want to know a secret?"

Amelie was holding her breath. Instead of speaking, she simply nodded.

"I've been–" Skye stopped mid-sentence. Someone was calling his name. He looked up, taking his eyes away from Amelie's. She had to fight the urge to grab hold of him and bring him back. "Did you hear that?"

"Skye? You in there?" It was Ben's voice.

"Must be a problem with the horses," Skye muttered as he moved toward the door.

Trying not to panic, Amelie followed him. The last time there was a problem with the horses, it had been a big problem – a fire that almost took her father's life and that had taken them five months to recover from.

Stepping outside, Amelie blinked into the darkness. Ben was standing next to someone. A tall, blonde woman who was smiling at Skye. Amelie looked from Skye to Ben, hoping that one of them would tell her what was going on.

"She said you were expecting her?" Ben stepped away

from the woman and towards Amelie, watching Skye as he spoke.

"Well," the woman said brightly, "I'm afraid I might have told a white lie about that but I wanted to surprise you." She was staring at Skye, and had moved closer. "Are you surprised?"

Skye swallowed hard. His jaw was twitching. At his sides, his fists were clenched shut. "You could say that."

Amelie gently put her hand on Skye's shoulder. "Skye? Are you going to introduce us?" She was doing her best to sound unbothered by the sudden appearance of a blonde American woman who, frankly, looked like a super model. But her voice came out a little more high-pitched than she'd hoped it would.

With fingers that, a moment ago, had been stroking Amelie's cheek, Skye rubbed the back of his neck. "Amelie," he said gruffly, "this is Molly O'Neal. We served together in the Veterinary Corps."

"Oh, hush. We were a little bit more than colleagues." Molly waved her hand at Skye as if he'd told a rather amusing joke then stepped forward to firmly shake Amelie's hand. "We dated for five years," she said, looking at Skye. "Heck, we were engaged for two of them."

CHAPTER TWELVE

SKYE

Skye was standing in the corner of his cabin's living room. On the couch, Molly was sipping a mug of coffee. She had crossed one long slim leg over the other and was watching him.

"You look like you want to bolt for freedom," she said, laughing.

Skye sucked in a deep breath and braced his hands on his hips. "Molly," he said, trying to remain calm, "what are you doing here?"

Blinking at him as if she had no idea why he wasn't thrilled to see her, Molly smiled. "I had some leave to take, and I've always wanted to see Italy."

Skye began to pace up and down. He'd come to Tuscany to get away from his old life. Never in a million years would he have expected it to follow him here. "And you didn't think I'd appreciate a bit of a warning?"

Molly's smile wavered. The corner of her lips twitched as if they were about to turn into a grimace. "I tried to tell you. When I called? You hung up before I had the chance." After frowning at him, she lightened her tone, the way she always did when she was trying to avoid an argument. "Besides, I didn't think you'd need a *warning*, Skye."

"Really? You didn't?" Skye was doing his best not to raise his voice, but the anxious hammering of his heart in his rib cage wasn't helping matters. Sitting down, because perhaps sitting would calm him down, he leaned forward onto his knees and met her eyes. "We didn't exactly part on good terms."

Molly put her mug down on the coffee table. For a moment, she stared at her hands, nervously rubbing her thumbs over her palms. When she looked up, her smile was gone and she sighed heavily. "I know," she said. "And I know it was my fault. I guess that's why I wanted to come. To see you in person and tell you I'm sorry for the way things ended."

As he examined her face, Skye softened a little. Despite the end of their relationship, they had been close once, and he knew when Molly was being earnest about something. "I'm sorry too," he said. "But you only called me a few days ago. Was this a last-minute thing?"

Molly tilted her head from side-to-side as if to say, *sort of.*

"You've come an awfully long way to apologise for

something that happened over eighteen months ago. You couldn't have emailed?"

Molly laughed and flicked her hair over her shoulder. Even now, he found her off-duty appearance totally at odds with her role in the military. "Like I said, I've always wanted to see Italy."

A long pause settled between them as they looked at one another. Flashes of their five-year relationship, which Skye hadn't thought of in months, danced in the back of his mind.

"So," Molly said, waving her hand at the cabin, "this is where you're living?"

Skye nodded. "And working."

"Tony told me your dad bought the place?" Molly paused, sensing perhaps that Skye wasn't yet in the mood for a catch up. Then she said, a little sheepishly, "I don't suppose you've got a spare cabin for an old friend?"

"I–"

"If you don't think it's a good idea, I can stay in town. There's a B&B–"

"It's fine." Skye had stood up and was already moving towards the door, pleased to have an excuse to leave for a few minutes. "We're closed to paying guests right now, so we have space. We've been renovating. I'll fetch a key for one of the empty cabins." He was at the door and didn't turn to look at her as he said, "Wait here, I'll be back soon."

Outside, after closing the door, Skye leaned against it and released a long shaky breath. He should have spoken to Molly properly on the phone; if he had, he could have avoided this. Of all the nights for her to turn up, she chose this one – the night he finally took Amelie on a date.

Thinking of Amelie, Skye's stomach tightened. He needed to find her and explain. He needed to tell her Molly wouldn't be staying long, and that she had absolutely nothing to worry about. However, as he looked back at the cabin, something in his gut told him he was wrong about that. There was something Molly wasn't saying; an apology for a break up that happened nearly two years ago wasn't the only reason she was here. But he couldn't begin to fathom what was.

CHAPTER THIRTEEN

AMELIE

"SHE LOOKS LIKE A BARBIE DOLL."

Amelie was leaning on the countertop at *Signiorelli's* watching Bea pour two steaming espressos into tiny white cups. Less than twenty-four hours since Skye's ex-girlfriend showed up in the middle of their perfect evening, she was in turmoil.

Handing Amelie one of the espresso cups, Bea tilted her head. "You are a beauty. No Barbie could compete with you."

Amelie smiled. She downed the espresso in one, then set the cup down on the wooden top. "Thank you. But you didn't see her. She's tall, and blonde, and she's got these *defined* arm muscles. Not too muscly. Not too skinny. Just... toned. You know?"

Bea folded her arms and widened her eyes. "You sound like a teenage girl going crazy over a boy."

"I know." Amelie buried her head in her hands and let out

a low groan. "But she's a super-model *soldier*, for heaven's sake. She understands Skye in a way that I don't. She knows what he's been through." Amelie paused and released a short sharp sigh. "And she has one of those sunny, nice-to-everyone Texan accents. *And* they were engaged! How do I compete with that?"

Sternly, Bea banged her palms on the counter. "There is no competition, Amelie. This woman–"

"Molly–"

"She and Skye broke up for a reason. Their relationship is over. It has been over for how long?"

Amelie narrowed her eyes and tried to work out where Molly O'Neal fitted in Skye's timeline. "At least eighteen months, I suppose."

"Well, there you go." Bea waved her hand then thrust a tall glass of water at Amelie to offset the coffee. "Skye's life is here now. With you."

Amelie nodded. "I suppose."

"No *suppose*. He lives here. She lives in America. You just have to grin and bear it until she goes home. She can't have too much leave. A week? Two?"

"I'm not sure." Amelie sighed and straightened herself up, then reached for her apron. "I avoided Skye when he came to talk to me last night."

A little softer now, Bea stepped around to Amelie's side of the counter and put her hands on her shoulders. "You and Skye are meant to be together. He is crazy about you. His ex-girlfriend being in town won't change that." Bea's eyes were sparkling. "I know," she said, "because I am very wise. If your mother were here, she would tell you the same thing."

Amelie laughed. "Yes, she would."

"Good. Now, do you want to sweep the floor or clean the wine glasses?"

Wrinkling her nose, Amelie pretended to consider the choice. "Floors," she said, already reaching for the broom. "I'll do the floors."

She had almost finished, and was unlocking the front door ready for the first of the day's customers, when a loud clatter from the kitchen made her jump. She turned around, expecting to see that Bea had left the bar and loudly begun work on the morning's pastries, but Bea was still in the room – standing by the coffee machine with a cloth in her hand.

"Did you hear that?" Amelie gestured to the kitchen. "I thought it was just you and me today?"

Bea shook her head, causing her unruly curls to sway from side to side. "It is," she replied. "Just you and me. Tula is on holiday." With the cloth still in her hand, she moved towards the door but Amelie sprang forward and stopped her.

"Wait..." She was speaking in a loud, urgent whisper. "Someone could have broken in. Perhaps we should call for help?"

Bea's lips crinkled into a laugh. "Amelie," she said, waving her hand dismissively, "this is *Legrezzia* – not London. We don't have break-ins or robberies. Tula probably got the wrong shift. Or I left the window open and a cat climbed in."

Amelie smiled and tried to look as though she agreed, but her heart was still beating hard in her chest. Following Bea, she slid her hand into her jeans pocket and gripped her mobile. Just in case. As the door swung open, the kitchen looked empty.

Bea stepped inside and waved her arms. "See. It was nothing. Just our imagination."

Amelie released the breath she'd been holding in her chest but, before she could begin to laugh at herself for being so jittery, her hand flew to her mouth. "Bea..." She pointed a shaky finger to the floor behind the kitchen island. Fumbling for her phone, Amelie stepped back as Bea turned around.

She was about to dial 118 when Bea shouted, "Markus?!" and dove down to the floor.

Amelie stepped around the island, clutching her phone to her chest.

"It's my nephew." Bea was speaking in Italian, kneeling opposite the intruder, who couldn't have been more than sixteen years old. "He's bleeding." She was stroking the boy's head. His eyes were closed and he had a nasty black eye as well as a cut on his forehead.

"Your nephew?" Amelie wasn't aware that Bea had any relatives; she'd always just been... Bea. No husband, no children, no siblings. Amelie forced herself to snap out of the panic that had taken hold of her. "Shall I call an ambulance?"

"No," Bea said firmly. "Find the first aid kit, please."

"Are you sure? He looks badly injured."

"No ambulance," Bea repeated. "Just the first aid kit, and lock the doors."

Amelie wavered; something was going on but now wasn't the time to find out what.

"Please, Amelie." When Bea looked up at her, there were tears in her eyes. Amelie nodded, grabbed the first aid box from its spot on the wall, then went out front to bolt the doors.

When she returned to the kitchen, Bea was cleaning the boy's head wound. He was conscious, but barely; his eyes flittering open every few seconds then closing again.

Amelie bobbed down beside Bea, presenting a fresh bowl of warm water and then placing her hand firmly on her boss's shoulder. "I really do think he needs a doctor."

Bea stopped and looked down at the bloodstained cloth she was holding. Switching back to English, she whispered, "We can't call anyone... he has run away. If the police find him, they'll take him back."

"Run away from where?" Amelie took Bea's hands in hers. "Bea, what's going on?"

"Markus is my nephew. He got in trouble a while back. He's been staying at a..." she searched for the word, "young people's prison. For rehabilitation. But he isn't allowed to leave. He must stay there. The fact he's here..." She looked down at Markus and swallowed hard. "Something has happened. And until I know what it is, I won't risk the police finding him."

Amelie chewed her lower lip and nodded slowly.

"He's not a bad boy, Amelie." Bea bit back a sob and pushed her hair from her face.

"Okay, but he needs help. Let's get him to the ranch. I'll call Skye. He'll look at him. I know he's a vet but–"

Bea was already standing up. "Skye. Yes. Thank you, Amelie." Swiftly, she took her bag from its hook near the back door and handed Amelie a set of car keys from inside it. "My car is at the house. Will you fetch it?"

Amelie nodded. "I'll be back soon."

After closing the door behind her, she tried to catch her breath. Leaving Bea with a beaten-up young man who'd, seemingly, escaped from a young offender's institute seemed like a terrible idea. However, Bea clearly trusted him, so Amelie broke into a jog and headed for Bea's small stone cottage which sat just a few streets away from *Signiorelli's*.

Once in the car, Amelie slotted her phone into the holder on the dash and called Skye.

"Amelie?" He sounded relieved to hear from her.

"Skye, something's happened. I can't really explain, but I'll be arriving at the ranch in about twenty minutes with Bea. Will you meet us at the gates?"

"Is everything okay? Are you all right?"

"I'm fine. But I need your help. I wouldn't ask if it wasn't–"

"Of course." Skye answered quickly. "I'll see you when you get here."

Considerably out of practise driving on small Italian roads, Amelie held her breath the entire way from *Legrezzia* to *Heart of the Hills*. In the back of the car, Bea was sitting with Markus' head in her lap. Her face was pale, and she was clearly fighting the urge to tell Amelie to drive faster.

As they'd dragged Markus out of the kitchen and into Bea's car, he had muttered something that Amelie hadn't been able to hear properly. Now, he was silent.

Glancing at him in her rear-view mirror, Amelie swallowed hard; what could have happened to leave him in such a mess?

At the gates, just as he'd promised, Skye was waiting for them. She stopped as close to the front steps as she could. Almost as soon as she'd climbed out of the driver's seat, Skye put his arm around her and asked, "Amelie, what's going on?"

"It's Bea's nephew. He's hurt." Before Skye could ask why they hadn't gone straight to a hospital, Amelie whispered, "He's supposed to be in some kind of institute. A prison. We don't know what's happened but he's pretty beaten up and until Bea's heard his side she doesn't want the police involved."

Skye sucked in his breath. Subverting law and order did

not sit well with him, and Amelie could see the conflict in his face as he weighed up doing the 'right' thing versus helping someone in distress.

"He's just a boy, Skye. He can't be more than sixteen. I promised we'd help."

After staring at her for a moment, Skye nodded and opened the back passenger door. "Can he walk?" he asked Bea.

"I'm not sure. He walked to the car but hasn't spoken since."

Turning back to Amelie, Skye told her to fetch Ben then climbed inside the car and began to check Markus' injuries.

When Amelie returned with Ben, who was looking just as concerned as Skye had, she saw that Bea was now outside the car, pacing, but Skye was still inside.

"Skye needs your help to get him into the house." Bea took hold of Ben's hands and gripped them tightly between her own.

Without asking any questions, Ben nodded; Amelie had given him the same bullet-point version of events that she gave Skye, and he didn't hesitate to lean inside and ask Skye what to do.

"He's going to be okay." Amelie put her arm around Bea's shoulders and rubbed the space between her shoulder blades. "Skye will sort him out."

Bea nodded. "He's not a bad boy," she said tearfully. "He got into trouble after my sister died but he's not a bad boy."

Amelie offered Bea a smile, then turned to watch Ben and

Skye help Markus out of the car. He was awake, eyes open, but he was unsteady on his feet. With Ben under one arm and Skye under the other, he began to walk. Amelie and Bea followed as the two of them practically carried Markus up the steps and into the house.

"Take him to the library," Amelie said, rushing ahead to open the doors.

As soon as Markus was positioned on one of the large sofas in the middle of the room, he closed his eyes again. Bea moved to sit down beside him but Skye stopped her. "I need my medical bag, Bea. Could you go to my cabin and fetch it?" He was handing her a key.

Bea blinked slowly and looked from Markus to Skye but then she nodded and, without saying anything, hurried out of the room.

"Skye..." Amelie took hold of Skye's elbow. "I could have–"

"I needed her to leave," he said quietly, before sitting down on the coffee table beside Markus and gently touching his shoulder. "Markus, buddy? I need you to open your eyes and talk to me."

For a moment, nothing happened. Then Markus' eyelids fluttered and he focussed on Skye's face.

"I'm not a doctor. I usually do animals, which means it's really important that you tell me right now if there's anything that could affect the way I treat you. Cuts and bruises, I can treat. But if there's anything else..."

Markus' eyes widened. In a hoarse voice, he said, "My English is not so good."

Skye's jaw twitched; his Italian wasn't great yet either. He'd been learning – Amelie had been trying to teach him – but he certainly wasn't fluent enough to communicate what he needed to.

Sitting down next to him, Amelie began to translate. When she got to 'anything else' she stopped and looked at Skye. "What do you mean by 'anything else'? I'm not sure what to say."

Ben cut in. "Skye needs to know if he's taken anything."

Amelie closed her eyes and nodded briefly. Of course – Skye needed Bea gone because he wanted to be sure that Markus was telling the truth. In Italian, Amelie asked Markus the question, making sure to meet his eyes as she said, "We will not tell your aunt, but you must tell us the truth."

"No." Markus spoke loudly. "*Non sono una cosi.*"

"He says he's not like that." Amelie looked from Skye to Ben. "I think he's telling the truth."

CHAPTER FOURTEEN

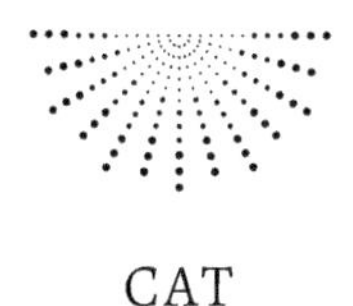

CAT

CAT TURNED AWAY from Stefan Hurst's door and shook her head at herself; why did she even care if he'd eaten today? If he couldn't be bothered to answer when she knocked, he could sort out his own meals. Even if it did mean disappointing Nonna.

She was stalking back up the path to the house when her phone beeped. Just as it had ever since she'd begun contacting Aida, her heart skipped a beat. She was beside the hedgerow that led into her mother's favourite part of the ranch – the Italian gardens near the pool – so ducked through the archway and sat down on one of the stone benches.

When she finally looked at her phone, she breathed in sharply. As she'd hoped, it was a message from Aida. She opened it gingerly, barely even daring to look because something in her belly told her that her birth mother would surely

– at some point – back away from her, tell her she was too busy or that it wasn't a good time for them to meet.

As Cat read Aida's words, a grin spread over her face.

Catherine, I am not working next Thursday. I am happy to meet in Sant' Anna. Let me know a time. Perhaps we should rendezvous at the fountain? I will wear a yellow sweater so you can find me.

Hugging the phone to her chest, Cat tried to calm down. Her heart was jittery, and she had no idea how she was going to last until Thursday without bubbling over from the anticipation.

After replying to Aida, saying she would wear her yellow earrings to go with the sweater, she called Ben. Eventually, he answered, but he sounded off somehow as he said, "Cat?"

"Is everything okay?" Cat stood up, instinctively starting back toward the house. Ever since last night, a feeling of foreboding had settled in her stomach; Skye's ex turning up was *not* a good sign. Her heart had almost broken in two as she'd watched Amelie absorb Molly's arrival, visibly sucking in her breath and trying not to let her feelings show on her face.

"You should get up to the ranch house. Something's happened..."

Cat didn't wait for Ben to fill her in, just hung up and broke into a run. By the time she reached the house, she was panting hard – but more from nerves than from exerting herself. "Ben?" she called into the entrance hall. "Amelie?"

"We're in here..." Ben's voice came from the library.

When Cat entered, she stopped in the doorway. A boy she didn't recognise was lying on the sofa. Her mother's friend Bea, from *Signiorelli's,* was kneeling beside him, and Skye was nearby speaking hurriedly into his phone.

Amelie and Ben both looked deathly pale. When Amelie saw Cat, she rushed to her and grabbed Cat's hands between hers.

"What on earth is happening? Who's that?" Cat stepped into the room and pulled the door closed behind her.

"Bea's nephew. He turned up at the café. He's badly hurt." Amelie pressed her lips together and glanced toward Bea, who was muttering something in Italian to the half-conscious boy in front of her.

"I can see that, but how?" Cat was trying to whisper but wasn't being very successful.

Amelie shook her head. "Not sure. Something about him being in a young offender institution."

Cat's eyes widened. "Okay," she said, holding up her hands, "should we be getting involved in this? The ranch is only just getting back on its feet, I'm not sure we need—"

She was cut off by Skye, who'd hung up and was walking over to them. "I spoke to Ethan, he said he'll call later when he's off shift and do a video consult. In the meantime, he's told me what to look out for. Probably best if I have some space." He looked at Bea, who didn't seem to have noticed he was speaking.

Taking the hint, Amelie took Bea's arm. "Come, Bea,

give Skye some space. Ben will stay to translate while Cat and I make you a hot drink."

Despite feeling as if she should jump up and down and ask everyone if they'd completely lost their minds, Cat smiled warmly at Bea and nodded. "Amelie's right. You're as white as a sheet."

Leaning closer to the boy, Bea whispered, "*Markus? Torno surbito.*" When he didn't reply, she stood up slowly, nodded at Skye, then reluctantly followed Amelie and Cat out of the room.

In the kitchen, Cat silently made three cups of tea and piled some extra sugar into each. As she set them down on the table, Amelie gave her a look which implied, *I'll tell you everything later.* Instead of asking the questions she was dying to ask, Cat simply slid into one of the chairs opposite her sister and sipped her drink while Amelie patted Bea's shoulders.

After what felt like forever, Skye and Ben finally appeared. Skye's sleeves were rolled up and he was pushing his curly hair back from his forehead. Instantly, Bea stood up and rushed over to him.

"He's okay, I think," Skye told her, although his face looked far from happy about the situation. "I'll speak to Ethan later, but he really should have some x-rays to be certain. I think he may have broken a rib."

Bea blinked hard and shook her head. She let out a small, quiet sob and Skye softened, reaching out to put his hand on her arm. "Can I go and see him?" Bea asked shakily.

Skye nodded. "I think you should. We need to know what's going on, Bea."

As Skye spoke, Cat glanced at Amelie; Skye was right, they needed to know what this boy had gotten himself into. But Cat knew Amelie's instinct, with things like this, was usually to trust first and ask questions later.

"I will speak to him," Bea said resolutely.

"Here, take him some water." Ben was pouring water into a large glass. When he handed it to her, Bea smiled thinly at him. Then she turned and marched out of the room.

CHAPTER FIFTEEN

SKYE

THE GOODWINS LOOKED NERVOUS. While Skye strained his ears for movement in the library, Amelie, Cat and Ben sat around the kitchen table nursing mugs of tea.

"Are you sure we shouldn't be calling the police?" Cat asked in a hushed voice.

"I told Bea we wouldn't." Amelie replied.

Cat nodded. Bea was an old family friend. Skye remembered her from when he'd visited *Heart of the Hills* as a child, but none of them knew anything about her nephew and he was fighting the urge to point out that Bea hadn't even mentioned his existence until today.

"This doesn't sit well with me either." Skye poured himself a mug of tea and walked over to stand beside Amelie. "But we should at least hear the kid's explanation before we decide what to do." He allowed his hand to rest on Amelie's shoulder, and almost smiled as she reached up to brush her fingertips against his. Briefly, his mind wandered back to last night. To the moment when he'd been certain that he was finally going to pluck up the courage to kiss her, and the moments after when he'd wished the ground would swallow him whole.

Right now, Molly – the woman he'd been engaged to, who he'd lived with, and who he fought alongside for over three years in the Veterinary Corps – was in Italy, sleeping off jet lag in one of the guest cabins. She was here and he had no idea how long she was planning to stay.

"Bea?" Amelie was looking toward the door.

As Bea walked over, Skye pulled out a chair for her.

Bea smiled at him. "Thank you, Skye."

For a moment, no one spoke until, gently, Amelie said, "Did Markus tell you what happened?"

Bea looked from Amelie to the others then closed her eyes. Wiping her hand across her forehead, she shook her head. When she looked up, it was clear that she was trying not to cry. Blinking back the tears, she took a deep breath, held it in her chest for a few long seconds, then released it. "Markus is my sister's son," she said.

Suddenly feeling out of place standing, Skye sat down between Amelie and Cat.

"He's seventeen. My sister, Mia, died when he was ten."

A ripple of sighs spread through the Goodwins. Skye felt his mouth go dry.

"He had no real father. His biological father left my sister when she was six months pregnant, and she remarried when

Markus was eight years old." Bea took a sip from her mug then set it down on the table. "I offered to take him when Mia died but his step-father, Antonio, wanted to keep him and Markus wanted to stay."

"Where were they living?" Amelie asked softly.

"Not far away. Near Florence," Bea replied. "It was fine at first but then Markus started to get into trouble. Nothing terrible. Just hanging around with the wrong kids. Skipping school. Smoking." She looked around the table, "No drugs though. Nothing like that. He was always a good boy, really."

Ben and Cat exchanged a glance which said they weren't entirely sure whether to believe this or not, but Bea didn't seem to notice.

Skye shuffled forward on his chair. "How did he end up in prison?"

Bea looked down at her hands. When she looked up, she seemed suddenly older than she had before. "He stole Antonio's car and took it for a joy ride. He was sixteen."

"And they locked him up?" Cat was frowning. "That seems a bit harsh."

"Yes. It was." Bea sighed and bit her lower lip. "His step-father, Antonio, is a policeman. He has a lot of influence and he wanted Markus to learn a lesson. He thought a shock might straighten him out. He persuaded the court to send Markus to the youth prison for six months."

Cat and Amelie were both shaking their heads but Skye frowned. "Six months? He's seventeen now. Shouldn't he have been out already?"

"He got into a fight not long after he went there and they extended his sentence. He was due to come home next month, though, and his behaviour has been excellent since the fight."

"So, what happened? How did he get in this mess?" Amelie glanced in the direction of the library.

"He said to me that he was on a day-release programme. He was supposed to be visiting an employer for an interview for when he is released. Just dishwashing at a café, but he was excited about it." Bea swallowed hard and touched her fingers to her throat. "He was attacked before he got there. He was at the train station. A group of men..." She shook her head.

"Why would someone do that?" Amelie said in disgust.

In his mind, Skye was reeling through several options, most of which involved Markus doing something illegal, getting in over his head, and ending up in trouble.

Bea tapped her finger on the table, now seeming more angry than upset. "From the moment he arrived, he was bullied because they knew he was the son of a police officer. Markus says the bullies found out where he was going for his interview and sent the men to beat him."

Skye bit his lower lip. It made sense, and he felt a little guilty for assuming the worst of the boy. If Bea's story was true, then what Markus had been through was more than any kid his age should have to deal with. "Do you believe him?" he asked her gently.

"Ninety percent," Bea replied, barely missing a beat. "But

even if he's telling the truth, if I call the prison, they will add time to his sentence. Antonio won't help him, not now, and he's almost eighteen..."

"What does that mean?" Cat asked.

"It means," Ben said solemnly, "that Markus would have to serve any additional time in an adult prison, right?"

Bea nodded slowly. "I think so, yes."

"That's crazy!" Amelie stood up from the table, a familiar flash of indignation rising in her cheeks. "It'll ruin his life. For what? For a *car*? Surely, his step-father would listen to reason if it was a case of Markus going to an adult prison."

"I don't think so. He's a proud man and he believes in the justice system. He truly believes that Markus needs this in order to turn his life around."

Amelie let out an angry groan and raised her hands to her head. As he watched her, Skye fought the urge to smile; this was exactly the look she'd had last summer, when they had been reunited for the first time in ten years. On the way to *Pisa* airport from London, Amelie's fiery attitude had persuaded the stewardess to allow a pregnant lady from the economy section of the plane to use the first class restrooms. Skye had been captivated by her then and he was captivated by her now.

"Listen." Ben cleared his throat and placed his palms down heavily on the table as if he was calling for everyone's attention. "Why doesn't Markus stay on the ranch for a few days? No one will know he's here. No one who would say anything, anyway."

"Stay here?" Cat looked decidedly unsure about the idea.

"Could he?" Bea was wringing her hands together.

Amelie, Cat, and Ben turned to Skye. He blinked back at them. "It's kind of your call, Skye," Amelie said gently. "You and Alec own the place now, and Mum and Dad aren't here, so..."

Skye bit his lower lip.

"What would your dad think?" Ben was leaning forward on his elbows but his mind was clearly already made up. "Because I know what our parents would say – Bea's been a friend to our family for years. Mum and Dad wouldn't hesitate to help her."

Turning away from them, Skye walked over to the large glass doors and stared out at the sun-dappled garden. He was trying to think clearly but he was struggling. Part of him – the part that had spent several years in the army and was used to discipline, hard work, and obeying authority – felt deeply unhappy about not coming clean to the police. At the same time, though, he felt a deep, gnawing ache in his stomach as he thought about a boy losing his mother at just ten years old. Skye's own mother passed away three years ago. He was still struggling to put himself back together, and he was a grown man. Markus was just a kid.

Skye felt a tentative hand touch his shoulder. Bea was shorter than him. A petite, middle-aged woman with an abundance of dark curly hair, and hazel brown eyes. "Skye. I don't want to put you in an awkward position. I know I'm asking a lot but, if Markus could stay, it would give me time to find out what really happened. If he is telling the truth, maybe I can talk to Antonio. Plead with him to see sense."

"And if Markus is lying?" Skye said gently. "What happens then?"

Bea folded her arms in front of her stomach and pursed her lips. "If he's lying," she said firmly, "I will call the police myself."

CHAPTER SIXTEEN

SKYE

By the time they had settled Bea and Markus into one of the cabins, it was mid-afternoon. The sun was waning and so were Skye's energy levels.

As they sat down in the porch swing on the veranda, Amelie said, "We've had an eventful twenty-four hours, haven't we?"

Skye grimaced and lightly touched her shoulder. "I'm so sorry, Am. I honestly had no idea that Molly was going to turn up."

Amelie nodded. Her strawberry blonde hair was loose and hanging in gentle waves over her shoulders; Skye loved it when she wore her hair loose. "She seems nice," Amelie said. After a brief pause, she added, "Has she told you how long she's staying?"

"We haven't talked properly." Skye rubbed the back of his neck; he could feel it beginning to flush. "Things between us didn't end well. We haven't spoken for over a year. From what I can make out, she feels bad about that and wants to…" He trailed off. He had no idea what Molly wanted, and realised how ridiculous that must sound to Amelie.

"She can stay as long as she likes, you know that." Amelie touched her fingertips to Skye's then smiled at him. "We'll just have to press pause on our second date for a while."

Fighting the urge to wrap his arms around her, Skye slotted his fingers between Amelie's and stroked the inside of her wrist with his thumb. She leaned in to rest her head on his shoulder.

A second date… she wanted a second date. That had to be a good thing.

"As soon as my ex-girlfriend and the ex-con are gone, we'll get straight onto it," he laughed.

"Ex-girlfriend? You mean ex-fiancé?" Amelie was looking up at him, and Skye looked away awkwardly.

"I…"

"It's okay." Amelie lifted her head from his shoulder and smiled, squeezing his hand tightly. "I'm not mad that you didn't tell me."

Skye released the air from his chest and bit his lower lip. He had no good explanation for why he hadn't told Amelie about Molly, except that Molly was so tied up with the Corps, and the Middle East, and Skye's decision to leave, that he couldn't possibly have told Amelie about one part without telling her the whole. Somehow, though, without him saying any of this out loud, Amelie seemed to understand. She was still holding his hand. The way she was looking at him made Skye want to pull her closer.

Before he could, Amelie's eyes moved away from him. Skye followed her gaze and fought back a sigh of frustration. In the distance, Molly had emerged from her cabin and was walking towards them.

Amelie stood up. "I'll leave you two alone."

"There's no need," Skye said, not letting go of her hand.

"Honestly, Skye, it's fine. I need to find Nonna and tell her what's going on before she accidentally stumbles across someone she's not expecting to find." Amelie glanced at Molly, gently tugging her fingers free from Skye's. "I'll see you later, okay?"

With that, she ducked into the ranch house and closed the doors behind her.

For a moment, Skye didn't look up. Then he braced his hands on his thighs and pushed himself to his feet. As Molly reached the steps that led up onto the veranda, Skye jogged down to meet her. "Sorry, Mol, I'm going to be busy the rest of the day."

"I–"

"We'll catch up tomorrow, I promise."

Molly said something in reply, but Skye was already walking away from her and whatever it was disappeared on the breeze.

It was hot. Too hot, and the sun was blinding him. When he looked away, he realised that Dallas was at his feet, ears pricked, waiting for him to tell her what to do. Her black fur glistened. He wanted to nestle his fingers into it, but that was for later. Right now, they were working.

Unclipping her from her harness, he told her what to do and watched her walk away. When she reached the building, panic began to rise in Skye's chest; something wasn't right. Dallas had stopped in the doorway. She wasn't moving. He tried to call her back but when he opened his mouth no sound came out.

Next to him, Molly was frowning. "What's wrong, Skye?"

Still, no sound came from his lips.

His heart began to hammer hard against his rib cage. He wanted to scream. It was building up inside him, and the sun was too bright. He couldn't see Dallas but he knew what would happen next.

Skye screwed his eyes shut, and then the explosions started. Bang. Bang-bang-bang. Bang-bang-bang-bang-bang.

"Skye?! Are you in there?!"

Skye bolted upright in bed. It was the middle of the night and pitch dark outside. His sheets were drenched with sweat, his heart beating so fast he could barely breathe. He scrabbled for the bedside lamp, and when light flooded his bedroom he leaned back against the headboard, panting.

"Skye?! Are you okay?!"

Amelie... she was outside, knocking on the door.

With shaking legs, Skye got out of bed and opened the front door to his cabin, ready to fold himself into Amelie's arms, aware that he wouldn't be able to stop himself from telling her what he'd seen while he was sleeping.

But it wasn't Amelie.

"I heard shouting." Molly was wearing pyjamas and a denim jacket, shivering in the cold night air. She looked past him into the cabin, then pulled her jacket closer and said, "Skye?"

"Bad dream." He scraped his fingers through his hair, still dazed, still trying to convince himself it wasn't real.

Without inviting Molly inside, he stepped back into the living room and left the door open. She followed him and headed straight for the kettle while he sat down on the sofa and put his head in his hands. He'd avoided her for an entire day but now she was here in his living room, making tea, and he couldn't escape it. He felt dizzy and a little nauseous.

"You know," Molly said brightly, as if it wasn't two o'clock in the morning, "I had to get a cab into the village to scout for food. This place is miles from anywhere."

Skye looked over at her. "Sorry. I didn't think..."

Molly shrugged, poured boiling water into two cups, then walked over to perch in the armchair opposite him. After handing him one of them, she asked, "You're still having nightmares?" and watched him carefully while she waited for his answer.

Skye sipped his drink. It was too hot but he didn't care. "That was the worst in a while," he said quietly.

Molly's forehead crinkled into a frown. "My fault?"

"No." Skye replied quickly but then tilted his head. "Maybe."

"I shouldn't have turned up like this. I'm sorry."

Skye rubbed the back of his neck. His breath was returning to normal. "My therapist will probably tell me it proves her point."

Molly didn't flinch at the mention of a therapist.

"She says I still haven't really dealt with what happened. That I need to talk about it with people close to me."

A sad smile crossed Molly's face as she met his eyes. "You never were very good at talking, though, were you?"

"Or you weren't very good at listening." As the words left his mouth, Skye winced. "I'm sorry. That was unnecessary. It was hard for you too."

Molly folded her arms in front of her chest. "I'm not here to argue, Skye."

"Why are you here?"

"I told you," she replied earnestly, "to mend some bridges. We were friends before we were anything else and I miss my friend."

Skye's head was spinning. Molly was right; they had been friends long before they became a couple but he knew – just *knew* – there was something else going on. Whatever it was, though, he couldn't figure it out right now. He needed sleep. A hot shower. To wash the memories from his skin.

"We'll talk tomorrow, okay?" He stood up and started moving towards the door, ushering her out.

Molly hesitated but then nodded.

As he watched her leave, Skye rubbed his temples and tried to ease the headache that was gripping his skull. His dreams were always the same, even though it hadn't happened that way. Always Dallas, walking away from him. Always out of reach.

Back inside, he climbed into a steaming hot shower and let the water pummel his shoulders. There was a time when he wouldn't have been able to do that; when the scars that peppered his back still stung at the slightest touch. Now, he felt nothing, but he knew they were there. They would always be there.

CHAPTER SEVENTEEN

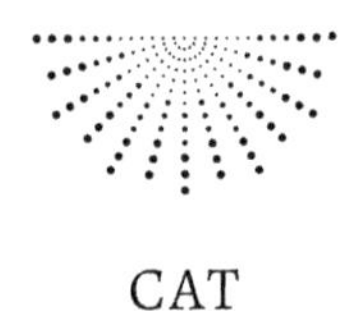

CAT

When Cat woke the next morning, at first, she forgot that a fugitive was sleeping in Cabin Ten and that it was her job to keep an eye on him while Bea figured out what had happened. When she remembered, and thought of Markus' poor bruised face, she shuddered.

Picking up her phone, she squinted at the brightness of the screen. It was only seven a.m. and still dark outside. Opening the shutters, just a little, she peered out at the ranch. Bea and Markus' cabin was pitch black, so was Molly's, but both Skye's and Stefan's had lights on.

Cat almost laughed; in just a few days, they'd gone from an empty ranch to a ranch with three unwanted guests: Markus, Stefan, and Molly. Cat sighed and shook her head. Poor Amelie; her and Skye's first date seemed like it had been utterly perfect right up until the minute Molly O'Neal arrived and started flashing her pearly white smile around the place.

Cat reached for the long grey cardigan she kept hanging on the end of her bed and pulled it on. Then she shoved her feet into a pair of fluffy cream slippers and headed for the stairs. When she reached Amelie's door, she paused and strained her ears for signs of movement inside. There were none, so she carried on but when she reached the entrance hall, she heard voices in the kitchen.

Pushing open the kitchen door, she found Amelie and Ben sitting at the table, a pot of coffee between them, both looking as though they hadn't slept a wink.

"What's all this?" she asked, sliding into a seat opposite Amelie. "A party and no-one invited me?"

"We're waiting for Ethan." Ben nodded at the iPad. "He ended up doing a double-shift but said he'd call any minute now."

Cat poured herself a coffee and yawned. "Markus is still here then?"

"As far as we know," Amelie replied. "I haven't heard from Bea since I checked on them last night."

"How does she think she's going to find out the truth about what happened?" Cat was looking at her siblings, hoping that perhaps one of them had realised this was a terrible idea. "What if the police turn up looking for him?"

"Bea's already told us to deny all knowledge if they turn up. She'll claim she stole a key and hid Markus here on her own," Amelie said stiffly.

"You think they'll believe that?" Cat raised her right eyebrow and tapped her fingernails on the table in front of her. Before Amelie could answer, the iPad began to ring.

After his initial, *The kid really needs to get to a hospital,* Ethan nodded solemnly and sighed. "Okay. I get it. He won't go to hospital. Skye suspects broken ribs. If that's all it is, they won't do much for it. Just painkillers and rest, but there could be any number of other things going on. Is there anyone we know locally who might help?"

"Don't think so," Ben said.

"Okay, well I'm going home for some kip. I'm not back on shift until tomorrow, so get Skye to call me when he's with Markus and I'll do my best to consult via video."

As the iPad screen went blank, the three of them sank into silence. Eventually, Cat waved her phone at her siblings and said, "In other news, I agreed a date with Aida. Thursday. In *Sant'Anna.*"

Cat watched Amelie carefully as she spoke, expecting to see a look of distrust flitter across her sister's face. Possibly because she was preoccupied, Amelie simply nodded.

"That's great." Ben squeezed Cat's hand. "Do you want one of us to go with you?"

Cat had considered this but, in the end, had decided she didn't. "No thanks, I'll be fine."

Amelie looked at her and smiled. "I'm really pleased for you, Cat." Then she glanced at the time on her phone. "*Signiorelli*'s should be opening soon and Tula's still on holiday, but I doubt Bea will want to leave Markus. I'll take them some food and tell her I'll manage things today."

"Will you be okay by yourself? You only started working there yesterday," Cat chuckled – Amelie was a lot of things but experienced in hospitality was not one of them.

For a moment, Cat thought Amelie was going to puff out her nostrils and fold her arms – offended by Cat's bluntness – but instead she smiled sheepishly. "I was just going to wing it," she said, shrugging her shoulders.

"I'll help. There's nothing much for me to do here today. The March arrivals are all sorted and Mr. Hurst can take care of himself. Seeing as he didn't bother to even answer the door to me yesterday."

"I'll check on him," Ben offered.

"Are you sure?" Cat was frowning. "He's not exactly a ray of sunshine."

As Ben nodded, Amelie and Cat got up from the table and agreed to meet on the veranda in an hour's time. At least *Signiorelli's* would stop her from spending the entire day thinking about Aida. *Always a silver lining*, her mother would say.

"You work here as well?"

Cat puffed her hair from her face and fumbled for her pen. *Signiorelli's* had been ridiculously busy all morning and she was starting to regret offering to help out. When she looked up, Stefan Hurst was staring at her.

"Mr. Hurst? No. I'm just helping a friend," she said, brushing down her black apron and trying to smile.

"I see."

"How did you get into the village? Taxis don't run on Sundays…"

"I walked," Stefan replied as if it should have been obvious.

"Walked? That must have taken you hours."

"I like walking, but I am rather thirsty now." Stefan nodded at Cat's notepad.

"Of course." She straightened herself up and tried to remember the waitressing skills she'd picked up when she worked at the gelato store in *Sant' Anna*. "What can I get you?"

"A coffee please. Black. No sugar. And a glass of water."

"Anything to eat?"

Stefan shook his head. "Just the coffee and the water."

Inside, Cat slapped her notepad down on the bar and growled. "Coffee and water for our guest, Mr. Hurst," she said to Amelie, gesturing to the table outside. Stefan had taken a book from his bag and already seemed thoroughly engrossed in it.

"You really don't like him, do you?" Amelie laughed, starting up the coffee machine.

"He's just so… abrupt. Barely a smile. No conversation."

"He's not bad looking though," Amelie said, peeping over the coffee machine towards the door.

Cat frowned and started to fiddle with a napkin on the bar. "*Pfft*. If you like beards."

"You do like beards..." Amelie handed her Stefan's coffee. She had raised her eyebrows and was smiling playfully. "Don't you?"

"Not ones that are attached to obnoxious, rude, humourless, Ger–"

Amelie began to cough, loudly. She was shaking her head.

"What? You think I'm exaggerating. Then you take this out to him and see what you think. Because, trust me, the best beard in the world couldn't make up for his utter *void* of personality."

Amelie hung her head and pursed her lips. As she did, a sinking feeling gripped Cat's stomach; someone was standing behind her.

"No need to bring the coffee outside."

As Cat turned around, wincing, Stefan reached past her and took hold of his drink.

Looking straight at her with his steely blue eyes, he said, "I came to ask if I may also have one of your salads?" He gestured to the blackboard menu at the end of the bar.

Cat nodded, unable to speak. Her cheeks were flaming. "Mr. Hurst, I–"

"The daily special will be fine."

CHAPTER EIGHTEEN

SKYE

JUST BEFORE MID-DAY, Skye found Molly near the yard. She was sitting on the bench next to the paddock, watching Jean paint the outside of the new barn.

"You're doing some remodelling?" she asked as Skye approached.

He leaned against the fence and put his hands into his pocket. "There was a fire last August. It took out the whole yard."

"That must have been difficult," she said, looking up at him purposefully.

Skye raised a hand to his eyes to shield them from the sun. Deliberately changing the subject, he said, "I haven't asked you yet how long you're planning on staying?"

"Just a week," Molly answered quickly, standing up and walking over to him. "I'll be out of your hair soon."

Sensing movement behind him, Skye turned to see Dot

the donkey padding gently across the field. When he reached them, he dipped his head and nuzzled into Skye's hand. "Hey, boy," Skye whispered, "meet Molly. She's a friend of mine."

When Skye turned to Molly, she was smiling. He wasn't sure whether he meant what he said; wasn't sure they could be friends, or whether he wanted them to be, but he sensed that – for whatever reason – this was what she needed to hear.

Perhaps she'd met someone else, Skye mused as they walked back up to the ranch house. Perhaps that was why she'd come; to tell him she'd moved on, that she was getting married, and to make sure he was okay with it. When he last spoke to Tony, he'd mentioned Molly was seeing someone. He'd said it carefully, as if Skye might have had some kind of breakdown over it because Molly had been the one to end things and not him. Skye had replied, "That's good. I'm pleased for her." And he had been. He and Molly weren't right for each other. Never were. Unfortunately, they'd only really noticed it when they stopped having the Veterinary Corps in common.

Skye glanced at her ring finger. It was empty, but that didn't mean he was wrong.

Half an hour later, Skye parked his truck in one of the side streets near the village square and told Molly they'd head to the deli for takeout.

"*Signiorelli's* is the only restaurant in the village."

"Ah, I ate there yesterday," she said, "It was adorable. I'm happy to eat there again."

"It'll be closed today. The owner's…" He trailed off. Molly didn't need to know about Bea and Markus. In fact, the fewer people who knew about Markus, the better.

However, as they rounded the corner, he noticed the German guy from the ranch sitting out front. The tables were all set and the sign on the door said it was open.

"Oh, great," Molly grinned. "I had the salad yesterday but today I'm thinking pasta. Got to do proper pasta in Italy, right?"

Skye nodded at her absentmindedly. Bea was up at the ranch watching over Markus, so who was running *Signiorelli's*? He gestured for Molly to sit down and ventured inside. When he spotted Cat behind the bar, he smiled. Of course, Cat was helping out. Then the kitchen door swung open.

"I'll take his salad over to save you the embarrassment…" Amelie was laughing, wearing an apron, and holding a plate piled high with salad. When she saw him, she grinned. "Well, this is a nice surprise."

Skye rubbed at his stubbled chin. "I didn't know you'd be here," he said stiffly.

Amelie laughed and furrowed her brow. "And you're disappointed?" She was smiling, but when she realised that Skye wasn't, her smile dropped a little. When she looked past him, out to the tables, he saw her muscles stiffen.

"I told Molly I'd show her the village. I didn't think…"

Skye could feel himself starting to blush, and the air between them was quivering with awkwardness.

Finally, Amelie blinked quickly and started toward the door. "It's no problem. Sit down and I'll take your order straight after I've delivered this to Mr. Hurst."

Skye followed her outside. He wanted to snatch hold of her elbow and make her look at him so he could tell her that he'd intended to take Molly for a walk around the village – not to the same place where he and Amelie had shared their first date – but Amelie wasn't going to give him the chance.

As Skye sat down next to Molly, his insides twisting with discomfort, she stood in front of them and took a pen from behind her ear.

"So, what can I get you?" Amelie was holding a pencil, ready to write down their order.

Skye looked at Molly and noticed she'd narrowed her eyes at Amelie. Since their brief meeting when Molly first arrived, they hadn't crossed paths, but now they were face-to-face and Skye wanted the ground to swallow him whole. "Oh, hi," Molly said in her sunniest voice, "I didn't know you worked here, Emily."

"Amelie," Skye said gruffly, reaching for a menu and tapping it up and down impatiently on the table. "Her name's Amelie."

"Gosh, I'm sorry. *Amelie*. What a nice name… you work here at the café? Not on the ranch?"

"It's a temporary thing," Amelie replied, waving her

notepad in the air. "I'm just helping out while they're short staffed."

"Well, it's such a quaint little place. I just love it..." Molly was being genuine; she wasn't the kind of person who tried to make others feel bad, but Skye could sense Amelie's embarrassment humming on her skin.

Cutting in, he said curtly, "We'll have coffee and whatever pasta dish you've got today."

Amelie quickly scribbled the instruction down, then nodded at them. "Great, I'll get Cat to bring you out a jug of water too." Before Skye could catch her eyes, she was gone.

After lunch, during which Skye spent most of his time trying to catch a glance of Amelie through the large front windows, he and Molly walked down to the river. It was quiet; grey clouds were gathering and Skye was almost certain there would be a brief rain shower soon.

They stopped and leaned on the old stone wall that ran along the river bank. Skye looked down. Below the bridge, there was a shallow, rocky stretch of river where a dog was playing fetch with its owner. The dog didn't look like Dallas, but that didn't stop him from thinking of her.

"You miss the dogs?" Molly had put her hand on his forearm and was looking at him with sincerity in her eyes.

Skye pressed his lips together. "Of course." He tried to laugh. "About the only thing I do miss."

"You don't mean that." Molly nudged him in the ribs. "You've got to miss the adrenaline, the–"

"No," Skye said quickly. "I don't."

Molly had knitted her fingers together and was now watching the dog in the river too. "Well, we miss you. All of us." She paused but didn't look at him. "You know, you could come back. If you wanted to."

"I don't want to, Mol – and you not getting that is the reason we stopped talking to each other. So, if you're here to make friends, maybe–"

"Okay. Okay." Molly raised her palms at him and dipped her head to meet his eyes. "I'm sorry. I was just testing the waters." She put her hands into her back jeans pockets and shook her blonde hair from her face. "You're happy here. That's great."

Skye turned away from the river and leaned against the wall. He was clenching his jaw, so he tried to relax it. "What about you?" he said, "are you happy?"

"Oh, sure." Molly answered quickly but shrugged as she spoke. "Everything's great."

Skye was about to tell her it was okay if she needed to tell him something – that it was a good thing if she'd moved on, and that she shouldn't feel bad about it because he had too – but before he could speak, thunder rumbled across the sky and it became almost instantly darker.

"Shoot. It's going to rain?" Molly squinted up at the clouds.

"Looks like we better make a run for it."

The words had barely left Skye's mouth when the clouds cracked open and huge, heavy raindrops began to fall. At first slowly but then faster and faster.

"Run? You're on! Race you to the car!" Molly shouted, already speeding off in the direction of the piazza.

Skye paused, shook his head, then smiled. Heading after her, he yelled, "That's a dangerous challenge, O'Neal! You've never beaten me yet..."

CHAPTER NINETEEN

AMELIE

"Quick! Get the cushions in," Amelie called to Cat as the heavens opened.

Thankfully, most diners had finished their meals and the few that were left were able to pick up their drinks and hurry inside.

As rain began to pummel the umbrellas and the cobbled piazza, Amelie rushed from one chair to another, scooping up cushions and throwing them at Cat so she could pile them up inside. She was putting down the umbrellas because the wind was getting up, brushing scraggly wet hair from her eyes, when she saw Skye hurtling toward her. At first, she smiled. His curly hair was wet and sticking to his forehead. He was laughing. But he wasn't looking at her; he was looking behind him.

"You'll never outrun me, O'Neal. Never!"

As Skye tore through the piazza, not even glancing in

Amelie's direction, Molly ran after him – her long legs carrying her at lightning speed past *Signiorelli's* and around the corner.

Amelie stood with one hand resting on the umbrella she'd only half taken down. It was still raining. Water was soaking through her clothes to her skin but she couldn't move. A feeling of utter dread had settled in her stomach. When Cat rushed outside to fetch her, it was as if she could see it etched all over Amelie's face.

"You saw them?" Amelie asked, pointing in the direction Skye and Molly had run in.

"Yes," Cat shouted above the rain, "but it doesn't mean anything. They were just trying to get out of the rain."

"They were laughing. Having fun." As Amelie spoke, her voice wavered. Quietly, she added, "She knows the old Skye, Cat. She knows things about him that I never will. She's—"

"His *ex*," Cat said firmly, tugging Amelie back inside. When they entered the warmth of the café, Cat put her hands on Amelie's shoulders. "She's his past. Exes can be friends. It doesn't have to mean anything that she's here."

Amelie looked down at her feet. She was standing on the welcome mat, dripping wet and starting to shiver. As Cat fetched her a tea towel to dry her hair with, she tried to think logically about the situation. She and Skye had been on a wonderful date. He'd been about to tell her something – she was sure of it – and they'd spent months liking each other. Plus, he hadn't said or done anything to make her think that he still had feelings for Molly.

"Let's invite her to dinner," Cat said, folding her arms in front of her chest.

"What?" Amelie was resting on a nearby table, still squeezing moisture from her hair.

"The best way to get the measure of this woman is to spend some time with her. So, let's invite her up to the house for a nice Goodwin family dinner."

There was a glint in Cat's eyes that made Amelie smile. "You wouldn't be planning to intimidate the poor girl, would you?"

Cat furrowed her brow and shook her head solemnly. "Of course not. Amelie Goodwin, I'm shocked you'd even suggest such a thing. I simply want to welcome her to the ranch." She untucked her arms and waved her hand in the air. "And maybe do some digging to find out what her motives are… but I'll be subtle, I promise."

As Amelie took out her phone to text Skye, before she had a chance to change her mind, she smiled to herself. The feeling in her stomach was still there, but Cat was right; what was that old saying? Keep your friends close and your enemies closer.

"It's okay," Bea reached for Amelie's apron and folded it neatly over her arm. "Nonna's with Markus."

Amelie glanced at Cat, who raised her eyebrows. Both

girls giggled. "Well, in that case, we know he's not a flight risk. No one can get past Nonna."

"Precisely." Bea clapped her hands together and tried to relax her shoulders. Smiling, as if she was trying to convince herself she was pleased to be at work, she lowered her voice and said, "I need to keep busy and keep up appearances. If Markus' step-father comes here looking for him, it will seem strange if I'm…" She wafted her hand in the air, searching for the English word.

"AWOL?" Cat added.

Bea grimaced. "Yes."

For a while, as she and Cat had worked side by side, serving customers who were hiding from the afternoon deluge outside, and planning what they could cook to knock Skye's socks off that evening, Amelie had forgotten *why* they were at the café. But suddenly, the gravity of Markus' situation had descended like a dark cloud.

"Did you speak to his step-father?" Cat asked, taking off her apron and placing it on the bar.

Bea shook her head. "I thought it was best to wait until he contacted me. If I start snooping, he will wonder why." When Cat frowned, Bea added, "Markus and I aren't in regular contact. There's no way I'd know he was missing unless I'd seen him."

At that, Cat nodded slowly. She and Skye were clearly still very uncomfortable with the idea of Markus hanging around the ranch but Amelie knew that both her parents *and*

Alec Anderson would want to help Bea and Markus, even if it was risky for them.

"All right, we'll head off." Amelie stepped in front of Cat and kissed Bea once on each cheek. "Please call if you need anything."

Bea nodded and cupped Amelie's face in her hands. "I will. Thank you."

Outside, as they headed for Cat's car, Amelie sighed.

"What is it?" Cat had looped her arm through Amelie's but now pulled away slightly.

Looking sideways at her sister, Amelie bit back a second sigh. "It's obvious you don't want Markus on the ranch."

"Do you blame me?" Cat widened her eyes. "He's an escaped felon. He has a very sad story but what if it's just that? A *story*."

"I trust Bea." Amelie could feel her cheeks starting to flush with indignation.

"So do I…" Cat exhaled loudly then softened her voice. "Amelie, I love Bea just as much as you do, but it's not just us and the ranch I'm concerned for – I don't want her to get into trouble."

"We have to let her handle it," Amelie said as they reached the car and Cat slid into the driver's seat.

"Yes," Cat said, gripping the steering wheel, "but she's not, is she? Yesterday she said she'd find out what was going on, but now she's saying she needs to wait for Markus' step-father to contact her."

Amelie bit her lower lip. Cat always said what she thought, a personality trait that made her a wonderful person to be around – because you always knew precisely where you stood – but also a difficult person to know – because she didn't much care for sparing peoples' feelings or treading softly.

"We'll give her a bit more time," Cat said as she started the engine. "Not too much time, though."

Amelie nodded and breathed in a long slow breath. "Okay," she said. "Okay. But for tonight, can we just worry about the fact I've invited Skye and his *ex-girlfriend* to dinner?"

Cat stifled a laugh and flicked on the radio. "It'll be fine," she said merrily, "totally fine."

CHAPTER TWENTY

AMELIE

A FEW HOURS LATER, as Amelie was having heart palpitations in the corner of the kitchen, Cat welcomed Skye and Molly into the room as if she was a waitress at a five-star restaurant.

"Good evening. So lovely to see you both."

Amelie looked over and caught Skye giving Cat a quizzical frown, but turned back to the risotto she'd foolishly decided to make before he could notice her staring.

"Cat, you've already met Molly."

Amelie's shoulders tensed. Was there a note of pride in his voice as he said Molly's name? No, she was imagining it. *Stop being ridiculous, Amelie.*

"I have, but I'm looking forward to getting to know her a bit better."

Cat had turned on the charm, and in that moment Amelie was so incredibly grateful to her sister that she found herself thinking she'd do pretty much anything Cat asked her to do for the rest of their lives.

"Amelie?"

Okay, maybe not. As Cat waved her over, Amelie hid her shaky hands in her apron. "Hi, you two," she said, completely unsure whether to greet Skye with a kiss on the cheek or a hand shake.

"Thanks so much for inviting me to dinner." Molly was beaming at her, all pearly white teeth and big lips and long-lashed eyes. "It's so kind of you."

"Honestly, it's our pleasure. Any friend of Skye's..." Amelie caught herself emphasising the word *friend* and stepping a little closer to Skye. Touching him lightly on the arm, she offered him her best smile and asked, "Wine? Beer?"

"Beer would be great." Skye followed her to the fridge while Cat took Molly's jacket and ushered her over to the table. "You know," he said, leaning in as Amelie handed him a bottle. "You *really* didn't have to do this."

Amelie tilted her head from side to side. Looking at Skye was calming the nerves in her stomach. His face was the same. Exactly the same, and when he stroked his fingers against hers, she had to fight the urge to throw her arms around his neck and kiss him right there in the middle of the kitchen.

"I wanted to," she said quietly. "Molly's your guest."

"She's just a friend, Amelie." Skye dipped his head to catch her eyes and slipped his non-beer-holding hand around her waist.

Amelie was staring up at him, allowing herself to swim in his sparkling green eyes, when she felt her nose wrinkle. "Can you smell that?"

"Amelie, I think the risotto—" Cat had gotten up from the table and was rushing to the stove.

"No!" Amelie hurried over and took the lid off the pan. "It was supposed to be simmering," she said, examining the heat setting while she nudged burned, dried-out rice around the pan. "I left the heat up too high."

"No problem, we'll just start again." Skye took the pan from her and started to scrape its contents into the bin but Amelie threw up her hands.

"That was the last of the arborio rice. I only bought one packet."

"We could do take-out?" At the table, Molly was holding a glass of white wine in her hand. "Is there a pizza place nearby?"

Cat winced sympathetically. "They don't really do take-out around here. The nearest is *Sant' Anna*, but we'd have to drive there to collect it—"

"It's okay, I'll rustle something up." Skye strode purposefully to the fridge and gestured for Amelie, Cat and Molly to sit back down. "You girls relax, I've got this."

As they sat down, Cat poured Amelie a glass then topped up Molly's and her own. "Well," Cat said loudly, tilting her glass at the other two, "here's to letting the bloke do the work while the ladies sit and enjoy the view."

Amelie almost choked on her drink as Cat began eyebrow-wiggling at Skye.

On the opposite side of the table, Molly laughed but kept her eyes carefully trained on her wine glass.

By the time Ben arrived, freshly showered after a full afternoon helping Jean with the new barn, Skye had concocted an incredible pasta dish using nothing but the sparse contents of the fridge. Amelie had suggested he raid Nonna's kitchen, but he'd looked terrified at the mere thought of it and had powered on with just tomatoes, mozzarella, parmesan, and herbs from the garden.

"Smells great." Ben sauntered in but frowned when he saw Skye stirring the pasta. "I thought Amelie was cooking?"

"I was," she said, guiltily. "But I burned it. Skye rescued us."

Glancing at Molly, Ben slid into the seat beside her and extended his hand. "We haven't really met properly, I'm Ben."

"Pleased to meet you, Ben." Molly smiled widely at him and Amelie caught her fluttering her eyelashes. Ben didn't seem to notice.

"Are we calling Ethan?" He gestured to the iPad on the countertop near Skye.

"Probably best let him sleep. He did a video consult for

Markus earlier and he's back on shift tomorrow morning," Skye said from by the cooker.

Amelie noticed Molly frowning as she tried to decipher who Ethan and Markus were, and couldn't help wishing Skye had kept Markus' name out of the conversation. She was about to move the conversation on when the reception bell rang and Cat groaned loudly.

"How is it possible that someone needs something? We're all here."

"I'll go." Amelie stood up and waved for Cat to stay seated. "Be right back."

Ducking into the entrance hall, she instantly recognised the figure standing beside the reception desk.

"Mr. Hurst," she said as she walked slowly over to him. "Is everything okay?"

"Not really. I was expecting dinner," he said curtly, tapping his watch as if to indicate that his food was unacceptably late.

"Oh, were you? I'm so sorry." It wasn't like Nonna to forget a guest but she was probably preoccupied with keeping an eye on the fugitive in Cabin Ten. Amelie glanced back at the kitchen. Cat would kill her... "Mr. Hurst, I'm afraid our chef is indisposed, but we're about to eat ourselves. Why don't you join us?"

Stefan shuffled uncomfortably. He was skinny, bearded and pale, but had oddly attractive eyes. "I'm not sure—"

"Come on," Amelie began to head back to the others and gestured for him to follow her. "We're very friendly. We won't bite." But when she entered the kitchen with Stefan in tow, Cat looked at Stefan like she wanted to do precisely that – bite him on the ankles and send him running back to his cabin.

Cat widened her eyes at Amelie.

"Mr. Hurst was expecting dinner. There must have been a mix up. I said he could eat with us." Amelie gestured to the chair that was usually reserved for Ethan's iPad head.

Cat looked exasperated. "A mix up? I tried to knock yesterday to ask about—" She stopped when Amelie offered a brief shake of the head.

"The more the merrier," Skye said loudly. "There's plenty." He smiled at Amelie as he put a huge bowl of steaming pasta down in the centre of the table. "Now, Mr. Hurst. What are you drinking? Wine or beer?"

CHAPTER TWENTY-ONE

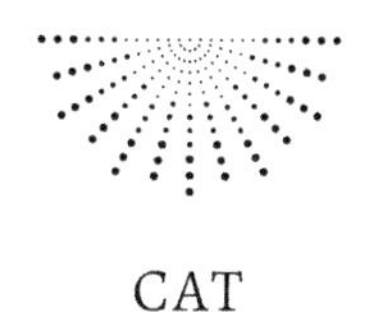

CAT

STEFAN LOOKED like a mole that had come out of its hole and was shocked to discover too-bright lights and too much noise. Blinking at Skye, eventually he said he'd like a beer, please. When it arrived, he sipped nervously at it like he'd never been offered one before.

Cat's entire body prickled with irritation. She'd gone to Stefan Hurst's cabin to ask him about meal arrangements and he'd ignored her, he hadn't mentioned anything about dinner when she saw him at *Signiorelli's,* and now he'd turned up looking bereft – as if she'd purposefully tried to starve him to death.

While Cat spooned pasta onto her plate and tried to stop simmering, Stefan sat down opposite her and smiled meekly. She smiled back, but hoped he didn't think she was pleased to see him.

Breaking through the silence, in her sunny Texan accent,

Molly said loudly, "I thought you guys were closed to guests?"

"Stefan had a bit of a mix up with his taxi. He was supposed to go to a ranch further north but the driver misunderstood and brought him here." Skye had sat down at the head of the table, and was holding his beer bottle with both hands.

"That's right,' Stefan said stiffly. "However, I liked it here, so I decided to stay."

After a slightly awkward pause, in which Stefan failed to elaborate or say anything that might initiate a real conversation, Ben lifted his wine glass and said, "Well, I think I should propose a toast… to new friends," he tipped his glass toward Stefan, "old friends," he looked at Molly, "and the chance to get to know each other a bit better."

As everyone else clinked glasses then dove into their meals, Cat watched Stefan. He had a strange look on his face. Sadness? Nostalgia? She couldn't quite work it out.

"Stefan, where are you from?" Molly smiled sweetly at him. She was eating quickly, as if her food was about to be snatched away from her.

"Germany," Stefan replied. "Frankfurt."

"Oh, I'd love to visit Germany. We travelled through once, didn't we Skye? Didn't have chance to see the scenery though." She looked at Skye for confirmation and he nodded.

"What is it you do there, Stefan?" he asked casually.

Stefan paused with his food half-way to his mouth and

cleared his throat. "I'm a writer." He almost sounded embarrassed.

"Really?" Amelie's interest had been piqued and she was sitting a little straighter in her chair. "What do you write?"

"Literary tomes that hardly anyone reads," Stefan replied.

Amelie laughed, but Stefan's voice had been so monotone that it was hard to tell whether he was making fun of himself or simply being factual in his answer.

"They are yet to be translated into English," he continued, returning to his food as if that was the end of the conversation.

Amelie opened her mouth, probably about to mention her publishing career back in London, or the fact she was trying to write her own novel, but then she closed it again and took a large sip of wine instead.

Cat was aware that she'd been the one to suggest getting everyone together but she was beginning to regret it. What had started as an opportunity to get the measure of Molly had turned into something else – something a little uncomfortable.

"What about you, Molly? You're still in the Veterinary Corps?" Amelie was watching Molly closely as she spoke, so probably didn't notice the way Skye's eyes darkened or the tightening of the muscles in his forearms.

"That's right." Molly cast a furtive glance at Skye. "After what happened, our old unit was disbanded, but I'm with a new unit now."

Amelie blinked quickly. In an instant, Cat could see from

her expression that she had no idea *what happened* and that it was a sore point between her and Skye.

"And you're on leave?" Cat interrupted, saving Amelie from having to think of something to say.

"Mmm hmm." Molly was looking down at her plate, nudging her pasta with her fork. "I had a few weeks to take, and I've always wanted to see Italy, so…"

"A few weeks? That's generous." Cat looked at Skye, half expecting him to say he didn't believe Molly's story.

Curtly, he said, "Very, and I should have mentioned that we're reopening to guests soon…" He trailed off, his hint that Molly shouldn't stick around too long hung awkwardly in the air.

"Oh, sure, of course. I'll be gone soon, I promise." Molly folded her arms in front of her chest and smiled again, but this smile was different – nervous and a little disappointed.

"Speaking of reopening…" Ben placed his hands palm-down on the table and looked at Cat, Amelie, and Skye in turn. "I've been thinking—"

"Uh oh," Amelie laughed.

"I've been thinking…" he repeated, slower this time, "it's Mum and Dad's anniversary soon. After everything that happened last year, maybe we should throw them a party? A surprise? Celebrate them coming home, the new barn, the Goodwin-Anderson partnership being born?"

At the thought of a party, Cat's heart began to flutter.

"Great idea." Skye nodded enthusiastically.

"Really great," Cat added, raising her right eyebrow. "Which is surprising for you, little brother."

Ben ignored her and took out his phone, opening up a list he'd already started making. "We could hold it in the new barn before we move the horses up to the stables. Invite people from the village. Get some music going, some food..."

"We could ask Ethan!" Amelie had picked up her phone and was waving it, ready to text their brother. "See if he can make it back. Mum and Dad would be thrilled."

"So, that's a 'yes'?" Ben waited expectantly for the girls to answer.

"As long as your dad will be okay with it?" Amelie asked, slipping her hand into Skye's.

"Dad? He can't say no to a party."

"Well, then," Cat said, sitting back and folding her arms. "It looks like we've got a party to plan."

As the others started chattering about who to invite and where to source a good but not too expensive band, Cat breathed in deeply. Their parents were due to return from holiday in three weeks, which meant they had three weeks to get the ranch ship-shape. Three weeks to get Ethan back to Italy. And three weeks to get rid of their unwanted guests. Molly had promised she'd be gone by then and Stefan had only asked to stay for a fortnight, so they shouldn't be a problem. But Markus? Cat shuddered as she thought of his beaten-up frame hobbling down toward Cabin Ten. Surely, Markus would be gone by then too? One way or another.

Excusing herself from the table, Cat stood up and went over to the coffee machine. Flicking it on, she briefly wondered whether Aida might want to come to the party. Then she almost kicked herself for thinking it; she hadn't even met Aida yet and bringing her birth mother to her parents' anniversary party probably wasn't her smartest idea.

"You okay?" Ben had followed her and was leaning back against the counter.

"Fine."

"Worried about telling Mum and Dad that you're meeting Aida?"

Cat twitched her lips from side to side. "A bit. Especially if we're having a party. I don't want to ruin the mood when they get back."

"So, tell them now." Ben gestured to Cat's phone, which was sitting on the counter next to the coffee machine. "Just text them. Get it over with. It'll give them time to absorb it and it'll give you time to focus on Aida." Ben squeezed Cat's arm and smiled at her. "They'll be fine with it, Kit-Cat."

"I just don't want to rock the boat when they're finally happy."

Ben pulled her in for a hug but, as he did, he pressed her phone into her hand. "Do it," he whispered. "It'll be *fine*."

CHAPTER TWENTY-TWO

SKYE

ONE WEEK LATER

"Mister Anderson?"

Skye brushed his hair from his eyes and turned around to see Markus walking toward him. Skinny, still covered in bruises, and with a constantly alarmed look on his face, he seemed far younger than his seventeen years.

Over the past week, he'd grown slowly stronger and, last night, Skye had told Bea that if Markus wanted to make himself useful while he was staying with them, he could help out at the stables.

In clumsy English, Markus said, "My aunt says you would like some help? With the horses?"

Next to Skye, Rupert puffed air from his nostrils and shook his fringe. Skye patted his neck. "If you're up to it?"

"Yes, thank you. I am much better."

Skye gestured to a broom. "You can sweep out the stalls," he said, pointing out a horseless one nearby. "But take it easy, yeah?"

Markus picked up the broom. Skye watched him closely. His ribs must still be sore but he wasn't showing it. Markus nodded at him, then walked over to the stall and began to quietly sweep it.

An hour later, Skye gave Markus a bottle of water and told him to take a break. "You've barely been out of bed for a week. You shouldn't overdo it."

Markus took a long swig from the bottle then wiped his mouth with the back of his hand.

"You're feeling all right?" Skye noticed he was speaking loudly, as if their communication problem was because Markus was hard of hearing rather than because they didn't speak the same language.

"All right," he replied. "Yes, thank you for your help." Markus walked over to a nearby cluster of trees and leaned against one. He was picking at the label on his water bottle.

Skye sighed and followed him; the kid looked completely downtrodden. Forlorn. Lost. "Listen, Markus..." He paused then rolled his eyes at himself. This wasn't going to work; his Italian was pretty weak and Markus' English didn't seem much better. Taking out his phone, Skye opened up his translation app and typed:

Can you tell me what happened at the prison?

He hit the translate button and handed the phone to Markus. Insanely quickly, Markus typed a reply.

My aunt told you why I went to the prison, I think?

He showed Skye the phone and Skye nodded. Then he continued:

I was going to a job interview. They released me for the day. Some other offenders at the prison disliked me because they found out my step-father was a policeman. They told some people they knew that I was going out for the day, and where to find me. The older men attacked me at the train station. Beat me. I woke up late. It was dark. I had missed my interview and my curfew to get back to the institution. I was scared about what they would do to me, so I got on a train. I travelled all night to find Aunt Bea. And now I am here. And I am stuck.

Skye watched Markus' face as the teenager typed his lengthy explanation. When Skye read it, Markus didn't watch him in return. Reaching the end, Skye exhaled slowly and sat up, pushing his fingers through his hair.

Has Bea spoken to your step-father?

Skye knew the answer; Bea told him three days ago that Antonio had finally called asking about Markus. She'd missed it because she'd been working but Antonio had left a very angry voicemail and Bea had been too scared to call him back since then.

I don't think so. He is not an easy man to talk to.

Skye shook his head. His jaw was twitching. Whatever had happened, Antonio's job was to be on Markus' side. To help him. Not to throw him to the wolves.

We will figure something out. Skye patted Markus'

shoulder as he showed him the translation. When Markus met his eyes, he nodded solemnly. "We will figure something out," Skye repeated.

For a moment, Skye thought Markus was going to smile. But he didn't. He looked utterly broken. As if someone had sucked all the joy and good feelings from his body and left him completely empty. Reaching for the phone, he wrote:

I hope we will, but I am afraid of what will happen if we don't.

Skye deposited Markus back at Cabin Ten and went straight to the ranch house to find Nonna. She'd promised him a cooking lesson and, even though he knew he should shower first, he was eager to get on with it.

When he knocked on the door of Nonna's kitchen, she grinned at him and folded her arms across her plump chest. "You are late." She tapped her watch.

"Only two minutes," Skye said, offering her a cheeky smile.

"Late is late," she said, still pretending to be angry with him. "And you have not changed from the horses." She wafted her hands as if he smelled terrible. "You cannot cook like this. Go…" She wafted him again. "Go, go."

Skye was laughing and heading back toward the entrance hall when Nonna added, "Wait. Drink this first. You've been working hard."

When he turned around, she was offering him a fresh glass of iced tea. "It must be warming up outside if you've broken out the iced tea," Skye said, closing his eyes as he took a sip.

"The sun is shining," Nonna said brightly, gesturing to the light that was streaming in through her kitchen windows. After a pause, she added, frowning, "Did I see you with the boy a short while ago? Markus?"

Skye bristled at the mention of Markus' name, and was almost tempted to ask Nonna to keep her voice down. "Yes," he said, biting his lower lip as he thought of what Markus had said to him. "He's not in a good place. Honestly, I don't know how we're going to get him out of the mess he's in."

Nonna put her hands on her hips. She was nodding and had sucked in her cheeks. "Is it our job to do that?" When Skye didn't reply, she softened a little and said, "I love the Goodwins. I will do anything for them, and Bea is an old friend. Her nephew… he seems like a good child. But—"

"But what if him being here gets the ranch into trouble?" Skye met Nonna's eyes and she blinked slowly at him.

"Precisely. Rose and Thomas had a terrible year last year. Things are good now. If we're caught hiding a runaway, what will that mean for them?"

Nonna was right. Skye knew she was, and he knew Cat felt the same way. Amelie, however, did not. As far as Amelie was concerned, it was easy; if the police came knocking, their story was that Bea had asked if her nephew could stay a while and do chores for some pocket money. No one would be able to prove they knew Markus was a fugitive.

Ben seemed to agree. But Skye wasn't sure what he felt about it. Part of him wanted to protect the ranch, his father, and the Goodwins, but he felt a powerful urge to protect the kid too. After today, that feeling was even stronger.

Putting his hand firmly on Nonna's arm, Skye said, "We'll stick to the story. It'll be fine."

Nonna pursed her lips. "Okay." She held up her hands. "I'll do what you say. You can trust me."

"I know we can." Skye bent down and kissed her on the cheek, even though he knew she'd bat him away because he smelled of horses and hay.

"Get away," she laughed.

"I'll shower and be back for that lesson. Fifteen minutes?"

"Don't be late. Oh, and Skye?"

"Ah ha?"

"Amelie asked me to tell you she's taking Molly for a trek in the woods."

"A trek? Amelie is taking *Molly* on a trek? When?"

Nonna looked at her watch. "Now."

As he headed back to his cabin, Skye's stomach twitched nervously. For the past week, he'd managed to keep Molly and Amelie apart. Molly had seemed happy to borrow the truck and go sightseeing on her own while Skye worked, and in the evenings she'd kept herself to herself. Skye had even begun to feel like she might be telling the truth; like maybe she really was in Italy for a holiday and nothing more.

But his current girlfriend going out for some one-on-one time with his ex-girlfriend… that was never going to be a good idea.

He paused at the door of the cabin and looked back toward the ranch house. Nonna would be cross with him for not going back but if he ran he could probably catch up with Amelie before they left…

CHAPTER TWENTY-THREE

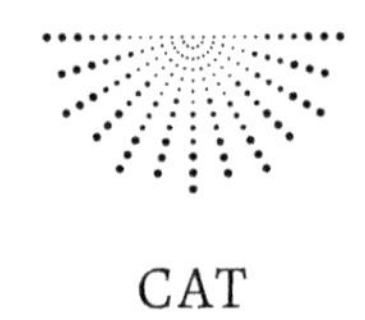

CAT

Cat was pacing up and down on the porch, half contemplating taking up smoking because it would have given her something to do with her hands, when she saw Skye stop outside his cabin, turn around, and jog in the direction of the stables.

Forgetting her nerves for a moment, she smiled. Molly had arrived at the ranch house a few hours ago, asking whether Ben might take her out on a ride but – probably because she was worried that Ben would succumb to Molly's charm at some point, and that it would prove horribly awkward for all concerned – Amelie had offered to take her instead.

Immediately, Cat had frowned at her; surely, she didn't want to spend the afternoon alone in the hills with Skye's ex-girlfriend? Amelie, however, had carried on smiling and insisted that it was fine – she'd like to.

As she and Molly headed off to change into suitable riding gear, Cat had briefly wondered what on earth Skye would say about it. Almost as soon as the thought occurred, it flittered away and was replaced by another: *Aida*.

Thoughts of her birth mother had been plaguing her for days. Late last night, unable to sleep, she'd finally gotten up and made a list of all the questions she wanted to ask. Now, as Skye disappeared from sight, she took the list from her pocket.

As she read through her scruffily scrawled bullet points, she fiddled with the earring in her left ear. Yellow. Like she'd promised.

"Can a kangaroo jump higher than a house?"

Cat looked up, surprised to hear someone else's voice and convinced she'd misheard what they'd said.

Stefan Hurst was standing in front of the railings, looking up at her, hands in his pockets.

"I'm sorry?" she asked, stuffing the list quickly back into her jeans.

Stefan's beard twitched. Was he smiling? "I asked – can a kangaroo jump higher than a house?"

"I…" Cat tucked her hair behind her ear. "I have no idea."

"But of course, it can. Because a house can't jump." For a moment, Stefan didn't move, then he began to chuckle.

"Wait…" Cat laughed. "Was that a joke?"

"Perhaps the translation wasn't correct." Stefan rubbed his beard. "It sounds funnier in German."

"No, no. It was funny," she said, "Very funny."

Stefan tilted his head at her then laughed at himself. "Well," he said. "It was the best I could do under such pressure."

"Pressure?"

"For a week, I have been trying to think of a way to prove to you that I am not… what were your words? *Obnoxious, rude, and humourless.* Which is quite a task, Miss Goodwin."

Cat's cheeks flushed and she stopped smiling. At the same time, both of them moved toward the steps. Cat waited for Stefan to reach the porch before saying, "Mr. Hurst, sincerely, I owe you an apology. I'm very sorry for what I said at *Signiorelli's* last week and for not being more welcoming when you joined us for dinner. There's no excuse for my behaviour. Things have just been a little hectic lately."

Stefan shrugged. Since the night he joined them for dinner, Cat had seen only fleeting glimpses of him around the ranch but today, for the first time, he seemed a little lighter than he had when he first arrived.

As Cat gestured to the porch swing and they sat down next to one another, Stefan said, "Please do not apologise, Miss Goodwin. You were quite right when you accused me of being rude."

Cat waited for Stefan to offer an explanation for his grumpiness. When he didn't, she said, "Well, maybe we should start over?"

Stefan nodded but didn't look in her direction. "Yes, maybe we should."

As she studied Stefan's slim frame and piercingly blue eyes, Cat noticed some of the tension in her chest start to dissipate. In three hours, she'd be in *Sant' Anna*, waiting for Aida. Picturing it had occupied her every waking moment that morning, but now she was at least thinking of something else for a few minutes.

After a moment's silence, Stefan braced his hands on his knees and stood up. "I am walking to *Legrezzia,*" he said. "I will see you later."

Cat stood up too and nodded. Before she could stop herself, she replied, "I'll be driving to *Sant' Anna* in about an hour. If you wanted to see somewhere new, you're welcome to come with me?"

Stefan glanced at the ranch gates. He looked as if he was thinking very hard about her suggestion. Cat was about to retract it because, really, why on earth would she want a stranger to accompany her on such a journey when she'd already told her family not to come? But then Stefan said, "Yes. Thank you. I would appreciate that," and it was too late to change her mind.

An hour later, as she'd suggested, Stefan met her back at the gates and climbed into the passenger seat of her parents' truck. Cat was used to driving smaller vehicles but straightened her shoulders, took a deep breath, and set off down the winding road that led away from the ranch.

Sant' Anna was an hour's drive away. For the first forty minutes, as trees and hills rolled past them and the sun shone brightly, she chattered non-stop. While Stefan listened quietly, she told him about local churches and the best places to eat, regaling him with every nugget of information she could think of.

But as she ran out of sight-seeing tips, and settled into silence, she began to sigh every few moments; trying to release the clots of air that kept lodging themselves in her chest. Eventually, Stefan looked at her. "Is everything all right, Miss Goodwin?"

Cat tried to smile but it wavered. The nerves in her throat turned into a swarm of dizziness, which quickly became nausea. "I'm sorry," she said, "I have to pull over."

She had barely stopped at the side of the road and flung open her door when she vomited. She was still hanging out of the truck when she felt a hand on her shoulder and saw that Stefan was offering her a bottle of water.

"Did you eat something bad?" he asked when she finally sat back in her seat.

Cat shook her head and wiped her mouth with the back of her hand.

Stefan handed her a tube of mints that he'd taken from his pocket, and the sight of them almost made her cry.

"It's nerves. I think." She took another sip of water then popped the mint into her mouth and crunched it to release the freshness.

Stefan didn't ask what she was nervous about. Instead, he

took his phone from his pocket and plugged it into the holder on the dash. "Close your eyes," he said.

Cat blinked at him, but he didn't reply, just waved his hand at her and began to scroll through his music collection. When he found the song he'd been looking for, he pressed play, turned up the volume, sat back, and closed his eyes.

For a long moment, Cat didn't move. It was almost the opposite of what she'd have expected him to play – a joyous, gospel track that felt almost like the blues music her dad used to listen to. A woman was singing loudly and there was a trill in her voice that sent a shiver down Cat's spine. She closed her eyes. There was nothing but a piano in the background but as the song reached its crescendo, a chorus of voices joined in, clapping, singing in harmony.

She had no idea how long the music played for. When the song eventually ended, she realised that she felt calm.

Without saying a word, Stefan turned off his phone and slipped it back into his pocket.

"Thank you," she whispered.

Stefan tilted his head from side to side as if to say *it was nothing*, then asked, "Are you going to be all right with the driving?"

Cat breathed in slowly. "Yes, I'll be fine." Then she started the engine and pulled back onto the road. "We're nearly there."

At the fountain in the centre of the piazza, Cat said goodbye to Stefan and watched him walk towards an antique bookshop nearby. He hadn't asked her what she was doing in town but had given her his number so she could let him know when she was finished.

She adjusted her bag on her shoulder and looked through the crowd. It was mid-morning, so most of the footfall from the market had died down and been replaced by people casually shopping or meeting friends for lunch.

Cat had no idea which direction Aida would be coming from, only that she'd be wearing yellow, which had made Cat smile; yellow was her favourite colour and, although she'd put on a cobalt blue jumper, she had added her sunshine yellow earrings as a finishing touch.

Adjusting the earring in her right ear, she breathed in slowly. Her nerves were returning. Her skin felt tight and hot, and she was worried that by the time Aida arrived she'd be in such a state that she'd be unable to speak to her.

Then, across the piazza, a figure emerged beside a large oak tree. It had come from the path beside the river; a woman dressed in a bright yellow dress and a long green coat.

Cat stood up. Her legs were trembling. She waved, and the woman waved back. She had dark hair. Dark like Cat's. As she drew closer, Cat looked away because she knew that as soon as she saw Aida's face, the tsunami of emotions building inside her would overflow and turn to tears.

"Catherine?"

Cat breathed a long, shallow breath, and raised her eyes.

The woman in front of her was smiling but her face was pale. As she extended her hand, Cat noticed it was shaking. “I’m Aida,” she said softly.

Cat looked at Aida’s hand. Her nails were painted emerald green, the same colour as her coat. “Aida…” she whispered. “I’m so happy to meet you.”

CHAPTER TWENTY-FOUR

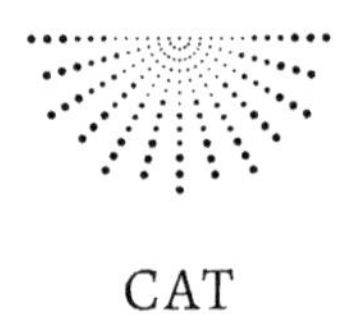

CAT

"Shall we find a café? Or would you prefer a walk?" Aida pulled her coat a little closer and looked around at the cafés and bars lining the piazza.

"Well, I could certainly use a glass of wine." Cat spoke without thinking. When she looked at Aida, she was smiling.

"Me too."

"The bar with the blue shutters is lovely, shall we try there?"

Aida nodded politely and adjusted her bag on her shoulder. Cat had never been told how old her mother was when she gave her up. Looking at Aida now, she couldn't imagine she was any older than in her late forties. Mentally, Cat added that to her list of questions.

When they were settled at a table in the corner of the bar, Aida shrugged off her coat while Cat asked the waiter for two glasses of red wine.

"You are right," Aida said, "it is lovely in here." She was looking up at the ceiling, at the fake foliage that hung down and made it feel like they were outside even though they were inside. Sunlight was filtering through the shuttered windows, and the gentle hum of the other customers – chattering, eating, drinking – relaxed the tension in Cat's muscles, just a little.

"Thank you for coming all this way." Cat said, seconds before the waiter returned with their glasses.

Aida accepted hers and placed it down gently in front of her, instantly starting to twirl the stem between her fingers. "Thank *you* for wanting me to." She smiled then raised her glass. "A toast, I think?"

Cat mirrored her gesture. "A toast to…"

"To second chances?"

"Yes. Second chances. *Salute*."

As they clinked glasses, Cat felt a warmth settle in her belly. Her nerves were melting away, and she hadn't even tasted her wine yet. There was something about Aida, her aura, her face. It was… comforting.

"So, Catherine, you said you are not working today. What do you do?"

Cat tucked her hair behind her ear so she could fiddle with her earring. "Well, until last year I managed a gelato store in town." She gestured toward the piazza. "Not far from here."

"I think I would get very fat if I worked in a gelato store," Aida laughed, patting her stomach.

Cat laughed. “It was certainly a challenge not to try every new flavour that came in the door…” She stopped and cleared her throat. “But my ex-boyfriend owned the store. When we broke up, I quit and moved back home to the ranch to help Mum and Dad. I work on reception now and, actually, I quite like it.” She smiled softly, trying not to feel awkward that she’d said *Mum and Dad.*

Thankfully, Aida didn’t flinch at the mention of them but she did say, “A ranch? Your parents have a ranch?”

“You didn’t know?” Cat asked, nibbling her lower lip.

Aida shook her head slowly. “I wasn’t told any details about the couple who adopted you. Except that they had wanted children for a long time and they were British but living in Italy.” She laughed and, though she’d been speaking in Italian up to now, added in English, “That is why I took night classes to learn English. Just in case…”

Cat began to blush. Sticking to Italian, she said, “You speak it very well.”

“Thank you.” Aida paused, taking another sip from her wine glass. “You must have many questions.”

Cat nodded. “Yes, but we don’t have to talk about them today.”

Aida smiled, almost instantly brightening. “All right. For now, then, tell me everything. I want to know all about you. Start from the beginning. School plays. Boyfriends. College.”

“Oh, I’m not sure you want to go down the boyfriends route. We’ll be here until next week if we have that conversation.”

"Then we'll just have to meet again next week, won't we?" Aida settled back into her chair as if she was waiting for Cat to begin her story.

"Okay... school plays." Cat frowned and began to laugh. "Actually, me and Amelie – my sister, she's adopted too – I remember we were in this awful production of *Romeo and Juliet*. I was ten, so she must have been about seven and *why* the school thought doing Shakespeare at that age was a good idea, I'll never know..." Cat paused, Aida's eyes had misted over and she was wiping them with a napkin she'd picked up from the table. "Sorry, shall I stop?"

Aida closed her eyes and shook her head. When she opened them, she said, "No. Please don't. But I'd love to see a picture of your sister if you have one..."

"Of course." Cat reached for her phone, swiped to a selfie she and Amelie had taken at Christmas, wearing silly paper hats and huge grins. "We look nothing alike, obviously."

As Aida looked at the picture, she touched it gently with her index finger. "Oh, but you do," she said. "You have the same sunny smile. I'd like to meet her one day."

Cat took the phone back and put it down in front of her. She felt like she might explode with a mixture of happiness and relief. "I'd like that too," she said.

"So, this play?"

"Well, we were doing this production of *Romeo and Juliet*, and I got the part of Juliet. Amelie was furious..."

Cat and Aida had been talking for almost two hours when Cat glanced at her phone for the time.

Aida noticed her and stopped talking, helping herself to some more of the antipasti they'd ordered because they'd both been too nervous to eat that morning and felt ravenous as soon as they sat down.

"Sorry," Cat said. "I can't believe how long we've been talking."

"Do you have to get back?"

Cat tilted her head from side to side. She didn't want to. She *really* didn't want to, but she and Amelie had been helping out at *Signiorelli's* in the evenings and she didn't want to leave her sister short-handed. "I've been helping a friend in her café. I don't have to be there until six but…"

Aida looked at the clock on the wall behind the bar. "Oh, well, then yes you must go." She tapped her wrist as if it displayed a watch, even though it was bare. "Besides, there is a bus soon that I probably should catch."

Suddenly, after spending the last couple of hours feeling as if she never wanted the afternoon to end, a sense of trepidation gripped Cat's chest. She inhaled slowly to try and dislodge it. "Okay," she said quietly. "And do you… I mean, shall we…?" She trailed off and reached for her glass, even though she'd switched to mineral water over an hour ago.

Aida took in Cat's expression then leaned forward and reached for her hand. Squeezing it, she said, "Yes, definitely. We could meet again next week?"

Cat couldn't help grinning. "Next week. Perfect."

"Let me get this," Aida said, waving to the waiter.

"No, no, really–" Cat put her hand into her bag but Aida shook her head at her.

"Catherine," she said gently. "I have missed many, many birthdays. I can treat you. Please, let me treat you."

Letting go of her purse and sliding her bag into her lap, Cat smiled. "All right," she said. "Thank you."

At the fountain, in the crisp late-afternoon air, Cat stood awkwardly with her hands in her pockets. When they first met, they shook hands. Now, she wasn't sure what to do. Aida, however, barely hesitated before pulling her into an embrace. Squeezing her tightly, she whispered, "I feel so lucky, Catherine. *Thank you* for replying to my letter."

"Thank you for writing it," Cat whispered.

Eventually, after several long moments, they pulled apart and Aida buttoned up her emerald green coat. "Are you heading in my direction?" she asked, gesturing toward the bus station.

"I gave one of our guests a ride into town. I should try to find him," Cat replied, taking out her phone to text Stefan.

"All right." Aida started to walk away. "Until next week."

"Until next week."

Cat watched Aida until she disappeared around a corner at the far end of the square. Eventually, she tore her eyes away and sent Stefan a message telling him she was ready to leave and would wait at the fountain. Barely a few minutes later, he appeared from the doorway of the antique book store near the blue-shuttered bar.

He waved awkwardly as he walked toward her. He was carrying a large canvas bag, which Cat presumed was full of books.

"You read Italian?" She asked when he was close enough to hear her.

"Not yet," Stefan replied, "but I thought I would try to learn."

Cat smiled, Aida's words bouncing through her head. *She learned English for me.*

"Did you have a pleasant afternoon?" Stefan asked politely as they started to walk back to the truck.

"Yes. It was lovely." Cat realised she hadn't told him why she'd been in *Sant'Anna* or who she was meeting but, just for a while, she wanted to keep the afternoon to herself. Relive it in her own mind before sharing it with anyone.

"I'm glad." Stefan didn't seem to mind that she hadn't shared any details with him. As they settled into the car and started off on their journey back to the ranch, he simply took his books from his bag and quietly sifted through them.

"What did you buy?" Cat asked as they turned onto the main road out of *Sant'Anna*.

"Tolstoy, Dickens, and Shakespeare," Stefan replied. "Texts I know well and brought with me, so I can compare German to Italian. It's the best way to learn a language."

"I thought the best way to learn was to just jump in and start speaking it?" Cat asked, adding in Italian, "*Non credi?*" When Stefan frowned at her, she translated for him, "Don't you think?"

He chuckled and rubbed his beard. "Probably."

"You're leaving soon," she said, drumming her fingers on the steering wheel. "Will you get through all of those before you go?"

Stefan straightened the books in his lap. "Actually, I was hoping I might extend my stay." He wasn't looking at her. "If that wouldn't be an inconvenience for you? I have been struggling with writer's block and the quiet is proving helpful."

Recalling the music he'd played her on the drive to *Sant' Anna*, Cat nodded; one good turn deserved another. "Of course," she said. "You're very welcome to stay."

Stefan smiled at her and returned to flicking through his books.

Turning off the main road and onto a smaller, windier one, Cat glanced at him and asked, "Which Shakespeare did you pick?"

"My favourite," he replied. "*Romeo and Juliet.*"

CHAPTER TWENTY-FIVE

SKYE

SKYE CAUGHT up with Amelie and Molly just before they left the ranch. They seemed surprised to see him but not necessarily pleased. Nevertheless, he insisted on tagging along, literally positioning his horse Shadow between the two of them and talking far too much about nothing in particular in an effort to prevent them from entering into too much of a conversation.

He wasn't really sure why he was nervous about them being alone; it wasn't as if he had anything to hide from Amelie, or from Molly. It just felt… unnatural. His past and his present interacting. Unnatural and worrisome.

As usual, though, Amelie proved his worries to be completely unfounded. She allowed him to tell Molly about the fire in the barn and about Alec's decision to buy the ranch, and then she cut him off. Just like that, she dived into the full details of how – not long after the fire – she'd backed out of her wedding day because Jed was, as she put it herself, a 'buffoon'.

Molly laughed at that, partly because of the word *buffoon* and partly because she was impressed Amelie had had the guts to cancel a wedding when the guests were arriving and the marquee was already up.

"He sounds dreadful," she said in her bright Texan accent.

"He wasn't dreadful." Amelie had, by this point, manoeuvred her horse Rupert so she was next to Molly and could talk at a normal volume instead of across Skye and Shadow. "He just wasn't the person I wanted to spend my life with." She glanced at Skye as she said that, and it made him look away.

Instead of being awkward about it, though, Molly smiled. "And you found someone you *do* want to spend your life with?"

"Sorry, is it strange to talk about this?" Amelie said, twirling her fingers into Rupert's mane.

"Yes," Skye laughed, blushing.

But Molly interrupted, "No, it's not. I'm glad Skye's happy." Peering around Amelie, she added, "Skye, really, I'm glad you're happy. We were friends before we were anything else, and all of it was so long ago now. Can we maybe do friends again?"

Skye looked at Amelie, she was nodding at him. "Sure," he said, "friends."

"Phew!" Molly laughed loudly. "Now that's out of the way, where's a good spot to speed up and let our hair down?"

A few hours later, having galloped through the meadows behind the ranch and trekked a little way through the woods, they arrived back at the stables. Amelie dismounted quickly, looking at her phone.

"Sorry, guys, would you mind seeing to Rupert? I have a shift in the café this evening. I'll be late if I don't get a move on…"

"Of course, go." Skye offered her a quick kiss on the cheek, which made Amelie smile, then waved for her to hurry.

"I'll see you tonight? After my shift?"

"Sure," he said, already looking forward to seeing her again. "Tonight."

As Amelie headed back up toward the ranch house, Molly leaned back against the fence and held her water bottle to her chest. "I had fun today. Amelie's nice. Real nice."

"Yeah," Skye smiled. "She is."

"Listen, Skye…" Molly cleared her throat and pressed her lips together. Skye knew that face; it was a face that said she had something to tell him and that she was nervous about doing so. He'd thought, while they were out with the horses, that being friends again and putting the past behind them might be the reason she was here. Now, he was doubting it.

"Ah ha?"

"Could we maybe get some dinner later? Or have a drink? There's something I want to talk to you about."

"Sounds serious." Skye tried to catch her eyes, but she wasn't looking at him.

"Can we?" Finally, she met his gaze. Her happy-go-lucky smile had disappeared and she looked genuinely worried.

"Sure. I need to spend some time in the stables, though. We can have a drink up at the ranch house later? Eight o'clock? Amelie finishes her shift at nine, so…"

"Great. I'll see you tonight."

As Molly turned and headed back toward her cabin, Skye passed his water bottle from one hand to the other. Finally, Molly seemed ready to tell him whatever she came here to tell him. When she first arrived, he'd convinced himself it was to do with her being in a new relationship but, especially after she realised he'd moved on and was happy with Amelie, there would have been no reason for her to keep that kind of information secret. Which meant it had to be something else. Something bigger.

Skye looked at his phone for the time.

In four hours, he'd find out. He just hoped he was ready for it. Whatever *it* turned out to be.

CHAPTER TWENTY-SIX

SKYE

SKYE FINISHED with the horses earlier than expected, but instead of suggesting to Molly that they meet before eight, he spent the time in his cabin. First, he showered, washing the remains of the day from his skin. Then he put on a clean pair of jeans, a white t-shirt and a thin, dark green sweater. Finally, he looked at the time. Seven p.m. It would be mid-morning in the States.

Scrolling through his contacts, Skye stopped when he reached Tony's name. They'd served together for three years but hadn't spoken since Skye left the Corps. Mainly because Skye refused to speak to anyone who reminded him of what had happened. If someone could shed some light on what was going on with Molly, Tony could.

Skye's fingers trembled as he tried to work up the courage to press 'call'. Eventually, he did it. When he held the phone to his ear and heard it ringing, he almost bottled it and hung up. Before he had the chance, Tony's voice on the other end of the line said, "Skye Anderson? Is it really you?"

"Hey, buddy," Skye tried to sound normal, casual, as if it hadn't been over eighteen months since they last spoke.

"*Hey, buddy*?" Tony wasn't going to let him get away with it, but was laughing. "That's what I get? Eighteen months with nothing and then *hey buddy*?"

Skye cleared his throat and grimaced. He was glad Tony couldn't see his face. He was pretty sure he was deathly pale. "Yeah, listen Tony, I'm sorry—"

Tony's voice softened. "Nah. Don't apologise. It's good to hear from you."

"Thanks." There was a pause while Skye tried to figure out what to say. Finally, he just blurted it out. "Did you know Molly's over here? In Italy?"

Tony made an *ahh* sound, as if he wasn't sure he should answer. "Yeah. I knew. How is she?"

"Good. Bit of a surprise to see her."

"I'll bet." Tony laughed, but he sounded uncomfortable. "So, have you two been catching up?" It sounded like a loaded question; a way to figure out whether Molly had confessed whatever she was there to confess.

"A bit. To be honest, though, she's been a little cagey. That's why I called. I feel like she's trying to tell me something..." Skye trailed off, hoping he was giving Tony the chance to admit what Molly felt she couldn't. When Tony didn't reply, Skye added, "You know, if you two are dating, it's fine with me."

Tony laughed, but it wasn't a jovial laugh, it was slightly melancholy. "Nah, man. We're not dating."

"Someone else, then?"

"Why don't you just talk to Molly?"

"I'm going to. Tonight. We're meeting for a drink, but I thought if I had a handle on what's going on..." Skye pinched the bridge of his nose and held the phone away from his mouth while he took a long deep breath. "Sorry, man, I shouldn't have called."

"Skye, it was good to hear from you. I'd like to catch up properly. But you need to talk to Molly, not me, about what's going on."

Skye nodded, even though Tony couldn't see him. "Sure. I get it. I will."

"You're doing okay, though? Over there?" Tony sounded like he wanted to start a real conversation, but Skye couldn't cope with that and worrying about Molly at the same time.

"Yeah. I'm doing okay. Listen, I promise I'll call again. Maybe you can come out sometime? Visit the ranch?"

Tony sighed a little then said, "Sure. Sounds good."

"Okay. Bye, Tony."

"Skye? Before you go – I tried to say it before but you never picked up my calls – I wanted to say that what happened in Bale was not your fault. No one blames you."

Skye squeezed his eyes shut and bit his lower lip. Images he didn't want to confront were starting to filter in. "I've got to go, Tony. Bye."

After hanging up, Skye counted from one to ten and tried

to focus on his breathing. His heart was hammering against his chest and his skin felt cold and clammy. He looked at the clock on the cabin wall. Seven forty-five. Time to get up to the ranch house.

As he passed the swimming pool and started on the path up to the house, he could see that Molly was already on the porch waiting. She was holding a bottle of wine. When he got close enough to hear her, she held it up and said, "I got this from the market the other day. I was going to sneak it home in my suitcase but thought…" She smiled and gestured to the house. "Can we borrow some glasses?"

Skye nodded and looked at the porch swing. Somehow, it felt too intimate. Instead, he took Molly to the dining area on the veranda and removed the winter cover from one of the tables. "I'll fetch chairs from inside, and some glasses," he said, hardly managing to look at her as he spoke.

"Sure." Molly leaned against the table. Skye could feel her watching him as he headed inside. When he returned, she helped him with the chairs then sat down and unscrewed the bottle while he returned for glasses.

The second they were properly seated, each with a wine glass in their hands, Skye dove in. "Okay, Molly, what's going on? Ever since you got here, I've felt like there was something you wanted to tell me. I've been trying to give you space. Let you say it in your own time. But…"

Molly looked down at her glass as Skye spoke. When he stopped, she nodded and met his eyes. "You're right. There is something."

"What is it?" Skye tried to smile, tried to tell himself it would be good news not bad. "Are you seeing someone? Because if you're worried about telling me, you shouldn't be. I'm happy for you. I spoke to Tony and he said you guys aren't an item but I always thought you'd be great together —" He was speaking quickly, his words almost falling over one another, and Molly was frowning at him.

"Why in the heck would I come all the way here to tell you I have a boyfriend?" She shook her head and laughed dolefully. "No, Skye, that's the kind of news I could give you by email."

Skye swallowed hard. What else could it be?

Molly reached for his hands and, before he could stop her, squeezed them. "It's bigger than that, Skye… it's Dallas."

"Dallas?" Skye felt as if his head had been pushed under water. When he'd first left the Corps, he'd seen his Belgian Malinois, Dallas, in his dreams – his nightmares – every night. For the past few months, he'd seen her less frequently and, although he hadn't missed waking up soaked in sweat, he'd missed her. Very much.

Molly bit her lower lip but didn't let go of Skye's hands. "Skye, we found her."

"Found her?"

"We were travelling through Bale on the way to Gira.

We're setting up a new..." Molly stopped and pursed her lips. "It doesn't matter. We were there, and I saw this dog at the side of the road. At first, I thought she was a stray but then I looked closer and..."

Skye took his hands back and scraped his fingers through his hair. "Is she...?" He couldn't bring himself to say it. "What happened to her?"

"She was in a bad way. Severely malnourished. Dehydrated. And an injury to her front leg had healed badly." Molly took out her phone and set it down on the table. "I have some pictures if you want to see them."

Skye felt like his heart was about to jump clean out of his chest. When Molly passed the phone, and he took in the images of the dog he thought he'd never see again, he began to cry. Without trying to hide it, he let the tears come and scrolled through. Picture after picture. She was skinny. So skinny. But her eyes were the same.

"We had to amputate. She was in a lot of pain," Molly said solemnly, reaching out to scroll on to another image. "She's doing better now the leg's gone."

Skye zoomed in. There she was. Dallas. Lying down, ears pricked, staring at the camera. She was missing her front leg, the right one, but she was there. "Where was this taken?" Skye couldn't look away from it. He wanted to hold the phone to his chest, but didn't.

"Back home in the States. Harrisburg."

Skye began to smile. Almost in slow motion, joy spread across his face. "Molly, this is unbelievable." He stood up and waved his arms in the air. "This is a miracle. A true to God, actual, miracle. She was out there for nearly two years! She survived for nearly two years…"

Molly smiled, but only a little. Her expression made Skye's stomach clench.

"This *is* good news, isn't it?"

Molly gestured for Skye to sit back down but, instead, he gripped the back of the chair and stared at her.

Skye paused, his initial elation giving way to a niggling sense of mistrust. "Why wouldn't it be good news, Molly? She's alive. You found her."

Molly breathed in through her nose, held the air in her chest, then exhaled slowly before saying, "Skye, she can't work any more."

"Of course, she can't." Skye was drumming his fingers on the chair.

"The dehydration damaged her kidneys. She'll need physio. A piece of shrapnel damaged her spine, and we've no idea if she'll suffer behavioural issues." Molly looked at her phone, the image of Dallas was still illuminated on its screen. She met Skye's gaze and swallowed hard. "Skye, the reason I didn't just email you when we first found her – apart from that you hadn't spoken to me for months – it was because I was hoping I'd find a solution. I didn't want to break your heart all over again."

"Find a solution to what?"

As if she was reciting a speech she'd rehearsed several times before, Molly said, "I came to Italy because I had to tell you face-to-face. They're going to put Dallas to sleep, Skye. The Kennel Master at Harrisburg agreed to wait until the end of the month because I've been talking to a charity who I thought might be able to help, but I got a final answer from them yesterday – the costs to rehabilitate her are just too high. They have too many other dogs to help." Her voice caught in her throat. "We can't save Dallas, Skye. I'm sorry."

Rage exploded in Skye's gut. "She was willing to give her life for us and this is how they treat her?!"

Molly winced. "I've felt all this myself, Skye. I've done everything in my power. I insisted we amputate to give her a chance. I insisted we bring her home. I tried my best to save her, but she's been home three months and her recovery is slow. Very slow."

"So, three months of care is the cut off point? She waited for us for nearly two years and we can't give her more than three months?"

Molly closed her eyes.

"I can't believe you waited all this time to tell me." Skye didn't know what to do with his arms or his hands. He wanted to punch something or tear something apart but there was nothing, so he kicked the nearby chair and let out a loud, anguished cry.

Molly stood up. She tried to put her hand on Skye's arm but he pulled away.

Skye was trying to calculate how many days were left until the end of February. "We need to delay them. Tell Harrisburg I'll take her. Who's in charge? Morcombe? Tell him I'll figure out the transport, the quarantine, visas, licenses, whatever. I don't care what it costs. I just need time." He was pacing up and down. "Heck, Molly, why did you wait? We could have started all this days ago! If you'd called me instead of wasting time flying over here – or if you'd told me when you arrived instead of spouting off *lies* about being here to make friends."

Molly's eyes had filled with tears and she was hugging her arms around her waist. "I've tried everything, Skye. I promise you. I've tried. But we're at the end of the road now and, to be honest, when I got here and saw how well you were doing, I thought about waiting until it was already done. Until she was gone. I thought about telling you afterwards instead of–"

Skye felt like his head was about to explode. "Why would you even *think* about not telling me?"

"Because I didn't want to see this look in your eyes! The hope. The thought that you might be reunited with her." Molly glanced at her phone then back at Skye. Trying to steady her voice, she said solemnly, "There is no way you can bring her here. She's too sick to travel. No vet would sign off on it. She'd need to remain in the States for at least six months, receiving specialist care…"

"If it's a matter of money–"

"It's not just money, Skye. It's resources. There are too many dogs and not enough people to help them."

"You flew her back to the States. She wasn't too sick to travel then."

"That was on military transport. And there's no way the military will..." Molly was wiping tears from her cheeks. Inhaling sharply and shaking her head, she said, "I'm sorry, Skye. I'm so sorry, but the decision's been made. Dallas is being put to sleep on February 27th. We can video call. You can see her. They said that's okay. You can even be on video with her when they–"

Skye held up his hand. He didn't want her to say it. Couldn't bear to hear her say it. For a moment, the two of them simply stared at one another.

"Skye..."

"I need you to leave. I don't want you here."

"Skye, let's talk about this."

Skye turned away from her. "Just go."

CHAPTER TWENTY-SEVEN

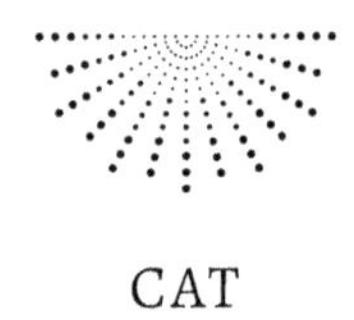

CAT

ALL EVENING, *Signiorelli's* had been too busy for Cat and Amelie to speak beyond Amelie asking if Cat's meeting with Aida had gone well and Cat replying, "Yeah, really well." Now, finally, it was slowing down. The tables were clearing, those drinking outside had started to wander home, and it was almost time to close. In the corner of the room, Stefan Hurst was bent over a large leather-bound notebook. He'd arrived not long after Cat's shift started and had been scribbling away in his book ever since.

"Can I get you anything else?" Cat asked tentatively, worried about interrupting him.

Stefan blinked at his page then tucked his pen behind his ear and looked up at her. "Sorry, are you closing?"

"Not yet." Cat gestured to his notebook. "You seem busy."

"I am," Stefan said, almost smiling. "Is it all right if I stay for a while longer? I can order another drink?"

"You don't have to order anything," Cat replied. All afternoon, even as she talked with Aida, she'd been hearing the music he played her. It was soothing. It quietened her mind, and she was immensely grateful to him for sharing it. "The table is yours for as long as you like. I can give you a ride back to the ranch if you want to stay until closing?"

Stefan took his pen from his ear and tapped it up and down on the page in front of him. "Yes, thank you, I'd like that."

Cat nodded, took Stefan's empty glass and salad bowl, and headed back to the bar. Having just finished wiping down a nearby table, Amelie was leaning back against the wall next to the coffee machine and brushing down her apron. She swiped some loose hair from her face and as Cat walked past, said, "So, what was she like? Do you want to talk about it? You've barely said a word all evening."

Stepping past Amelie and depositing the dirty dishes on the tray beneath the counter, ready for washing later, Cat's shoulders tensed. "I guess it depends whether *you* want to talk about it." When she turned around, she raised her eyebrow at her sister. "I'm happy, Amelie. It was good. Really good. So, I don't need Debbie Downer to pour cold water over it." She knew she sounded antagonistic, too defensive, but couldn't help it; for a while, at least, she wanted to bathe in the warm fuzzy feeling that had settled over her. She wanted to live the fairy tale she'd been imagining since she was a little girl. Her mother was back in her life and she was nice, beautiful, *normal.*

Cat expected Amelie to bite back but her sister simply twitched her nose from side to side and said, "I'm glad it went well. *Really* glad. Did she look like you?"

Cat hesitated for a moment, then put down the glasses she'd been holding and took out her phone. "We took a self-ie," she said, her heart fluttering. "Here…"

As Amelie peered over Cat's shoulder, her eyes widened. "Wow, she really does look like you. Or you look like her, I guess."

"It's bizarre, Am. It was so easy. Like we'd known each other forever. She wanted to hear everything, all about me and what my life's been like. About the ranch, and you guys, and Mum and Dad." Cat thought she saw Amelie's smile start to drop, but continued anyway. "We were together all after-noon, and she wants to meet again next week."

For a moment, Amelie didn't say anything, but then she wrapped her arms around Cat's neck and squeezed her tightly. "I'm glad," she said. "Really glad." After a pause, she added, "Did you talk about… the past? What happened when you were taken into care?"

Tensing up, Cat pulled loose from Amelie's grasp and folded her arms in front of her chest. "I knew you wouldn't be able to resist," she said, rolling her eyes.

"Resist what?"

Cat sighed and returned to clearing away the glasses. "No, we haven't talked about it. She offered but I didn't want to. We've got plenty of time for that and I want to judge her on what I find *now* not what happened back then."

Amelie opened her mouth to reply. Before she could, the bell tinckled and the door swung open behind her. Turning away from Cat, she greeted the short, dark-haired man who'd entered and asked if he'd like a seat inside or outside.

"Neither," he replied in Italian. "I am looking for Bea Romano."

Behind the bar, Cat fumbled with the glass she was holding and put it down loudly on the counter. Amelie was smiling but had slotted her fingers together behind her back and was squeezing them so hard that Cat could see her knuckles whitening.

"Bea's not here at the moment," Amelie replied. "Can I take a message?"

The man reached into his pocket, a gesture that made Amelie take a step back. Drawing out his phone, he swiped it open then turned the screen toward Amelie. "Have you seen this boy?" He looked at Cat. "And you? Have you seen him?"

Cat bit her lower lip then put on her best 'service' smile and walked over.

Amelie was shaking her head. "No, I'm sorry, I haven't seen him."

Cat peered at the phone. It was showing a picture of Markus, floppy haired, a little younger, and not covered in bruises, but it was definitely Markus. "I'm sorry, I don't think so. But we do get a lot of customers." Cat gestured to the half-full room and tried not to start nervously tapping her foot.

"I'm the boy's step-father. He's missing. Bea is his aunt."

Amelie's eyes widened. Cat forced herself to do the same. "I didn't know Bea had a nephew," Amelie said.

"When will she be back?" The man put away his phone and glared at them.

"She's staying with a friend for a few weeks," Cat said quickly, the lie rolling off her tongue before she'd had a chance to think it through. "We're covering the café while she's gone."

"Her friend's not well," Amelie added. "So, we're not sure how long she'll be gone."

"I see." The man looked from Cat to Amelie. Cat could feel Stefan watching them from the corner of the room but carried on smiling.

"Would you like to leave a message?" She asked politely, praying Amelie held her nerve a little longer.

"Do you have a telephone number for her? The one I have seems out of date. She is not answering."

"I'm sorry, I'm not sure we're in a position to share Bea's personal information," Amelie said, surprisingly smoothly. Cat nodded in agreement.

"All right. Then tell her Antonio is here and needs to speak with her urgently about Markus. I will be in town for a few days in case she *returns* sooner than expected."

With one final look around the café, as if he thought Bea might be hiding in a corner somewhere, Antonio pulled the door open and strode outside. Cat and Amelie watched as he crossed the piazza and headed down the side street which led to the only B&B in *Legrezzia.*

When he was out of sight, Cat allowed herself to breathe. Reaching for Amelie's hand, she put her other hand on her chest. She could feel her heart thud-thud-thudding. "Amelie," she whispered, "that was…"

"I know." Amelie was deathly pale. "What do we do now?"

CHAPTER TWENTY-EIGHT

AMELIE

"I'LL PACK UP HERE. You go check on Bea and Markus. Tell them what's happened." Cat's fingers were trembling and Amelie felt a little shaky herself.

"Are you sure?" She was already taking off her apron.

Cat tilted her head at the door. "Maybe, I don't know, make sure you're not followed or something?"

Amelie almost laughed but then bit her lower lip. "Really?" She looked at the spot where, a few moments ago, Markus' step-father had been standing and swallowed down the lump which had formed in her throat. Lowering her voice, she said, "You think he suspects something?"

"He's a policeman," Cat shrugged. "Maybe. We weren't exactly smooth, were we?"

Amelie shook her arms to release the tension that had gripped her shoulders. "Okay. I'll be careful." She didn't even know what being careful meant; should she check behind her as she walked? Take a different route home? Stop if another car got too close on the way back to the ranch?

Cat opened her mouth to speak, but then gave a little shake of her head and pressed her lips together.

"What?" Amelie narrowed her eyes. Her sister's face had sharpened.

"It's just..." Cat was picking at a loose splinter of wood on top of the bar. When she looked up, she said, "It's getting serious now, Am. If Antonio finds out where Markus is then we could all be in trouble. The ranch could be in trouble."

Amelie flicked her index finger against her thumb. "I know." When she looked up, she smiled thinly. "I'll talk to Bea. We'll think of something. You're sure you'll be okay here?"

Cat glanced at the table where Stefan Hurst was still nose-deep in his notebook. "Stefan said he wanted to stay until closing. I offered him a ride back to the ranch, so I won't be alone."

Usually, Amelie would poke fun at Cat for that; she'd say something about her warming to Stefan, changing her mind about him, perhaps even liking him. Tonight, however, neither of them was in the mood for jokes.

Leaving *Signiorelli's*, for the first time in a long time, Amelie felt nervous to be walking alone at night. She'd felt this way in London almost daily. When she first left Tuscany to study in England, leaving a big bar or club on her own had caused her to have a near panic attack each time. When she'd had to navigate busy tube trains full of drunk, leery passengers. When she'd had to walk the short, dark stretch from the underground station to her student apartment. But she'd never, ever felt that way in *Legrezzia.* With its cobbled streets, warm street lights, and friendly faces, it had always felt a completely safe place to be. Even after dark.

Tonight, though, she found she couldn't reach the truck soon enough. When she did, she turned on the lights and checked the back seat in case someone was lurking there, as if she were starring in some gritty crime drama.

"Oh, come on, Amelie. Get a grip," she muttered to herself as she turned the key in the ignition. "Get a grip."

Back at the ranch, Amelie parked up near the house and headed straight to Cabin Ten. The lights were on, but when she knocked it took more than a few seconds for Bea to answer.

When she did, she looked worried. Putting her hand to her chest, she breathed, "Oh, Amelie, it's you," and stepped aside to let Amelie in. "It's late."

"I brought leftovers," Amelie said, holding up the paper bag of treats she'd brought from the café. "Some of the pastries were going spare."

Bea smiled thinly and took the bag. "Thank you." She held it for a moment, with both hands, as if it was something precious, then took it to the kitchenette and turned on the kettle. "Coffee? Tea?"

"Tea would be lovely." Amelie looked around the room then added, "Bea, is Markus here?"

"He is taking a bath." Bea looked up briefly then, taking in the expression on Amelie's face, did a double take. "Is everything okay?"

Amelie walked over to the kitchenette and perched on one of the tall stools behind the counter. Resting on her forearms, she said quietly, "Markus' step-father came to the café."

Bea was holding two mugs and put them both down with a thud on the counter. "When?"

Amelie looked at the clock. "About an hour ago. After he left, I came straight here." She almost laughed at herself as she added, "Don't worry. He didn't follow me or anything."

Bea's eyes widened. When she shook her head, curls fell over her face. Brushing them away, she said, "What did he ask you? What did he say?"

"He asked where you were. We said you were staying with a sick friend, so that he didn't hang around expecting you back. He showed us a picture of Markus and asked if we'd seen him. We said no. Then he left."

"Did he believe you?"

"I think so." Amelie tried to picture Antonio's face. In truth, she couldn't tell what he'd believed. "He said he'd tried calling you but that you hadn't answered."

Bea took her phone from her pocket and looked at it. "I have been avoiding him. I know I said I'd sort it out but…" She glanced toward the bathroom door and shook her head.

"I don't know how, Amelie. I don't know how to help Markus out of this mess. I believe he is telling the truth, but I'm not sure that's enough."

Amelie hesitated. What she was about to say felt utterly ludicrous. "Bea, Antonio couldn't... I mean, he couldn't trace your phone could he? I'm just wondering if maybe you should switch it off for a while?"

Bea's expression paled. With shaky fingers, she turned her phone off and tossed it onto the table nearby. "He wouldn't," she said. "Would he?"

Amelie patted Bea's arm. "It's okay, Cat and I can handle the café for a while. You just stay up here, out of sight, until he leaves town. Maybe when Mum and Dad get back, or Alec, they'll know what to do." As the kettle boiled, drowning out her voice, she pulled her cardigan closer around her waist and tried to smile. "Alec has all sorts of contacts. You never know..."

Bea nodded but didn't smile back as she deposited the teabags in the mugs. When she turned around to fetch the milk from the fridge, she stopped. Her shoulders started to shake. Amelie jumped up and ran around to the other side of the counter. Pulling Bea in for a hug, she said, "It's going to be all right. Antonio's got no reason to connect you with the ranch. Markus is safe here."

Bea patted Amelie's back, then stepped away. Smiling ruefully, she said, "Do you see how crazy this is? Telling lies to the police. Hiding from the police. Worrying that the police are tracking my *phone*? All because Markus was beaten. Because Markus was hurt and no one is willing to stand up for him."

"You're standing up for him," Amelie said.

"But it's not enough, Amelie, is it? I believe Markus. I believe he'll be in danger if he goes back to prison, and I believe the authorities will want to make an example of him. Add time to his sentence. I don't care about myself but I care for that boy, and he doesn't deserve this." Wiping away a tear, Bea shrugged hopelessly in a way that made Amelie's heart hurt. "He doesn't deserve this."

CHAPTER TWENTY-NINE

SKYE

Skye was fuming. He could feel his blood pumping through his veins. Throbbing. Pulsing in his temples and in every muscle in his body.

But beneath the fury was pain. A pain he'd been trying to ignore for so many months and which had now been exposed.

"Damn, you, Molly!" He yelled, even though he was alone in his cabin. "Damn you!"

When he heard a knock on his cabin door, at first, he thought it was his heart hammering in his chest. When he realised it wasn't, he strode toward it and flung it open.

"I told you to leave!"

He'd expected to see Molly, but it was Amelie who was standing in front of him. He blinked at her and braced both hands on the doorframe, blocking it with his upper body. Amelie was looking at him with wide, worried eyes and had taken a step back as if she expected him to lunge for her.

"I said I'd drop by after my shift. I know I'm late, but I had to see Bea. Markus' step-father turned up…" Amelie trailed off and folded her arms in front of her chest. She wasn't wearing a jacket and it was cold outside. "Skye, are you okay?"

Skye opened his mouth to speak but no sounds came out. Instead, he shook his head.

Without saying anything, Amelie put her hand on his shoulder, nudging him to drop his arms to his sides, and guided him inside. As Skye sat down on the edge of the sofa, she made tea. When she handed it to him, he felt like he might start crying and pressed his lips together, sucking in his cheeks.

Amelie sat next to him and angled herself toward him, wrapping her fingers around her own mug and blowing across the top of it to cool the hot tea. After a short silence, she said, "I know you struggle sometimes with memories of the past. I try not to ask about it. I want you to talk to me when you're ready, when it's the right time, but…"

Skye nodded. He could hear her words, but he could also hear the conversation he'd had with Molly. It was playing on a loop in his head, making it hard to concentrate.

"I've never seen you like this," she said, inching closer so she could put her hand on his knee. "So, I think, maybe this time I will ask… what's going on, Skye? Is it to do with Molly? Has her being here brought back bad memories?"

Skye almost laughed. *Memories*. His head had been full of them ever since he left the Corps, but none were as vicious as the ones that were circling tonight. Eventually, he cleared his throat and reached for his phone. Handing it to Amelie, he said croakily, "My dog, Dallas. This was us. Two days before..." He stopped speaking and put his head into his hands.

Amelie studied the picture. "I don't think I've seen a picture of you in uniform before," she said, smiling warmly. "You look handsome. Dallas is beautiful."

"I was Dallas' handler. I'd been with her since she was a puppy. Other dogs in the unit, I cared for them, of course, but Dallas... she was family."

"*Was*?"

Skye screwed his eyes shut. "I thought she'd died." When he opened them, he tried to keep his voice steady. "But Molly told me this evening that they found her. Back in Bale. For eighteen months, she'd waited for someone to return for her. *Eighteen* months. She was in a bad way, but they brought her home to the States."

Amelie was watching Skye very carefully. Setting down her mug on the coffee table, she said, "Is she okay now?"

"No." He could barely make himself say it. "That's why Molly came here. She wanted to tell me face-to-face that they're..." He looked up at the ceiling and tried to blink his eyes free of tears. "That they're..." As his voice cracked, Amelie moved closer and clasped his hand in hers. Finally, he looked at her. "They're going to put her to sleep. At the end of the month."

Amelie breathed in slowly. "Because she's sick?"

"She could get better but it would take months and the army won't pay for that." As Amelie opened her mouth to speak, Skye shook his head. His skin felt hot and cold at the same time, and there was a tight, bubbling sensation in his stomach. "I can't stand it, Amelie. I feel like I'm going to explode. She's back. She's alive. If Molly had called me instead of coming all the way out here, I could have gone to the States. I'd have had time to figure something out…"

Softly, Amelie said, "Surely, Molly wouldn't let them put her to sleep if there was another option?"

Skye tugged his hands free and braced them on the back of his head. "She said she contacted charities but they couldn't help."

"And what about Dallas?" Amelie ducked to meet Skye's gaze. "You love her. I can see that. You love her so much, but what's best for her, Skye? If she's in pain—"

"You think I'd make her suffer if I didn't believe there was a chance she could get better?"

"No, I'm not saying that… maybe you need to talk to Molly again? Ask to see Dallas' notes?" Amelie shook her head and a strand of hair fell across her face. "I don't know, I don't understand how this works but–"

"No. Clearly, you don't." Skye heard how bitter his words sounded but didn't try to take them back.

Amelie blinked at him and straightened her shoulders. Again, she reached for him and squeezed his knee. "Skye, take a minute. Breathe. Let this sink in…"

"Take a minute?" Skye stood up so abruptly that Amelie

jolted backwards. "Dallas doesn't have a minute. She has twenty-one days Amelie! Twenty-one days." He turned around, scanning the room for his laptop. When he saw it, on the dining table near the double doors, he marched over to and flung the lid open.

Amelie was watching him from over by the sofa.

"You can let yourself out," he said abruptly. "I have to get started."

"Started?"

Barely looking up, he concentrated on typing in his password and opening up his emails. "I'm not letting her go, Amelie," he muttered. "I'm not letting her go. Not this time."

CHAPTER THIRTY

CAT

"ARE you sure it's okay for me to stay?" Stefan asked, looking up from his notebook.

Cat still couldn't quite believe that he wrote his books by hand, with pen and paper rather than a laptop. Before Antonio arrived, she'd been watching him; watching his hand move quickly across the page, his eyes bright, occasionally stopping to chew his bottom lip and think about something before continuing.

"Of course," she said, trying not to let him see that she was, in fact, desperate for him to stay. Desperate not to be alone.

Stefan had been looking down at his notebook, reading something, but now raised his eyes and met hers. "Thank you," he said, in perhaps the most sincere tone Cat had ever heard. "Thank you, very much."

Turning away from him, Cat headed back to the bar and

started wiping it down. She'd already taken care of the kitchen, unloaded the dishwasher, and brought the glasses back through to hang on the rack behind the bar. Wiping one, she tipped it upside down, so it could hang by its stem, then lifted it to the light to check there were no streaks; Bea was very particular about streaks.

Thinking of Bea, Cat's heartbeat quickened. If Antonio was intending to hang around, Bea would have to stay out of sight for a while and so would Markus.

She was deep in thought when, behind her, the door clattered open. As her entire body jumped with nerves, the glass slipped from Cat's fingers and shattered loudly on the floor.

"We're closed," she said in Italian, waving her arms at the man who was lingering in the doorway.

The man opened his mouth to reply, but Cat rushed forward, indicating the closed sign on the door.

"Closed!" she repeated. "Please, leave."

As the man stepped back outside, looking confused and rather put-out, Cat shut the door behind him, locked it, then leaned against it and tried to catch her breath.

From his table in the corner of the room, Stefan was watching her. Slowly, he put down his pen. "Catherine? Are you all right?" He stood up and walked over to her, putting a smooth hand on her forearm.

Cat shook her head. "Sorry, I'm just a little jittery. It's been a strange day."

Stefan studied her face for a moment, then tipped his head toward the bar. "Perhaps a glass of wine would help?"

Cat's first instinct was to say no but, almost as quickly as the thought came to her, she changed her mind. "Yes. I think it would."

"Sit down, I'll fetch it." Stefan gestured to his table then strode over to the bar and picked up an already-opened bottle of Bea's House Red and two unpolished glasses.

As she took a seat opposite Stefan's empty chair, Cat tried not to touch the papers that were spread out across the table; they felt precious, and personal, and she was glad she didn't speak enough German to understand any of it because that would have felt like an intrusion.

Handing her the wine glasses, Stefan scooped the papers out of the way, tucked them into his bag, then set down the bottle.

"Just a small one," Cat said, holding out her glass, "I have to drive back home."

"I didn't think you Italians paid much attention to drinking and driving rules?" Stefan said, smiling slightly with the corner of his mouth.

Cat tilted her head at him and tucked her hair behind her ear. "Well, my parents are British, so maybe I'm a bit more cautious."

"Ahh, you are British, that explains the accent." Stefan sat back and took a sip of his drink. He looked relaxed. Happy. His face softer and his shoulders less hunched than they had been when he first arrived in *Legrezzia.*

Cat looked down into her glass, twisting the stem gently between her fingers and watching the movement of the dark red liquid. "Actually," she said, "I'm not British. I was born in Italy. My parents are from England, but I'm adopted."

"I see, and you were adopted at a young age?"

Usually, when she told people she was adopted, they were too awkward to ask questions about it, but Stefan didn't seem awkward at all. Cat smiled, "I was six when I was adopted but I'd been in care for a while before that. I was two years old when I was removed from my biological mother."

Stefan put down his glass and watched her as if he could sense that she wanted to say more.

"Actually," Cat laughed a little, "that's why I was in *Sant' Anna* – I was meeting my mother. Hence the panic attack on the drive over."

"It was the first time you had met her?" Stefan asked, sipping his wine.

Cat nodded. "The very first time. She contacted me a while ago, but I only just decided to go through with it. I wasn't sure if I wanted to. Amelie thought it was a bad idea–"

"Why a bad idea?"

"She's adopted too, except she's never wanted to know anything about her birth parents. I always have, and…" Cat shrugged. "I guess she doesn't get it." When Stefan didn't ask another question, Cat continued, "She was nice. My mother. She looks like me."

"You were together a long time. You must have had a lot to talk about?"

"Mainly, we talked about me. She wanted to know what

I'd been doing all these years and, well, I'm thirty-three now, so there's a lot of years to catch up on."

"Thirty-three?" Stefan brushed his hand through his hair and chuckled. "I feel very old all of a sudden."

Cat narrowed her eyes at him. "Old?"

Whispering, Stefan leaned forward. "I am forty-nine years old," he said, as if it was a deep dark secret. "It will be my fiftieth birthday in August."

"Forty-nine?" Cat waved her hand at him dismissively. "That's not old. I never date men my own age – there needs to be at least a fifteen-year age gap to balance out the emotional maturity."

Stefan laughed and rubbed his beard. He'd trimmed it and Cat could see that, beneath, he was blushing. She started to blush too. Why on earth had she mentioned dating? What did that have to do with anything?

Clearing her throat, she tried to change the subject. "So, I'm guessing your parents are German? Not British?"

"Ah, yes. German." Stefan glanced at her then back at his wine. "However, my father recently died. Three months ago."

"Oh, Stefan, I'm sorry." Cat reached for his hand but instead of putting her fingers on top of it, placed them beside it on the table.

"This is why my sister booked me a holiday. She thought it might help free me from my..." He paused, searching for the world. "Malaise?" Gesturing to his bag of papers, he continued, "I have been unable to write since my father passed."

"But today you seem to have found your groove again?" Cat asked, finishing off her small glass of wine and folding her hands in her lap.

"Yes, I think I have." Stefan smiled at her.

"You like writing in cafés?" Cat stood up, collecting their empty glasses and getting ready to take them back to the bar. Stefan followed suit, lifting his bag onto his shoulder and tucking in his chair.

"Not usually, but I like this one."

As he spoke, Stefan met her eyes, and Cat wished her hands were free enough for her to tuck her hair behind her ear; something about the way he was looking at her made her skin feel hot and her stomach flutter. It was unexpected, and she wasn't sure what to do about it.

"Was it the meeting with your mother that caused you to feel… *jittery*?" Stefan was looking at the broken wine glass on the floor behind the bar.

Cat put their empty ones on the counter and took a dustpan from beneath it. As she began to sweep up the mess, she contemplated telling Stefan about Markus. But, despite Stefan opening up to her, and the fluttery feeling in her stomach, Cat didn't feel like it was *her* place to decide whether Stefan should be brought in on Markus and Bea's secret.

"Yes," she said, standing up, "and no. I can't really talk about the other reason."

"I understand." Stefan put his glasses back on and adjusted his bag on his shoulder.

Cat smiled and took off her apron. Brushing down her red

sweater, she tried to relax her shoulders. "Ready?" She looked back at the un-put-away glasses. "I'll finish this tomorrow."

"I am ready." Stefan followed her to the door, standing aside as she turned off the lights and took her coat from the hook by the window.

Walking across the cobbled piazza toward the side street where Cat had parked her parents' truck, she looked sideways at Stefan and pushed her hands into her coat pockets. "Will you come again tomorrow? To write?" She paused. "I can save you the corner table if you'd like?"

Stefan glanced at her. His lips twitched into a smile. "Yes," he said. "I would like that. Very much."

CHAPTER THIRTY-ONE

AMELIE

Sometime after four a.m., Amelie fell into a deep sleep. Before that, she'd been floating just below the surface of sleep, her thoughts still racing. Thoughts which had managed to cut through her usual meditation app, a hypnosis track, and every deep breathing technique she'd learned when she'd attended a relaxation seminar back in London.

All night, she'd bounced from thinking of Bea and Markus, to Cat and Aida, to Skye and Dallas. Finally, at three a.m., she'd texted her mother. Mum wouldn't have her phone switched on, so wouldn't be disturbed, but the knowledge that she would call Amelie in the morning helped her to eventually settle.

Just after sunrise, her phone rang.

"Mum?" Amelie spoke sleepily into it as she rubbed her eyes. Glancing at the shutters, which were only allowing the smallest whisper of light to pass through their slats, she added, "It's early. You're on holiday. Aren't you supposed to sleep in?"

Groggy from only a few hours of proper rest, Amelie reached for the glass of water she kept by her bed and took a long drink.

"I've spent a lifetime waking up at dawn to see to the horses, sweetheart. Holiday or no holiday, it's hard to retrain your internal clock." Her mother's voice was warm and soothing. Like a hot bath easing the ache of tired muscles. "Is everything all right? Your message said you need to talk." Mum laughed, and Amelie pictured her pinching the bridge of her nose. "Which always fills me with fear… you're not arguing with your sister again are you?"

Amelie laughed too; she loved the fact that her mother still pictured Amelie and Cat as the teenagers who bickered whenever they were out of their parents' earshot. "No, Cat and I are fine." She paused. "Well, sort of fine."

She knew Cat had told their parents about meeting Aida, and she also knew Cat would *hate* for Amelie to discuss it with them behind her back, but she needed help and her parents were the only ones who could give it.

"Is Dad there?"

"He's here. Do you want to speak to him?"

"Can you put the phone on loudspeaker?"

"Ah. I think so…" Her mother's voice faded and Amelie heard her parents mutter between themselves as they tried to figure out how to follow her request. Finally, her father said, "Amelie? Can you hear us?"

"How's that?" added Mum.

"Perfect." Amelie shuffled up straighter and tapped her fingernails against the back of her phone as she held it to her ear.

"What's going on, Am?" Dad asked, his voice gravelly and gruff; the way it always was when he hadn't yet consumed enough coffee.

"I don't even know where to start," Amelie sighed.

"The beginning?" Mum nudged.

"I'm sorry to do this when you're on holiday. There's stuff going on…"

"Start at the beginning," Mum repeated herself then, to Amelie's father, said, "Thomas, call reception and ask for some coffee. I get the feeling we'll need it…"

An hour later, Amelie said goodbye to her parents, making them promise not to even *think* about returning home early, and assuring them that she felt much better after their conversation.

"Okay, sweetheart. Call us any time." Mum said, blowing kisses at her down the phone.

"Any time, Am," her father added. "And we'll see you in a fortnight."

"See you soon. I love you both." Amelie blew a kiss back and ended the call. She felt better. Her parents had told her, in no uncertain terms, that the best thing she could do for Cat was to let her figure things out with Aida on her own.

"I know you want to protect her. We do too," Mum had said, "but this is something she needs to do. If you stop her, she'll resent you for it. So, just listen to her, be there for her, and try not to worry too much. She's a big girl."

As Amelie replayed her parents' words, she pulled her blue cardigan from the bedpost and shrugged herself into it. She had known, in her gut, that she needed to stop trying to protect her sister and just be there for her. But putting it into practise was a different matter. Hearing her parents tell her what to do stopped the what-ifs and the maybes from circling in her head and put into focus the fact that Cat was going through something and that Amelie's job, as her sister, was to be there to catch her if she needed catching. Not to stop her from falling in the first place.

Downstairs, in the kitchen, she flicked on the kettle and took two mugs from the cupboard, anticipating that Cat would – at any moment – appear from upstairs.

In fact, Ben was first to show his face. He walked sleepily over to her, already reaching out his hand for a coffee cup.

"Morning," he said. "Cat told me about Antonio showing up. Are you all right?"

Amelie poured them each a coffee and leaned back against the worktop. "Fine. A little shaken. Worried about Bea and Markus…" She paused as Ben opened up the big glass doors and took a breath of dewy morning air. "I told Mum and Dad," she said quickly, biting her lower lip.

"You did?" Ben was more surprised than annoyed.

"I was panicking. I didn't know what to do. Now that Antonio's in town it all feels more…"

"Serious?" Ben asked, sipping his coffee.

Amelie nodded. "Sheltering Markus puts us all at risk–"

"You don't need to justify it to me," Ben said. "I think you were right to call them."

"You do?"

Ben looked at her over the top of his coffee cup and blinked in agreement. "What did they say?"

"They said we should let Bea and Markus stay as long as they need to and simply deny all knowledge if anyone asks. They're going to call Alec and ask if he knows a good lawyer."

"So, keep doing what we have been doing and wait for Alec to save the day again?" Ben laughed a little.

Amelie bit her lower lip. "Yes. Except, Bea can't continue to go to the café now that we've told Antonio she's not in town. Cat and I will have to do some more shifts, which means it'll just be you and Jean to sort out the barn and the horses."

Ben shrugged. He was wearing an oversized grey t-shirt, the kind he'd slept in since he was a teenager, and a pair of torn old jeans that made Amelie imagine her father telling him to smarten himself up. *Doesn't matter if you're mucking out horses or taking guests out trekking, you dress to do the ranch proud,* he'd say. Even though it was the middle of winter and there were no guests to be seen. "It'll be fine,"

Ben said. "Skye's around too, even though he's been a bit distracted lately."

Amelie wrinkled her nose and folded her arms in front of her stomach.

"What?" Ben narrowed his eyes at her. "You two aren't in a fight already are you? Is it Molly? Because you know Skye only has eyes for you, Am."

"No, it's not Molly." Amelie walked over to the doors to stand opposite Ben. "Actually, I suppose maybe it is."

He waited for her to explain but as Amelie told him what she'd told her parents, about Dallas and about Skye's determination to help her, his expression changed. Brushing his fingers through his hair, he exhaled loudly. "That's rough. Is Skye all right?"

"Not really. When I saw him last night, he was almost manic. Molly's been trying for the past three months to help Dallas and hasn't succeeded, but Skye thinks he can do something."

"Or feels like he *has* to do something."

"Exactly. The guilt was written all over his face. He feels like he let her down by leaving her out there."

"She survived for eighteen months on her own?" Ben asked, shaking his head.

"Eighteen months," Amelie replied. "And now the army is going to…" She couldn't bring herself to say it. "Dad thinks I should tell Alec. Says he'd want to know but–"

"But you feel like you'd be betraying Skye if you did that?"

Amelie sighed and shifted from foot to foot. The floor was cold. Usually, she liked it that way but today it was creeping up into her calves and making her shiver. "I'm going to go talk to him," she said, marching quickly over to the sink and ditching her coffee cup. "He might feel differently now it's all had a chance to sink in."

"Let me know if you need anything," Ben called after her.

"Can you just check in on Bea before you go see to the horses?" Amelie asked on her way out of the room.

"Sure."

"Tell her Cat's got the café covered today and I'll take the evening shift with Tula."

"Okay. See you later."

Amelie waved briefly as she headed through the doorway, then jogged upstairs, pulled on some jeans and a sweater, and hurried back down. There was nothing she could do to help Bea and Markus, or to help Cat, but she could help Skye. She had to be able to help Skye.

CHAPTER THIRTY-TWO

AMELIE

PASSING THE RECEPTION DESK, Amelie paused and looked at the keys hanging behind it. She wanted to believe that Skye would be in his cabin waiting to let her in to sit and talk with her about what was going on but, deep down, a part of her knew he wasn't going to be there. So, trying not to notice the guilt throbbing in her stomach, she took the key to Skye and Alec's cabin and carried it with her as she jogged past the swimming pool and the Italian gardens.

When she reached the cabin, she knocked on the door. There was no answer. Next, she looked through the windows, peering in with her hands cupped around her face, but the entire place was in darkness. Usually, Skye would be up by now, getting himself ready to go to the stables with Ben. The fact he wasn't standing in the kitchen drinking coffee gave her a sinking feeling in her gut. After taking the key from her pocket, she slipped it into the door and knocked as she pushed it open

"Skye? Are you here?"

No one answered.

Quietly stepping into the room, Amelie flicked on the light and watched as it illuminated the living space of the cabin that Skye and Alec had shared since they moved to *Heart of the Hills* last year.

Moving through to the hallway, she pushed open each door and checked the bedroom and bathrooms. All of them were empty, and Skye's bed clearly hadn't been slept in.

Back in the open-plan living area, she spotted a half-full coffee cup on the side near the sink. She touched her fingers to it. It was cold.

On the table, Skye's laptop was sitting open exactly where it had been last night. Amelie walked over to it and nudged one of the keys. It blinked to life, displaying an opened inbox and several typed documents.

At first, Amelie looked away. She shouldn't be here; she shouldn't be intruding like this. But the feeling in her stomach wouldn't go away. Skye was in trouble and she needed to do something to help him. So, she pulled out a chair, sat down, and peered at his emails. The top three had been received in the early hours of the morning, all responses to people Skye had emailed about Dallas. Clearly people he knew or had worked with when he was in the Veterinary Corps. Clearly people he'd thought could help him.

As Amelie read through the series of sympathetic but

factual responses, her throat tightened and her eyes filled with moisture. Every single person had said the same thing; they had already spoken to Molly, they had already tried their best to help, there was nothing else they could do.

The very last email, which had come from someone who seemed more sympathetic than the others, was open in a separate window and Skye had begun to reply to it. It was an angry reply, not considered, not formal like the other emails he'd sent. This one was raw. She could feel his pain vibrating through the screen as she read his words, *'She's family, Sir, I can't lose her again…'* But he had stopped mid-sentence and hadn't completed the rest of the message.

Amelie looked up at the clock. There was a chance Skye had headed down to the stables early, perhaps wanting to distract himself, but as she took out her phone to call him, it began to ring.

"Hello?" She answered quickly and tried not to sound too worried.

"Amelie? It's Molly." Molly's usually bright voice sounded a little shaky

"Molly?"

"Did Skye tell you what happened?"

"He did. I'm in his cabin now but he's not here. I don't know where he is." Amelie paused. Part of her wanted to race to the stables to see if Skye was there but another part felt that maybe, just maybe, Molly could tell her something that would help her get through to him. That maybe Molly could help her understand what he was going through.

“Molly, can we talk?”

Without hesitating, Molly replied, “Come to my cabin. I’ll make coffee.”

“I shouldn’t have told him the way I did.” Molly was perched on the wall outside her cabin nursing a cup of coffee. Amelie was sitting in a chair opposite her, leaning forward onto her knees. “I should have called him instead of coming all the way out here,” Molly said.

“Why didn’t you?” Amelie was trying not to sound judgemental, but she hadn’t been able to figure out why Molly would come all the way to Italy to deliver the news rather than simply tell Skye over the phone. Or why, for that matter, she’d waited so long to tell him once she was here.

Molly sighed and tugged at her long blonde ponytail. “If I’d called, if I’d managed to persuade him to talk to me, or if I’d put it in an email, Skye would have insisted on travelling to the States. No matter what I said, he’d have thought he could save her. When I came here, I was waiting to hear back from one last charity. I knew what they were going to say, but I wanted to wait until it was concrete, so I could tell Skye categorically – face-to-face – that Dallas can’t be saved. So I could stop him from… *hoping*.”

“Is hope such a bad thing?” Amelie asked, chewing her lower lip.

“It is when it’s destined to be shattered,” Molly replied

solemnly. Taking a deep breath, she put her coffee down on the wall beside her and shook her head. "I don't know how much Skye's told you about what happened in *Bale*..."

Amelie blinked quickly, remembering Skye's nightmares and the way he'd trembled on the beach last summer. "Not much."

"It was rough. We lost three dogs and two soldiers. He blamed himself. He wanted to return to duty, but he was injured. It happened around the same time he lost his mom and I think losing Dallas was just... too much."

Amelie's shoulders drooped and she rubbed at her thighs even though she wasn't cold.

"I handled it all wrong. I didn't know how to help him." Molly bit her lower lip. "I don't know, maybe I thought at least I could help him now... make up for the way I behaved back then." She gave a wry smile. "He already hated me, so I figured it didn't matter if he hated me a little more. I just didn't want him to feel that elation, that joy, at the thought of being reunited with her, only for it to be broken into a million pieces. I didn't want him to try and save her and to fail."

"I get it." Amelie's skin was hot and prickly. Skye's grief was almost palpable in her stomach. Without even seeing his face or being near him, she knew what he must be feeling, and she could barely breathe under the weight of it.

Standing up, she shook her arms to free them from the itch that was making them ache. "You're sure you've tried everything?" She knew what Molly's answer would be, but asked the question anyway.

Molly nodded slowly. "She's too sick to travel, she's too sick to rehome, and they don't know what long-term physical or behavioural issues she'll have if she pulls through. As her handler, Skye has a right to adopt her but that's complicated by the fact he's living here now and by her injuries. The charities I asked won't go near it. It's too costly and they have too many other dogs to help. I've spoken to *everyone* I can think of. I had one last shot, a charity down South who thought they might be able to step in. But they emailed me yesterday to say it's the end of the road."

"They thought they could help but changed their minds?" The sadness in Amelie's belly was rapidly turning to fiery indignation at the idea that all of these people were simply washing their hands of a dog who risked her life for her country.

Molly waved her hand dismissively. "They thought they might be able to find a temporary foster in the States, someone to look after Dallas until she was fit enough to travel. But the medical side is too complicated. She'll still need a lot of veterinary care, at least for another month, and they don't have anyone equipped to do that."

As Molly spoke, Amelie's heart began to beat a little faster. Her temples were throbbing, and she was still groggy from lack of sleep, but an idea was on the tip of her tongue. "What if we paid for veterinary care until she was well enough? Organised it privately?"

Again, Molly shook her head. "It'd be eye-wateringly expensive. I know Skye's dad would probably pay, but Dallas would still need an approved foster carer and because of the potential behavioural issues no one I spoke to was willing to take the risk."

"Behavioural issues?"

"She's a war veteran, Amelie. Dogs can suffer PTSD just the same as humans, except they have sharper teeth and bigger bites."

"Right." Amelie looked down at her phone. She only knew one person in the States, but one person was more than no people. As she said goodbye to Molly and promised to let her know when she tracked down Skye, Amelie already knew what she was going to do.

She was barely at the bottom of the path before she raised her phone to her ear.

"Ethan? It's me. Listen, I need your help. It's a long shot, but you're the only person I could think of to call."

CHAPTER THIRTY-THREE

AMELIE

"AMELIE, I'm a human doctor not a dog doctor, and I have *zero* contacts in the military." To start with, Ethan's tone was typically flippant but when Amelie released a deep sigh, he softened a little. "Okay, tell me again from the beginning…"

For what felt like the hundredth time, Amelie relayed what Skye had told her. Ethan listened, just as Ben and her parents had. When she stopped, he let out a long low whistle. "Right. Okay. I see why the dog's important."

"I knew it was a long shot, I just needed to do something and you're the only person I know in America, so this is my something." Amelie was walking down to the stables but, unlike most mornings, had barely even noticed the gentle swaying of the grass beside the path or the way the sky was changing from pink to blue as the sun rose above the horizon.

"I get that." Ethan sounded like he was outside. Amelie looked at the time.

"Where are you?"

"Elena and I just had dinner," Ethan replied, a tinge of coyness in his voice as he said Elena's name.

"Isn't it the early hours of the morning for you?"

"I just finished a long shift. Found her lingering outside waiting to take me for food."

"Because he's been working too hard and hasn't eaten properly in days!" A bright American voice, which Amelie didn't recognise, made her smile. She'd never seen Ethan in love, but she could hear it in his voice. He loved this woman, and she loved him enough to take him for food in the middle of the night. At least one of the Goodwin siblings was content.

"She sounds very lovely," Amelie said.

"She is..." Ethan's voice disappeared and the phone beeped. When Amelie looked at it, she saw he was inviting her to switch to video. Patting at her hair nervously, because she hadn't expected to be e-meeting her brother's girlfriend for the first time when she'd barely slept or showered, she accepted it and got ready to smile.

She waved as Ethan came into view. He seemed to be walking through a park. Dimly lit, twinkling stars up above, very romantic.

He waved back then moved the camera to one side.

Elena, who Amelie recognised from the pictures she'd seen online, stepped into view, and smiled broadly at the camera. "Hi, Amelie, lovely to meet you."

"I'm sorry to interrupt your date," Amelie said, feeling

underdressed compared to Elena's big bright earrings and stylish red coat.

"No problem. Is everything okay?" Elena looked to Ethan as she spoke, and he repeated a shortened version of what Amelie had told him.

"So, they need a foster for Dallas, but it's got to be someone who can provide veterinary care," Ethan explained.

"The foster carer would have to be willing to take on possible behavioural issues, too. Until she's well enough for Skye to bring her to Italy," Amelie finished.

Amelie watched as Ethan narrowed his eyes at Elena. "What?" he asked her. "That's your thinking face."

Elena glanced at the camera then back at Ethan. "It's just…" She paused and twitched her lips from side to side. She and Ethan were sitting on a bench now and he'd put his arm around her. "My cousin is a vet…" Elena shrugged tentatively and, speaking to Amelie, said, "She has her own practice. I could ask…"

"Yes!" Amelie almost shouted down the phone. "Yes, please, Elena. Thank you."

"I don't know if she'll be able to help," Elena warned. "But I'll ask her."

Ethan was looking at Elena as if she was the sun, and the moon, and everything in between. When he pulled his eyes away and directed them back to Amelie, he was smiling. "Well," he said, "turns out, I'm as useless as expected but my girlfriend is amazing."

"Not amazing yet." Elena nudged him. "I only said I'd ask."

Ethan nodded then said to Amelie, "Maybe don't tell Skye yet? Until we've spoken to…" he looked at Elena. "What's your cousin's name?"

"Nell," Elena laughed. "Her name's Nell."

Amelie bit back a smile. "Of course, thank you Elena, thank you so much."

After hanging up, Amelie walked a little more quickly to the stables. Passing the new barn, she headed for the old stables at the far end of the ranch. The new ones were almost ready. After their parents' surprise party, they'd be able to move the horses back up to the yard nearer the house and things would finally feel as if they were getting back to normal.

She paused as she reached the old broken-down barn that Skye had shown to her, and gently brushed her lips with her index finger as she remembered their almost-kiss. It felt like a lifetime ago now; so much had happened since Molly arrived.

When she'd thought about Skye living close by, building his own house on the ranch, being there every single day, she'd also thought about whether it might one day end up being *her* home too. The idea had made her feel a little giddy, like an excited schoolgirl picturing a wedding with the boy of her dreams. But before any of that could happen, she needed to make sure Skye survived the next few weeks.

If Elena's cousin couldn't help Dallas, then Amelie would

not let him go through this alone. She'd be there for him. She was just praying he'd let her.

"He's not here, and Shadow's gone too." Jean the stable manager looked furious, and Ben was clearly trying to calm him down. "He can't just take off with no warning. He certainly can't just take a *horse* without telling anyone. We have a sign-out sheet precisely so we don't waste time worrying that a horse has been stolen or has escaped." Jean looked pointedly at the clipboard and pencil which hung from a rusty nail on the side of one of the stables.

Ben patted Jean's shoulder. "I know, Jean. I'm sorry. Skye's just going through something."

At that, Jean huffed loudly and stalked off, muttering something under his breath about Americans and people with no experience thinking they owned the place.

"Technically, they do own the place," Amelie said to Ben, raising her eyebrows.

"He's just anxious about the new barn and the reopening," Ben said, grabbing the sign-out sheet and scribbling Skye's name on it. "I'm writing this in, but I don't know for sure he's taken Shadow. I'm just assuming he has because they're both missing, along with one of the overnight trekking tents."

"A tent?" In that exact moment, Amelie knew where Skye had gone.

Before Ben could answer, she was grabbing the sheet and writing her own name on it.

"Can I take Rupert?"

Ben opened his mouth to object but then sighed and said, "Yeah, sure, why not? It's not like we still have renovations to manage, a new barn to finish, a party to plan, and an escaped convict staying on the ranch."

Amelie tilted her head at her little brother and squeezed his arm. Ben was *never* sarcastic, so he must really be worried. "I thought you said you'd be okay today?"

"When I thought Skye was here to help. Now it's just me and Jean."

"Get Markus to pitch in. The least he can do is earn his keep, and he's been helping Skye," Amelie said as she guided Rupert from his stall and gave him a kiss on the nose.

"Am, you know a storm's forecast, right?" Ben looked up at the sky but Amelie shook her head at him.

"It looks fine to me. I'll try to get Skye back here tonight. If I can't, Cat might have to do a double shift at the café, but I'll text her en route." Amelie finished fastening Rupert's saddle and swung up into it with ease.

As Ben tossed her a bottle of water, he said, "On route to where?"

"The creek," Amelie replied. "He'll be at the creek. I'm sure of it."

CHAPTER THIRTY-FOUR

SKYE

SKYE HAD BARELY SET up his tent when the woods beside the creek became suddenly darker. Looking up between the branches, he saw that storm clouds had rolled in over the valley. Usually, he'd have checked the weather before heading out on an overnight trek. This morning, he hadn't even thought about it. He'd just been desperate to escape. To get away from his own darkness. And the only way he could think to do that was to disappear into the hills.

This was where he'd come before Amelie's wedding. When he thought she was about to marry Jed and when he needed to do something, anything, to stop his heart breaking.

Now, here he was again.

"Just you and me, Shadow. You and me." He patted Shadow's neck and momentarily wondered how the horse would react if a thunderstorm started. "Hope you're better with thunder than I am, boy." He shuddered as he thought of it; the way the ground would shake. The sound of the thunder.

Trying to shift his mind to something else, he sat down beside the creek and started setting up a fire. The spot he'd picked was sheltered, hopefully sheltered enough to protect the flames from the rain if it came.

As he began to stoke the fire, he looked over at the water that was softly flowing over rocks and rushes. It was far too cold for a swim but looking at it made him remember the times he and Amelie had spent there after the wedding. Back when they'd been unsure whether to touch, hold hands, and act like a couple or whether to just be friends because it was too soon to be anything else. He'd never expected that feeling to last for so many months.

From September until winter crept into the hills, they'd come up to the creek at least once a week. They'd swum together, talked, lazed on the rocks, reading and bathing in each other's company. But they'd never kissed. He'd thought about it almost every time he was in her presence. Finally, when they'd had their first real date, all those days ago now, he'd thought it was about to happen.

Now, he was on the verge of ruining it all. He could feel it.

He was so suffocated by the weight of his fear and his sadness that he didn't know how he was ever going to pick himself up. He didn't know if he'd have the strength to wrap his arms around Amelie, to romance her, to date her, to convince her to marry him one day. He felt the way he'd felt back in America. Before he came to the ranch. Before Amelie and Italy softened his pain. Except, this time, he had nowhere else to run to. This time, there was no escaping it.

CHAPTER THIRTY-FIVE

AMELIE

Amelie had been riding for over an hour and was about a mile away from the creek when the clouds split open. Rain fell in stinging sheets onto her skin, onto Rupert, onto the path in front of them. It was so heavy she could barely see, but Rupert knew where they were going.

Bravely, he trudged on, barely seeming to notice the rain or the thunder that was rumbling above their heads. It was so dark it felt like the middle of the night and the storm showed no signs of stopping.

Finally, Amelie spotted a flicker of light up ahead. "Over there, Rupert," she called over the rain, but he was already heading toward it.

When they reached the tiny, almost extinguished campfire, Amelie climbed down from Rupert's back and tied him up beside Shadow. Shadow looked nervous, but seeing Rupert seemed to calm her.

"Skye?" Amelie moved closer to the tent that she recognised as one of the ranch's. It had been set up beneath the shelter of the trees, but its canopy was slick with rainwater. "Skye? Are you in there?"

She was bending down, about to unzip the entrance, when she heard a voice behind her.

"Amelie?"

She stood up and whirled around. Skye was holding a pile of firewood. His shirt was soaked and sticking to his skin, his curly hair slick against his forehead. "Not really the time to be building a fire!" She waved her arms to indicate the water dripping from her fingertips and laughed.

For a moment, Skye didn't move but then he tossed down the wood and hurried over to open the tent.

"I went to find dry kindling," he said as they clambered inside. "But I think the fire's a bit of a lost cause."

Amelie stood hunched beneath the roof of the tent, reluctant to sit down for fear of getting everything wet.

"Here…" Skye fished a towel from his backpack and handed it to her then took one for himself.

As she pulled her hair loose and tried to squeeze it dry, Skye watched her. "It's freezing in here," he said, reaching for his bag. "I have spare clothes…" He pulled out some joggers and a large burgundy sweatshirt. "I'll um…" He gestured to the entrance and turned around, so he was facing away from her.

As Amelie tugged off her damp jeans and swapped them for Skye's joggers, she watched his shoulders rising and falling. Anxiousness was practically vibrating on his skin, and she hated that she didn't know what to say to him. When she'd bundled her clothes into the corner of the tent and was securely inside Skye's sweatshirt, she finally said, "Are you okay with me being here?"

Skye paused for a moment, then turned around.

Before he could answer, she added, "I mean, I guess if you'd wanted to be completely alone, you'd have picked a better hiding place." She sat down and tucked her knees up under her chin. "You're becoming a little predictable, Skye Anderson."

Skye's mouth twitched into a smile and he rubbed the back of his neck with his towel. "I guess I am."

Amelie looked around the tent. She wanted to tell him about Ethan and Elena. She wanted to offer him a glimmer more hope than he had right now, but Molly's words echoed in her ears; what use is hope if it's destined to be shattered?

Instead, she patted the ground next to her. "Do you have snacks?" she asked, pointing to his bag.

"Actually, yes, I have cookies and..." Skye crouched down and began to rummage in the bag. He pulled out a flask and presented it to her. "And tea."

"You had time to make a flask of tea but no time to tell me you were running off into the wilderness?" She watched him carefully as she poured them each a cup from the flask.

Skye replied quickly, as if he was deeply worried he'd upset her, "Nonna makes it for me every morning. She leaves it outside the cabin."

"It's okay, Skye. I was joking." Amelie touched his knee, but the contact made him flinch and the flinch turned into a shiver. "Do you have any more clothes?" She gestured to his bag.

He pulled out a second sweater, and a pair of jeans, and stood up.

"I won't peek, I promise." Amelie put her hands over her eyes and dipped her head, but made an exaggerated show of trying to sneak a look past her fingers.

Skye smiled at her. A smile that, despite the circumstances, made her heart race. "Make sure you don't," he said, turning around.

Concentrating on her knees, Amelie heard Skye pull up his fresh pair of jeans, waited a moment, then allowed herself to look up. He was turning his sweater the right way around, getting ready to lift it over his head, and his back was exposed. Amelie stifled a gasp. Raised, reddish-purple scars were peppered across his lower back, snaking like veins toward his left side. Until now, she'd never seen them. She knew they existed – Skye had told her about them – but even when they swam together in the creek he'd kept them covered by a t-shirt, and she'd been careful never to catch sight of them when he didn't want her to.

As if he sensed she was watching, Skye turned around. Before he could pull his sweater on, Amelie stood up and took hold of it. "You don't need to hide this from me." She rested her hand gently on his side.

Skye closed his eyes. His broad shoulders were trembling.

"Do they hurt?" Amelie kept her palm pressed against his skin. She wanted him to know that none of it mattered to her. The scars, his past, what he did or didn't do; none of it mattered to her.

"Sometimes. Mostly, they're okay." Skye's voice cracked as he spoke and he looked away, brushing his fingers through his still-damp hair.

Outside, the rain was falling harder on the tent's canopy. So hard it almost drowned out their voices.

Skye put on his sweater and smoothed it over his stomach and sides. As Amelie sat back down and pulled a blanket round her shoulders, he sat beside her and crossed his legs.

"I talked to Molly," Amelie said, trying to interpret his expression as she spoke. "She told me a little of what happened. Not all of it."

If Skye was upset that she'd spoken to Molly behind his back, he didn't show it.

"Skye, I've always said that I'll be here when you're ready to talk–"

"I know."

"You don't have to tell me, but if you want to…" She slipped her hand into his and squeezed his fingers. "It's just you and me. Whatever you say here, it can stay here."

Skye tried to smile. "In the tent?"

Amelie laughed and bit the corner of her lip. "Yes… what's said in the tent, stays in the tent. Ranch rules."

Skye inhaled deeply and reached out to touch the corner of Amelie's blanket. He took it between his fingers and scratched his fingernail over the threads. "So, there's a saying. A saying I've never liked very much: *paws before boots*."

Amelie frowned.

"It means that, as much as we want the dogs to be safe, the aim is for them to save *human* lives. Handlers are trained to provide first aid. The vets are there to provide medical care, and we love these dogs, but their job is to do dangerous things. We know that going in." Skye's voice seemed stronger and his tone was different. He was speaking like a solider.

"We were travelling. We received intel about a planned attack, so I ordered the convoy to change routes. An IED went off. Took out four vehicles."

Amelie swallowed hard; she couldn't even imagine... "That's how you were injured?"

Skye screwed his eyes shut. A tear escaped and rolled down his cheek. He touched the scar on his forehead then wiped his eyes. "When I woke up, they told me we lost three dogs and two men. They told me Dallas was..."

Amelie sat up on her knees and wrapped her arms tightly around Skye's upper body. His shoulders began to shake.

"It's okay to be sad, Skye."

He tried to pull away but she held him closer.

"It's okay to be sad."

"Amelie–"

Sitting back, Amelie cupped his face in her hands and dipped her head to meet his eyes. “It’s *okay* to miss her.”

As she let go of his cheeks, Skye looked away. “I missed her so much.”

“I know.”

“And now she’s back, and I’m going to lose her all over again.”

Amelie stopped herself from saying what she wanted to say – that everything would be okay. Instead, she slipped her hand into Skye’s and let their fingers wind together. “I know, and I’m so sorry.”

CHAPTER THIRTY-SIX

SKYE

As rain and wind battered their tent, and thunder rumbled through the valley, Skye and Amelie slept. When Skye woke, with his body curled around Amelie's, light was filtering in through the minuscule gaps between canvas and floor, and he could once again hear the rush of the creek outside.

Amelie yawned and rubbed her eyes sleepily. Her hair was loose and had dried in wispy waves. Skye liked it like that. Turning toward him, she stroked his upper arm. "How long were we asleep?"

"An hour maybe?" Skye asked.

Amelie sat up and reached for her phone, which was sitting beside her soggy pile of clothes. He watched as she looked at it. She blinked several times and seemed to be reading something and rereading it.

"Skye…" Her eyes had widened.

"What is it?"

"Ethan," she said breathlessly. "It's Ethan. He said he can take Dallas."

Skye frowned. His entire body was suddenly crawling with pins and needles and his mouth was sandpaper dry. "Take her?"

"I needed to do something to help and I didn't know what else to do, so I called Ethan. I didn't actually think he'd be able to help but–" Amelie was speaking quickly. She handed Skye the phone but he couldn't focus on it so she took it back and paraphrased. "His girlfriend Elena – her cousin is a vet in New York. If we can cover Dallas' medical costs, Elena and her cousin will foster Dallas and care for her until she's well enough to travel. We just have to get approval from…" Amelie waved her hands in the air. She was grinning. "Whoever we get approval from."

Skye's breath was coming thick and fast. He was dizzy and the tent was too warm. He needed air. Fumbling with the zip, he pulled open the entrance and stepped outside. Everything smelled of rain. The air was cool, and water was dripping from the trees. Nearby, Shadow and Rupert were nibbling on some grass by the river.

"I'm sorry." Amelie lightly put her hand on his shoulder as he bent forward to catch his breath. "Maybe I shouldn't have gotten involved? I just–"

Before she could finish, Skye grabbed hold of her. Lifting her into the air, he whirled her around and let out a yell that made the trees vibrate. "Haha!"

When he put Amelie down, she was laughing.

"Amelie Goodwin, you're the best thing that ever happened to me."

"Skye…"

"I love you."

"Skye, you don't have to say that. You're emotional and–" Amelie shook her head. Her hair fell across her face. Skye brushed it back and let his fingertips linger on the soft fine hairs at the base of her neck.

"I love you, Amelie, and I should have said it sooner."

Amelie blinked up at him.

He loved her. He loved that she was shorter than him. He loved the freckles on her nose and the colour of her eyes. He loved the way she stood up for anyone she felt was being downtrodden, and he loved that she was the only person in the world who could take away the ache in his heart simply by being there.

"I love you too," Amelie laughed. "I loved you from the second we sat next to each other on the plane."

Skye wrapped his arms around her waist. When she returned her eyes to his, he smiled and traced his thumb over her lips. She leaned into his touch. "Remember what I said to you on your *un*-wedding day?"

"You said the day we finally kissed would be the day you told me you were falling for me…"

"Problem is, I skipped *falling* and went straight to *fallen*."

Smiling, Amelie stood up onto the tips of her toes and wrapped her arms around Skye's neck. "Then you've got some making up to do, haven't you?"

CHAPTER THIRTY-SEVEN

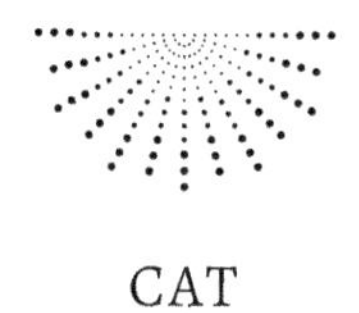

CAT

ONE WEEK LATER

"It's Valentine's Day, you're seeing Aida on Valentine's Day?" Amelie was standing in front of her wardrobe holding up dress after dress while Cat paced up and down by the window.

"Well, I'm supposed to be. But I haven't heard from her yet." She shook her phone as if it might prompt a text message to come through that had been stuck in cyber space.

Amelie bit her lower lip.

"You think she's ghosting me, don't you?" Cat asked. "Well, she's not. I spoke to her three days ago on the phone. We video chatted for two hours."

"I didn't say anything," Amelie finally settled on a light blue knit dress that flared out at the waist.

"Nice," Cat said absentmindedly, "I like that one. It goes well with your tan boots."

Picking up the boots, Amelie pulled them on over her leggings then swapped the tunic she'd been wearing for the dress. Smoothing it down, she asked, "Okay?"

Cat nodded. "You look great."

Amelie exhaled loudly, her nostrils flaring a little, and sat down hard on the end of the bed. "If you spoke to Aida a few days ago and she said she was okay to meet then maybe she's just having phone problems."

"Maybe…" For the hundredth time that morning, Cat refreshed her inbox in case Aida had emailed instead. "So, I should just go to *Sant' Anna* and wait where we said we'd meet?"

Amelie tilted her head from side to side. Unexpectedly, she replied, "Yes. You should." She glanced at the clock. "Which means you should get going."

Cat nodded. She'd gotten dressed hours ago, but something about Aida's sudden lack of communication had made her hold off on leaving. Since their first meeting, the two of them had texted daily and chatted several times on the phone. For Aida to go quiet on the day they were supposed to meet was… odd. Not necessarily concerning, but odd.

"All right," she said, hugging her sister and kissing her on the cheek. "Have a lovely time with Skye. Do you know where he's taking you?"

"No idea," Amelie said. "I think it's outdoors, though, because he said to wear something warm."

"Hope it's not riding." Cat raised her eyebrow at Amelie's dress. But as her sister's face turned to alarm, she squeezed her arm and added, "I'm joking. It won't be riding."

In response, Amelie rolled her eyes and shooed Cat toward the door. "Go on, go. Have fun with Aida. I'll text you when I'm back."

"Ditto." Cat blew Amelie a couple of kisses, headed back to her room to grab her purse, then shoved her phone into her pocket, took a deep breath, and told herself to stop panicking. Aida would be there. Just as she'd promised she'd be.

She was half way to *Sant' Anna*, and had stopped for fuel, when Aida finally texted. Climbing back into the driver's seat, Cat breathed a sigh of relief as she opened the message. When she read it, however, her fingers tightened on the steering wheel.

Cat, I am very sorry. I cannot make it to our meeting today. I will call to rearrange.

Cat read the message three times before throwing the phone onto the seat next to her. Tears had sprung to her eyes and she was clenching her fists. Without meaning to, she punched the steering wheel. It felt good, so she did it again, and again, and again. When she stopped, a middle-aged woman with a child was watching her. She took the child's hand and hurried her into their car as if Cat was about to jump out and start screaming at people.

Wiping her eyes with the back of her hand, she turned the key in the ignition and pulled out of the petrol station. By the time she reached the ranch, her tears had dried up but the seasick feeling in her stomach hadn't gone away.

She'd just parked up by the house when Ben came rushing outside. He was pulling a checked shirt on top of a white t-shirt and almost tripped on the front steps.

"What's wrong?" Cat asked, a knot of worry forming in her throat as she climbed out of the truck.

Heading for his moped, Ben grimaced and shouted, "I have a date, and I only went and forgot!"

"Forgot?" Cat frowned. "A date with who?"

"The girl from the deli. Camille." Ben ruffled his hair with his fingers and stooped to peer into the moped's mirror.

"A lunch date?"

"Cinema. I'm picking her up in town and…" Ben shook his head. "I don't have time to talk about it, Cat, I have to go."

"Right."

"Aren't you meeting Aida today?" He climbed onto the moped and pulled his helmet on.

"Later." Cat nibbled the inside of her cheek, the way she always did when she was telling an untruth. "You better go. Have fun."

"Will do. Bye."

As Ben sped out of the gates, Cat sat down on the bottom step. Behind her, the house was empty except for Nonna, who would be preparing lunch for Stefan, Bea and Markus.

Cat raised a finger to her ear and fiddled with her yellow earring then she rolled her eyes at herself and sighed. "Valentine's Day is always terrible," she muttered, unpinning her earring and holding it in the palm of her hand.

"Always?" A voice from behind made her jump. She turned to see Stefan walking slowly down the steps with his hands behind his back.

Shaking her head, she smiled. "Yes. Always."

"Even if someone brings you flowers?" Stefan sat down beside her.

Laughing, Cat said, "*If* someone bought me flowers that would be lovely, but I can safely say that not once, in thirty-three years, have I been given flowers on Valentine's Day. Except the time my dad bought me a rose because he felt sorry for me – the year my high school boyfriend ditched me for *Leoni Mancelli*."

"Leoni Mancelli?" Stefan was hiding a smile beneath his beard.

"Awful girl. Too pretty," Cat said, tutting.

"Well, then, I am pleased to say I have broken a habit..." Stefan took his hand from behind his back. He was holding a tiny bouquet of daisies. "Not roses, but..." He handed them to her.

As Cat took them, she dropped the earring she'd been holding and bent to pick it up. At the same time, Stefan did too and their foreheads bumped awkwardly. Rubbing her head, but grinning, Cat sat back on the step and held the flowers to her chest.

"Ouch." Stefan was holding her earring with one hand and rubbing his temple with the other.

"Yeah," Cat said. "Ouch."

Chuckling, Stefan handed back her earring. His fingers brushed against her palm and sent a jolt of fizziness from her wrist all the way to her head.

"Thank you." She sniffed the daisies, even though she knew they wouldn't smell of anything. "You've made what would have been an awful day much, much better."

"Awful because it is Valentine's Day or awful because of another thing?" Stefan asked, standing up and offering her his hand.

As he pulled her to her feet, Cat tightened her grip on the flower stems and found herself saying, "Why don't we go inside? I can put these in water, make you a coffee and bore you with my dreadful morning."

"I would like that." Stefan smiled and straightened his cardigan. "Very much."

CHAPTER THIRTY-EIGHT

AMELIE

THEY HAD BEEN WALKING for over an hour. Skye was lost but pretending he wasn't. Every now and then, he checked his phone but whenever Amelie asked where they were going, he told her it was a surprise.

Eventually, she stopped and put her hands on her hips. "Skye, if you tell me where we're going, I can probably get us there. I've known these woods since I was a kid."

They were in the forest south of *Legrezzia.* In summer, it was a beautiful place to spend the day but now, in mid-February, it was shadowy and too cool to be comfortable.

Skye let out a frustrated growl. "I should be good at this," he said, waving the phone.

"In here, everything looks the same. There aren't many navigation points." Amelie held out her hand and waggled her fingers. "Where are we going?"

Adjusting the straps of the backpack he was carrying on

his shoulders, Skye finally gave in and passed over the phone. "The old church," he said. "I read an article about it…"

"Why didn't you say so?" Amelie didn't even need to look at the phone.

"You know how to get there?"

"I do but I'm not sure you're going to like it." Amelie winced a little as she spoke.

"We're in the wrong place, aren't we?"

She nodded, wrinkling her nose. "I'm afraid so. We're in the wrong woods. We could veer east and circle around the town, up through the hills, but–"

"But I'm guessing that would take all afternoon?" Skye asked, pushing his hair from his face and exposing the scar above his eyebrow.

Amelie walked over to him and squeezed his arm then, slipping her hands around his waist, said, "It doesn't matter. We can just have the picnic here." She gestured to the ground, which was sodden with fallen leaves and smiled as if she genuinely thought it was a good idea.

Skye laughed and shook his head. "Very romantic."

"Or we could go back to the truck. Drive to the river?" Amelie took hold of Skye's hand and tugged it as she began to walk. "It was a lovely idea. We'll try again in spring. For my birthday, maybe?"

Skye put his arm around Amelie's shoulders and pulled her closer. She fit almost perfectly under his chin, a feeling she never grew tired of. "I'm sorry."

"Don't be sorry. It was a lovely idea. Come on…"

Half an hour later, they arrived back where they'd started and climbed back into the truck. "You know what?" Amelie turned in her seat so she was facing Skye. "I'm kind of starving, and it's nice here." She looked out at the trees. "Why don't we just put on the radio and picnic in the truck?"

"We can't spend our first Valentine's Day in my truck, Am," Skye laughed.

"Why not?" She stroked the top of his hand. "It's a nice truck. We're together. We have music and…" she reached up and flicked on the overhead light, "mood lighting, and I'm guessing Nonna's packed us up some treats in that backpack."

Skye pulled the bag onto his lap and unzipped it. "Actually," he said, wiggling his eyebrows at her, "I prepared every single thing in this bag. Nonna didn't even help."

"Oh, well now I really am dying to eat. You'd better show me what you've got…" Amelie sat back and folded her arms.

As Skye took out delicious looking treat after delicious looking treat, Amelie realised she couldn't stop smiling. "You know what?" she said as she took an arancini from a small plastic box. "I've eaten in hundreds of fancy restaurants."

"With Jed?" Skye asked, his upper lip twitching.

"Well, yes, but I wasn't going to say that," she tutted at him. "My point was… I've eaten in some of the fanciest restaurants in London, but I think this is the most romantic meal I've ever had."

Skye smiled the sideways smile which made his cheek dimple and which, in turn, made Amelie's heart flutter. "Is that right?"

"It is."

"I'm about to make it even more romantic," Skye said smoothly.

"Oh yeah?"

He plugged his phone into the holder on the dash and opened up a playlist. Its title was *For Amelie*. "Ready?"

Amelie grinned. "Ready." But just as Skye pressed play, the phone began to ring. *Ethan Calling.*

Skye's eyes widened. Shoving aside the tub of arancini, he accepted the call and Ethan's face came into view. He was in his apartment. Elena wasn't there, but Amelie could see a picture of her pinned to the fridge behind him.

"Hey guys, sorry to interrupt on Valentine's," Ethan said. He looked tired. It was early in the morning in New York and Amelie knew he'd been working too hard lately.

"No problem." Skye was leaning forward as if he wanted to jump into the phone. "You have news?"

"Not really, except that there is no news," Ethan said. "We still haven't had an answer from the Kennel Master at Harrisburg but your friend Molly's arriving today. We're going to get together and see what we can do."

Skye's demeanour had changed. In a split second, he'd

become twitchy and his face had turned grey around the edges. "Ethan, we've only got fourteen days."

"I know." Ethan moved position and looked sincerely into the camera. "I promise, we're doing everything we can on our end."

"What can I do?"

Ethan shook his head. "We've got your letter. Your video testimonial. The rest is just–"

"Red tape and paperwork." Skye rubbed his hands over his face as he answered.

"Seems like it." Ethan tried to sound a little more jovial as he added, "But Molly will get things moving. She seems like the type of woman who's good at getting things done."

As Skye looked away, out of the window, Amelie took the phone from the dash and smiled at her brother. Skye was still mad at Molly. He hadn't even said goodbye to her, despite Amelie trying to persuade him to, but they needed Molly's help and Skye knew that. "Thanks, Ethan. Let us know when Molly arrives." Amelie paused, because it didn't come naturally for her to be sincere with her usually-sarcastic younger brother. "What you're doing… it means a lot."

"It's nothing." Ethan shook his head then said, "Tell Mum and Dad I'm sorry I can't be there for the party. Work is…" He breathed out loudly and puffed his lips the way the horses did when they were over tired. "But Elena and I have both booked some time off in the summer."

"You have? That's brilliant."

"We'll try and call in on the party." Ethan gestured to the phone. "Video call, obviously."

"That would be great."

"Okay, see you soon."

"See you, buddy," Skye interjected, offering a small wave as he temporarily snapped out of his web of thoughts.

"Happy Valentine's, little brother." Amelie blew Ethan a kiss then ended the call.

Beside her, Skye was silent for a long moment before turning back to the playlist he'd made her.

"Skye, we don't have to do this now." The food he'd so lovingly prepared seemed a lot less appetising than it had a few minutes ago.

"I'm sorry," he said quietly, sitting back in his seat. "I'm not sure I'm going to be good company after that. I've been trying not to think about it but–"

Amelie turned off the music and squeezed Skye's hand. "It's okay, really. Let's head home and get some coffee. Ben had a date with that girl from the deli… we can go tease him about it. Get some juicy details."

"You're sure?"

"We're going to have lots and lots of Valentine's Days together, Skye Anderson. You can make it up to me next year."

Skye smiled at her and, even though the smile didn't quite reach his eyes, he said, "Next year. It's a date."

CHAPTER THIRTY-NINE

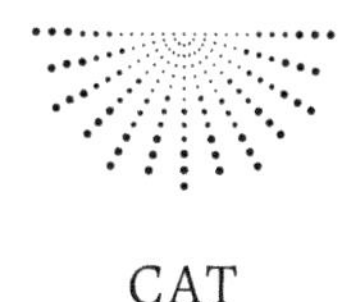

CAT

CAT WAS in the kitchen making a bad attempt at recreating their mother's blueberry muffins when Amelie and Skye arrived back from their date. She'd expected them to be all giddy, full of smiles and flirtatious glances. But when they entered the kitchen, Skye said he'd changed his mind about coffee, gave Amelie a brief peck on the cheek, and left.

"What was that about?" Cat held out the mixing bowl so that Amelie could run her finger around the edge of it.

"Tastes good," Amelie said, avoiding the question.

Cat put the bowl down and gestured to the table. "Sit. Tell me what happened."

With a sigh, Amelie did as she was told. "We got lost. Skye was trying to find the old church up in the woods but he wouldn't tell me where we were going and we ended up miles from anywhere. We went back to the truck but then we got a call from Ethan."

"About Dallas?" Cat had brought over a muffin tray and was pouring the batter into the holes.

Amelie nodded. "He's struggling to sort everything out. It all seems to be taking forever and, well, Dallas doesn't have forever, does she?"

Cat closed her eyes. She couldn't imagine what Skye was going through, didn't want to imagine it. "I'm guessing that ruined the romantic mood?" she asked.

"Just a bit." Amelie folded her arms in front of her chest and stretched out her legs beneath. "I don't mind. I'm just worried about him."

"You've done everything you can," Cat said, returning to the oven and slotting the muffin tray onto the middle shelf. "These will be ready soon. Sugar always helps."

Amelie smiled, but the smile turned to a frown as she said, "Aren't you supposed to be with Aida?" She checked the time. "You can't have been together long if you're back from *Sant'Anna* already?"

Shrugging and willing her face not to betray the sickly sensation in her stomach, Cat turned on the kettle. "She had to postpone. A work thing. She was trying to get out of it but…" She trailed off, she'd never been good at lying to Amelie and was glad she was facing the cupboard, taking out coffee mugs, as she spoke.

"Sorry, Cat." Amelie was either too distracted by Skye to question Cat's explanation or had decided to be more supportive. Either way, Cat wasn't going to object.

"So," she said, gesturing to the mugs as she turned

around. "Just us girls. We could do ice cream and a movie? Like the good old days."

"You mean like the year we both had a horrendous crush on *Gianni Rosetti*?" Amelie pulled an 'eeew' face as she spoke.

"Ha! I'd almost forgotten him… didn't we both sent him a Valentine's Day card?" Laughter bubbled up in Cat's throat as she pictured teenage Amelie and Cat sitting at the kitchen table trying to outdo one another's cards.

"Yes, we did. Except he sent one to–"

"Carina Cornell!" Cat performed a pouty hair flick and put her hands on her hips as if she was modelling for a beach-wear catalogue.

Amelie was laughing hard. Sitting up, she squeezed her side and said, "Oh, don't, you're giving me a stitch."

"Okay, okay." Cat waved her hands. "Let's ditch the coffee. We'll get wine, and a cheesy rom com, and a *bucket* of ice cream, and–"

Amelie stood up, gesturing to the backpack Skye had left her with. "And Skye's snacks will go to waste if we don't eat them, so…"

Cat grinned at her sister. Perhaps it wasn't going to be the worst Valentine's Day after all.

The next morning, Cat was woken by a foot digging into her side. Forcing her eyes open, she blinked at the tangle of limbs on the bed. Amelie was asleep beside her and Ben, who'd arrived home from his date just after midnight, was upside down with his head hanging off the end of the bed and his feet far too close to Cat's face.

Giving him a shove, she sat up. Ben groaned, wobbled, and fell to the floor with a thud. Rubbing his neck, he looked up at her. "Harsh," he said croakily.

Cat nestled back into her pillows and folded her arms. "You deserve it after what you did to poor Gina."

"I didn't *do* anything."

"Exactly!" Cat laughed. It turned out that Gina from the deli had been in love with Ben for pretty much forever. When he asked her out for a Valentine's Day date, she thought he was about to confess he was mad about her too.

"I was being a gentleman. I don't like her like that, so I'm not going to kiss her on Valentine's Day, am I?"

"But you did take her on a date on Valentine's Day…" Amelie had stirred and was peering at her brother through narrow sleepy eyes.

"Yes, but I didn't realise she thought it meant something. I just thought…" Ben let out a frustrated growl and clambered back onto the end of the bed. "Okay, I'm an idiot. Can we talk about something else now?"

Cat and Amelie were both laughing at him, and Amelie was about to hit him with a pillow, when they heard footsteps in the hallway.

"Girls? Ben?"

"Mum?!" Amelie jumped off the bed and ran to the door.

Flinging it open, she squealed and hurled herself forward, wrapping her arms around their mother and pulling her close.

A smile spread across Cat's lips. "You're early," she said as Amelie finally let go and allowed Mum into the room.

"It's almost midday." Mum looked at her watch and tapped it. "But it looks like you three had a late night?"

As Mum sat down on the edge of the bed, Cat realised that the uneasy feeling which had been lodged in her stomach for days had begun to soften. Their parents were home, back where they belonged, which meant that everything – Markus, and Skye, and Aida – would soon be fixed.

As Amelie and Ben followed Mum downstairs, Cat told them she'd be there in a minute; while Amelie had been regaling Mum with tales of Ben's date, Cat's phone had beeped.

Closing the door and leaning against it, she opened the message.

Cat, I'm very sorry about yesterday. Can we try again? I am free this afternoon. We could meet at the beach near Cecina if you can make it there? I will bring some food for us?

Cat's jaw tensed. She tapped her fingernails on the phone screen. Then she shook her head and shoved the phone into her pocket. Aida would just have to wait for a reply.

Downstairs, she found her parents, Ben, and Amelie

sitting around the kitchen table. Nonna was making tea, the doors were open, and the sun was shining into the room.

"Did you have a lovely time?" Amelie was asking.

Turning to their father, Mum smiled and squeezed his hand. She was looking at him with wide, soft-around-the-edges eyes that made Cat feel like they were intruding on a private moment. Dad brushed a hand through his thick grey hair and nodded. "We had a wonderful time."

"But it's good to be home," Mum added. "A lot has been happening, I think?"

As Cat sat down, taking a cup of tea from Nonna and wrapping her hands around the mug, she listened to Amelie tell their parents the latest update on Skye and Dallas.

Their father, who'd always loved animals more than he'd loved people, looked like he wanted to either cry or shout. "What about Alec? When's he back?"

"Tomorrow. He's agreed to pay for whatever Dallas needs. We just have to convince the army to say yes to Elena and her cousin providing foster care." Amelie was wringing her hands together. "Which isn't easy, apparently."

Dad bit his lower lip. "No. I can imagine."

"And how is Bea? Has Alec's lawyer been in touch?" Mum had lowered her voice and was leaning onto her forearms. She was wearing a teal sweater that brought out the silvery blonde shades in her hair.

Cat nodded. "They're meeting with him after the weekend. We haven't seen Antonio since he showed up at the café but..."

"I'll go and see them." Mum stood up.

From the corner of the room, Nonna called, "Rose, you haven't eaten."

But Mum shook her head. "I'll have something when I've seen them. Thank you."

"Then I will come with you," Nonna said, loading some of the pastries she'd been preparing onto a separate tray. "You can talk to Bea and Markus while you eat."

At that, Mum smiled. Blowing them each a kiss, she took her coffee with her and promised she'd catch up with them later.

Cat was watching Nonna and Mum leave when her phone beeped for a second time. She glanced at it then turned it face down on the table. When she looked up, her father was frowning at her.

"You're not answering it Kit-Cat?"

"It's Aida," she said quietly; it still felt like a betrayal to even mention Aida's name to her parents. "She's asking to meet me today but…"

Dad exchanged a look with Amelie. "Have you seen her much since your first meeting?" he asked, as if it was a perfectly normal conversation to be having.

"No," Cat said. "We were supposed to meet yesterday but something came up."

"If you want to meet her, Cat, it's okay. We can catch up on your news this evening." Her father was smiling as if he really meant what he was saying but it made Cat's temples throb to think about what he was feeling beneath the surface.

"You're sure?" She looked at Amelie, who was concentrating very hard on her pastries.

"Of course," Dad said, squeezing her hand.

"What about the party?" Cat looked at Ben, but the second the words left her mouth she slapped her hands over her lips and gasped. Wincing, she glanced at her father.

"Party?" He looked at each of them in turn. "What party?"

"Cat!" Amelie was staring at her.

"Cat, seriously?" Ben shook his head and laughed dolefully. "All this time and you blow it at the last minute?"

"I'm so sorry," Cat felt like crying. The emotions bubbling away in her stomach were too much. "Dad, forget I said anything. Please?"

"It's no use, we've got to tell him now." Amelie got up from the table, her chair scraping against the floor. Marching over to the sink, she tossed in her cup and sighed. When she turned around, she said, bluntly, "Dad, we were planning a surprise party for you and Mum. To celebrate your anniversary, and the barn, and–"

"Fresh starts," finished Ben.

Their father was smiling broadly. "Well, that's wonderful," he said, chuckling. "Your mother will be thrilled."

"Except now it's not a surprise," muttered Amelie.

"It'll still be a surprise for her," Dad said. Patting Cat's arm, he added, "At least now I know, I can find an excuse to keep her out of the barn until tomorrow." Looking at the others, he said, "Really, kids, no harm done."

But as Amelie sat back down and began to tell their father what arrangements were in place, and Ben painted a graphic picture of how stunning the new barn was going to look with the lights and decorations they'd organised, Cat stood up. "Sorry, I'll be back."

In the entrance hall, she leaned against the wall and took out her phone.

Aida, I can be in Cecina in a couple of hours. I will let you know when I am on the way.

CHAPTER FORTY

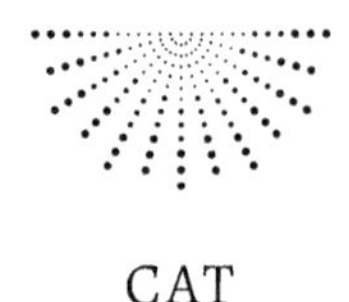

CAT

CAT WAS ABOUT to climb into her parents' truck when she spotted Stefan walking past the pool. They'd spent an hour together yesterday, drinking coffee and talking about his books. She'd told him about Aida. He'd told her a little about his own parents. Without really thinking about it, she jogged over to him.

"Catherine," he said, smiling at her, hands in pockets. "You look nice."

Cat looked down at herself. She'd put on a navy and white striped sweater, jeans, and a pair of knee-high navy boots, but she was barely wearing any makeup and felt anything but *nice*.

"Thank you."

"You are going somewhere?" Stefan looked past her at the truck.

"I'm going to *Cecina* to see Aida." She folded her arms

then put them back down by her sides, unsure what felt the least uncomfortable. “Would you come?”

Stefan blinked at her as if he’d misheard. “Come? With you?”

“Sorry.” She waved her hands at him. “Sorry, it’s a silly idea. Why would you want to do that?” She laughed at herself and started to walk away. “I’m sorry, Stefan, I’ll see you later.”

“Wait…” Stefan caught her arm. His fingers lingered for a moment, then he took them away and met her eyes. “Of course, I will come with you.”

“Really?”

“May I have a moment to make sure my cabin is locked up?”

Cat nodded. “Take as long as you need. I’ll wait in the truck.”

As Stefan walked away, she released a long slow breath. She had no idea why, but the thought of having him with her – his calm, unassuming presence just *there* beside her – helped quell the nerves that were wracking her stomach.

In the driver’s seat, she put the key in the ignition but didn’t switch on the radio; she knew what music she needed to hear and it was only Stefan who could play it for her.

"I can wait in the truck, if you prefer it?" Stefan asked when they pulled into the parking area opposite *Cecina's* small sandy beach.

"I'd like you to come." Cat glanced at him. "I know it's strange. I can't explain it. I just feel nervous this time. Not *good* nervous." She tapped her fingers on the inside of the door just below the window. "Her tone changed. The first time we met, and for a few days after, she was polite, kind… sunny. When she cancelled yesterday, she was distant. Matter of fact. Then today…" She braced her hands on the steering wheel and exhaled slowly.

Stefan began to open his door. "Let's go and find out, shall we?"

On the beach, Aida was waiting for them in the shelter of a small cove. She'd brought a picnic blanket and two paper bags that looked like they were from a local deli. She waved and, when she realised Stefan was walking beside Cat, her smile widened.

"Cat, you brought a friend?" Aida extended her hand and Stefan shook it. He was barefoot, his trousers rolled up a little, and was carrying his shoes and socks.

"Yes," Cat answered, studying Aida's face.

"A *boyfriend*?" Aida whispered. Despite the fact she was speaking in Italian, Stefan seemed to absorb the gist of what she was saying and looked down at his feet, shuffling them deeper into the sand and wiggling his toes.

Cat ignored her. "This is Stefan. He's German, so we should stick to English if that's okay? Stefan, this is Aida."

"It is nice to meet you," Stefan said politely.

Aida nodded. "You too." Turning back to her picnic blanket and the paper bag, she said, "I bought some things from my favourite shop. I hope there is enough for three."

"Oh, I don't have a big appetite." Stefan patted his slim stomach and held out his hand for Cat's as she lowered herself onto the blanket.

"A gentleman," Aida said, observing the gesture with a smile. "That is very rare these days. You should hang onto him." Laughing at herself, she pointed at Cat's hand and said, "Hang onto him? See, you are doing it already."

Cat narrowed her eyes and began to chew the inside of her cheek. There was something different about Aida today; she was twitchy and brash. The opposite of the reserved, softly spoken woman Cat had spent an afternoon with in *Sant' Anna*.

Stefan sat down next to Cat and looked out at the rolling waves. "I love the beach," he said. "I grew up on a farm very far from the beach. We didn't go often when I was a child."

"A farm. How lovely." Aida was unloading the bag. Before revealing any food, she took out two large bottles of wine and two small plastic cups. "You and Caterina have a lot in common."

Cat swallowed hard. Caterina was the name on her birth certificate, but she hadn't used that name in years. A prickly heat was working its way up her throat. Through tight lips, she said, "*Catherine*. My name is Catherine or Cat. Never Caterina."

Aida had been unscrewing one of the bottles but stopped. Her eyes widened, and then she laughed. "Of course. I'm sorry." Shrugging she added, "Caterina – Catherine. They are the same, no?"

Sucking in her breath, Cat tried to breathe through the fire in her belly and concentrate on the sound of the waves. She felt like screaming. She felt like running back to the truck and leaving this woman – this Aida imposter who had taken the place of the woman she'd met by the fountain – and never looking back.

Stefan saved her from the impulse.

"My family kept pigs," he said loudly, cutting through the tension. "But having spent time on the Goodwins' ranch, I think I much prefer horses. The smell is much better." Stefan reached for the wine and poured two glasses.

Cat smiled at him, hoping he could see from her expression how grateful she was to have him there. When he offered her a glass, she shook her head. "I better not, I'm driving."

"Oh, please," Aida said, holding up her cup. "Just a small one."

"We can share," Stefan said softly.

Cat met his eyes. "Thank you."

"*Saluti*!" Aida tipped her cup at them. Then downed her drink in one.

Three hours later, as the waves inched further up the beach, and the sky darkened with rain clouds, Cat stood up. "I think we should get going," she said to Stefan.

"Yes," he said, clambering to his feet. "I believe we should, but what should we do with your mother?"

Cat put her hands on her hips and let out a large puff of air. Looking up at the sky, she blinked away the urge to yell.

On the blanket, Aida was asleep and snoring. She had finished both bottles of wine almost single handedly, had asked Stefan lots of inappropriate questions about his love life, why he wasn't married, and what his intentions were towards Cat, and then she'd passed out.

"Don't call her that," Cat said. "I don't even want to think about that."

"Of course. I'm sorry."

Cat looked at him. He was watching her with sympathetic eyes. "No, I'm sorry. I didn't mean to snap at you. This whole thing is just…" She couldn't find the words.

"Do you know where she lives?"

Cat shook her head. "No, but I suppose we could check her purse for ID."

Gingerly, as if he was a thief who was about to be discovered, Stefan picked up Aida's handbag and held it open.

Cat dipped in her hand and drew out Aida's purse. "Here," she said, pulling out a driver's license, "*Via Aurellia 213*."

Stefan rubbed his beard. "I do not know where that is."

"Neither do I," Cat said, "but my phone will." Looking

down at Aida, who was snoring and had her arm across her eyes, she sighed. "Let's pack up this rubbish and then we'll try and wake her."

As Stefan piled their empty food cartons and the two wine-free bottles back into the paper bag they'd come from, Cat shook Aida's shoulder.

"Aida? We need to get you home? Can you get up?"

But Aida simply groaned and rolled over as if she was asleep in bed.

"We will carry her," Stefan said, stooping down and pulling Aida upright. "Take her other arm."

Cat copied his movement and between them they managed to drag Aida to her feet. Her head rolled and, in Italian, she muttered, "What are you doing to me? Leave me alone."

Eventually, they made it back to the truck and heaved Aida into the back. Strapping her in, Stefan offered to ride beside her. "In case she is…" He gestured to his mouth.

"Oh God, I hope she doesn't vomit." Cat's jaw tensed as she slotted her phone into the holder on the dash. "Her place is a ten minute drive away."

In the back of the truck, Stefan offered her a sympathetic smile as Aida slumped over and rested her head on his shoulder.

Cat gripped the steering wheel. "Okay, let's go."

When they reached *Via Aurelia,* Cat parked the truck halfway up the kerb and looked at the small modern apartment block opposite. "That's it," she said.

Dutifully, Stefan helped her pull Aida out of the truck and support her as she stumbled across the road. As they moved, she began to cry and started to mutter almost unintelligible apologies, mainly directed at Stefan.

At Aida's front door, Cat took her keys from her handbag and pushed it open. She hesitated before going inside. "This feels wrong. I barely know her. I shouldn't be in her apartment."

Adjusting Aida's weight on his shoulder, Stefan used his other hand to pat Cat's arm. "It is all right. We are helping her, not intruding."

Cat nodded and breathed in deeply.

Stepping into the hallway, she tried not to look at the walls, or at the console table with a small neat vase of flowers on it, or at the pictures on the walls – generic art prints of beach scenes and forests.

They passed two doors, which Cat nudged open in case they led to a bedroom. One was a closet. The other was a bathroom.

At the end of the hall, a third door opened onto a tiny kitchenette and living area. A small grey sofa sat opposite a walnut coffee table and an old TV. Breaking free from Stefan, Aida wobbled over to it and flopped down. Pulling the blanket from the back of the sofa, she draped it over her shoulders and nestled down into the cushions.

"See yourselves out," she said, eyes barely open.

Cat stood back and wrapped her arms around herself. Forcing herself to turn away, she went to the sink and filled a glass with tap water. On the draining board sat three empty wine bottles.

Cat closed her eyes and braced her hands on the edge of the sink. She opened them when she felt movement beside her. It was Stefan, gesturing for her to give him the glass.

As he took it over to the sofa, Cat picked up the bottles and threw them into the bin. They clunked loudly but she didn't care. Brushing down her jeans, because they were still carrying remnants of sand from the beach, Cat looked around for a spot to leave Aida's keys.

When her eyes landed on the fridge, her breath caught in her chest. Pinned to it, with a small teddy bear magnet, was a picture of Aida and a young woman. Cat stepped closer. At a glance, the woman could have been her; mid-length dark hair, the same body shape, the same smile, a similar age. But it wasn't her.

She touched her finger to the picture then tugged it loose.

"Are you ready?" Stefan was standing by the door to the hallway, hands in his pockets, looking like he was waiting for a bus.

Cat tightened her grip on the picture but, instead of putting it back, she shoved it into her pocket, turned away from the fridge, and placed Aida's keys loudly on the coffee table on her way out.

CHAPTER FORTY-ONE

AMELIE

"IT'S PARTY TIME!" Ben yelled through the house as he hurtled down the stairs.

It was early and Cat was behind the reception desk trying to sort out a problem with a wine delivery at *Signiorelli's* while Amelie finished off a hand-written sign that would direct their party guests to the new barn.

Their father was under strict instructions to keep Mum out of the way until seven p.m., so had taken her out at the crack of dawn on the promise of going to look at a new filly one of the nearby ranches was having trouble handling.

"Haven't we taken on enough problematic horses?" Mum had grumbled, referring to Andante, the horse which had caused her father's riding accident a couple of years ago and led to untold problems in the eighteen months afterwards.

"I promise, she's worth a look," Dad had said, winking at the kids as he'd ushered their mother out of the door.

Watching them leave, Amelie had almost been glad that Cat had spilled the beans; it would have been difficult to keep both parents occupied and out of the way. With Dad on their side, they could at least guarantee that one parent would be surprised by the party.

"I'm going to go put this up," she said, peering through the window to check their parents were out of sight.

"Okay." Cat had put down the phone and was absent-mindedly tapping a pen up and down on an empty notepad.

"Everything all right?" Amelie leaned onto the desk and smiled at her sister.

Cat looked tired. She'd arrived back from *Cecina* early yesterday evening, and Amelie was certain she'd seen Stefan Hurst exiting the truck with her. Instead of coming to sit with the rest of them in the library, and telling them about her afternoon with Aida, Cat had disappeared upstairs saying she'd gotten a little too much sun on the beach and needed to lie down. Which was clearly a lie because the sun had barely peeked out from behind the clouds all day.

Amelie had almost gone after her, but Mum and Dad had given her a look that said, *Just leave it, Am. She'll talk when she's ready.* So, she had… she'd left it. But now, she was beginning to wonder whether she'd done the right thing.

"Cat?"

Cat looked up and blinked at her. "Hmm?"

"Are you all right?"

"Oh, fine," she said, forcing a smile. "Just tired and

worried about *Signiorelli's*. With neither of us on hand today…"

"Tula's capable. She'll be fine. She said her boyfriend's helping."

Cat nodded. "Right. I forgot." Then, looking at the door, she said, "Weren't you going to hang the sign?"

Amelie bit her lower lip. "Yes, I was." She patted the desk and dipped her head to meet Cat's eyes. "I'll be back in a minute, then maybe we can have breakfast? Talk?"

"About what?" Cat had folded her arms in front of her chest.

Amelie shrugged. "About yesterday? What happened with Aida? Why I saw *Stefan Hurst* getting out of the truck with you?" Amelie raised her eyebrows, trying to lighten the mood, but Cat's face crumpled and she batted her hands at her eyes. Rushing around to Cat's side of the desk, Amelie dropped her makeshift sign and wrapped her arms around her sister. "Oh, Cat, what happened?"

"I can't…" Cat tugged herself free and shook her head. "I can't talk about it today, Am. I don't want to spoil the party. Tomorrow, okay?"

Amelie took a step back and examined her sister. She looked shaky, and Amelie knew that feeling – like the smallest act of kindness would cause you to crumble. "Okay," she said firmly. "Tomorrow, but don't think I'll forget."

Cat's lips curved into the smallest of smiles. "Tomorrow. Promise."

Outside, Amelie paused on the top step of the veranda and breathed in deeply, closing her eyes; something had happened with Aida. She'd known that it would and, yet, the fact she was right gave her absolutely no pleasure.

She'd reached the top paddock and was pinning up her sign, while going through various iterations of a conversation with Aida Borrelli in which she demanded she leave Cat alone, when she spotted Skye leaving his cabin.

He waved at her and broke into a run when he reached the top of the path.

"Nice," he said, admiring her large swirly writing. "*This way to the farm*?"

"Barn!" She thumped him gently on the shoulder but melted as he tucked her under his arm. "This way to the *barn*."

"Oh, right." Skye kissed her forehead. "Good job you're not trying to write this novel of yours by hand."

"What novel?" Amelie sighed a little; so much had been happening lately that she'd barely given writing a second thought. "I'll probably just end up working in *Signiorelli's* for the rest of my life."

"Would that be such a bad thing?" Skye asked as they instinctively started to walk toward the barn to check Jean's progress with the decorations.

"Yes. No. I don't know." Amelie laughed. Trying to stop her thoughts returning to Cat and what had happened yesterday, she said, "When's your dad back? Will he be here in time for the party?"

"He said he'll be here mid-afternoon," Skye answered but then, slowing down, he said, "Actually, Am, about the party…"

"Ah ha?" She slowed her pace to match his and rested her head on his shoulder.

"I might have to leave early." Skye's muscles had tensed.

"Early?" Amelie stopped. "Why?"

Sweeping his fingers through his hair, Skye broke eye contact with her and looked at his feet instead. "I'm flying to New York."

"New York?" Amelie rubbed at her forehead as if it might erase the creases that had formed.

Returning his gaze to hers, Skye took hold of her hands. "I can't sit tight and wait for Molly and Ethan to fix things. I need to know I've tried. I need to know I've done my part."

"But… tonight?" Amelie tugged her hands free because her palms were beginning to feel clammy. "You're going tonight? You couldn't go tomorrow?"

"The next option was three days away. I can't wait that long."

Amelie started walking again but then stopped. "When did you decide this? Why didn't you tell me?"

"I booked the flights last night. I'm telling you now." Skye took a few big strides to catch up with her and put his hands on her shoulders. "I'm sorry, Am. I have to do this."

As she looked at him, the hot prickly feeling on her skin slowly faded. "No, I'm sorry. I get it. I was just surprised and–"

"And you'll miss me?" Skye asked hopefully.

"Maybe." Amelie looped her arm around his waist and breathed in his cologne. "Definitely."

"Hopefully, I'll be back in a week with good news," Skye said as they continued toward the barn.

"A week?"

Skye tilted his head from side to side. "Longer, maybe. I don't know."

As they reached the barn and Skye jogged over to where Jean was balanced precariously on a ladder, stringing fairy lights, Amelie tried to smile. *Longer. Maybe.* What did that mean?

She flexed her fingers, trying to release the tension that had gripped her upper body. It was no good; the thought of Skye leaving, and of not knowing how long he'd be gone for, made her want to go and lie down in a dark room with the covers pulled over her head.

He had to go, she understood that, but she had no idea how to be okay with it.

CHAPTER FORTY-TWO

AMELIE

AT SEVEN P.M., their parents arrived home. Amelie, Ben, and Cat were waiting at the top of the path and saw their father, as he'd been instructed, drive straight down toward the barn instead of parking near the house.

When he reached the second paddock, he stopped the truck, walked around to the passenger side and opened the door.

"Thomas?" Mum said as Dad helped her down. "What's going on?"

"You'll see." He had covered her eyes with a scarf but, as he guided her forward, he pulled it free.

"Surprise!" Amelie waved her arms. Cat and Ben followed suit.

As their mother took in the sight of her three grown-up children, the decorations they'd strung along the fences, and the illuminated barn, her mouth dropped open and her hands went to her chest.

"Happy Anniversary," Cat said, opening her arms to give their parents a huge hug.

"Anniversary?" Mum looked from Thomas to Cat, then at Amelie and Ben.

"The kids did it all," Dad said. "I was just accidentally in on the secret."

As their parents walked toward the barn, music began to play. Jean's fairy lights had been lit up around the door and, from inside, they could hear the chatter of the guests who'd snuck in just after six p.m. and who had been waiting ever since.

"We wanted to celebrate you both," Amelie said, looping her arm through her mother's.

"And the new barn," Ben added.

"And new beginnings." Cat nodded toward the spot where Skye and Alec were waiting, just outside the barn doors.

When Amelie looked at her mother, she saw that her eyes were sparkling with tears.

"I don't know what to say…" She looked down at her clothes and shook her head. "Oh, look at me, I'm not dressed for a party."

"Ah!" Cat said triumphantly. "We thought of that. Follow us."

Tugging their mother away, Amelie and Cat left their father with Ben, Skye and Alec, and took their mother to one of the new, unused stables at the rear of the yard. Hanging up at the back was Mum's favourite blue dress, a mirror, and a necklace. On a stool nearby, they'd placed her small makeup collection, a hair brush, and a pair of tights.

"And..." Cat stooped down and, from beside the stable door, picked up a pair of red court shoes. "To match Dad's cowboy boots," she said.

At that, with tears still streaming down her cheeks, Mum tipped her head back and laughed. "I wondered why he wore those darn things today!" She said, moving into the stable and brushing her fingers over the fabric of her dress. When she turned around, she opened her arms wide and said, "Oh, girls, my girls."

Together, Amelie and Cat folded themselves into their mother's embrace and the three of them stood for a moment, not saying anything.

Kissing them each on the forehead, Mum stood back and breathed in as if she was trying to pull herself together. "Right. Okay. You girls go and wait with your father. I'll make myself presentable."

"Don't be too long," Amelie said as they headed for the door. "You've got party guests waiting to greet you."

Outside, Amelie squeezed her sister's hand and breathed a long sigh. "She's pleased," she said.

"Of course, she is," Cat grinned, looping her arm through Amelie's.

Over by the fence, their father was standing alone, like a

high school student waiting for his prom date to arrive. Before they reached him, they saw a figure in the distance.

"I thought everyone was already here?" Amelie said as a weight settled in her chest.

"They are."

"Hello! Welcome," Dad was waving at whoever it was, but the feeling in Amelie's chest hadn't shifted; she knew that person. It was a man. A shape she recognised.

As the man stepped into the light, Amelie stopped and grabbed Cat's hand. "Antonio," she whispered, but Cat had already seen him.

"Go," Amelie said, waving Cat toward the barn. "Tell Bea and Markus to hide. I'll hold him off."

"Hide?" Cat's eyes widened. "They're inside? I thought we agreed they should stay in their cabin?"

"Mum would have wanted them here," Amelie said meekly; it had been Dad's suggestion and she'd felt unable to say no to it.

"Amelie!" Cat groaned, pinching the bridge of her nose.

"Cat, we can discuss this later. Just go." Amelie made a shooing gesture and moved away.

As Cat disappeared into the barn, Amelie stepped up next to her father and whispered, as quickly as she could, "It's Markus' step-father. Bea and Markus are inside."

Without even flinching, Dad nodded coolly and said, "Okay, kiddo. Leave it to me."

Not allowing Antonio to make the first move, Dad strode

forward. "I'm sorry, sir, this is a private party and you're on private ground. Can I ask your name?"

"I'm here for my son." Antonio was shorter than Amelie's father but his voice was deeper and his expression angrier.

"Your son?" Dad blinked at him. "Forgive me, I'm not sure who–"

"Don't give me that. I've been watching this place for days." Looking at Amelie, he said, "I know the girls working in the café are connected to the ranch, and I know Bea's cell phone was here around the same time my son went missing."

"You mean your step-son? The one you allowed to languish in prison because you thought it would teach him a lesson?!" The words came out before Amelie could stop them.

At the same time, Cat and Skye came outside, and Amelie heard her sister mutter, "Amelie…"

"No, I'm sorry." Amelie strode forward so she was standing next to her father. Her heartbeat was throbbing so loudly she was certain everyone else could hear it. "I'm not letting this man march in here and–"

"Amelie…" Bea's voice made her turn around. As soon as she saw her, Amelie's legs began to tremble. What had she done? Why did she *say* that? "Hello, Antonio." Bea walked over and folded her arms in front of her chest.

"Bea," Antonio practically growled. "Where is Markus?"

"He's safe," she said. "But he won't be if you drag him

back to that place. Do you know what they did to him? Do you know what he suffered in there because he was the family of a policeman? Because he was *your* family? Because *you* sent him there?" Looking Antonio up and down, she said, in a voice full of disdain, "My sister would be ashamed of the way you have treated her boy. She would turn in her grave if she knew what he'd been through since she died."

For a long moment, no one moved. Bea's words hung in the air, quivering, turning everything colder. But when Amelie looked at Antonio, his eyes had changed.

"I know."

Bea frowned at him.

"I *know,*" he repeated. "I let him down…" Shaking his head, he said, "You think I'm here to take Markus back to prison?"

"Aren't you?"

Antonio laughed dolefully. "I am here to *help* him." Waving his arms, he added, "Why do you think I'm here alone? If I wanted him back in jail, why wouldn't I just send the police straight here when I realised where he was?"

Before Bea could answer, Nonna's voice boomed out of the barn. "Child, come back! You should stay inside…"

When Amelie turned around, she saw Nonna tugging helplessly on Markus' arm as he marched outside. "It wasn't Bea's fault," Markus said, finally freeing himself from Nonna's grasp and running to stand beside his aunt. "I didn't know where else to go. I made her help me." He gestured to Amelie, Cat, and Skye. "I made all of them help me."

"Markus..." Antonio reached out as if he wanted to put his hands on Markus' shoulders but stopped when Markus flinched. Holding up his palms, he said, "Markus, I am sorry. I am so sorry for the choices I made, but I'm here to help you."

"Help me?" Markus looked at Bea then back at Antonio. "You want to *help* me?"

"I want to try. If you'll let me."

No one spoke. Markus was examining Antonio's face as if it was entirely foreign to him. Finally, Bea took Markus' arm and started walking away from the barn. Gesturing for Antonio to follow them, she said curtly, "Come. We'll talk in our cabin, away from the party."

"Bea, are you sure?" Amelie lurched forward, ready to stand between Markus and Antonio if she had to.

Bea nodded. "We will be all right."

"I will come with you." Nonna was standing with her hands on her hips but was pointing her index finger at Bea. Turning to Amelie, she said, "Girls, the food is ready inside for your mother." Then marching over to Bea and Markus, but glowering at Antonio, she said, "I will come with you and I will call Mister Goodwin if there is any trouble."

Bea smiled gratefully. Markus nodded.

As they walked away, Bea and Markus tight beside one another, Nonna's stocky frame forming a barrier between them and Antonio, Amelie's temples began to throb. "What just happened?" She turned to Cat and Skye. "Is he saying he's going to help keep Markus out of prison?"

Skye shook his head. "You all were speaking Italian, so I have no *clue* what just happened."

"I think he is, yes," their father said. "At least, I hope so."

"Did I miss something?" Mum's voice drifted across the yard and caused everyone to turn around. She was wearing the dress Amelie and Cat had chosen for her, and she looked beautiful.

"I'll explain later, my love." Their father's eyes glistened with pride as he held out his arm for their mother. "We're the guests of honour. We should get inside."

Mum grinned. A true, happy grin that made Amelie's heart almost burst with joy. No matter what else had happened in the last year, her parents were back where they belonged – together – and now it was time to celebrate.

CHAPTER FORTY-THREE

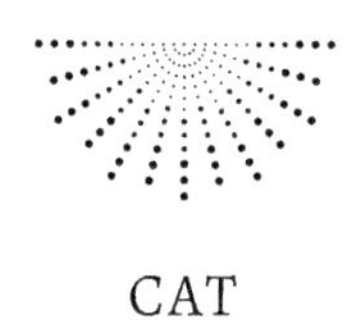

CAT

As Amelie took to the dance floor with Skye, Cat scanned the room for Stefan. She spotted him over by a hay bale that had been fashioned into a seat. He was wearing a smart blue jacket and smiled when he saw her. But before she could walk over to him, her phone rang. She took it out of her handbag and stared at it. *Aida Calling.* She hung up but, immediately, it rang again.

Holding up her index finger to indicate 'one minute' to Stefan, she tilted her head at the door and he mouthed 'OK'.

Outside, she headed for the picnic bench beneath the trees and sat down. Her phone rang again. She held it in her hands, watching Aida's name on the screen but unable to answer.

Finally, she picked up.

"Hello?"

"Cat? Thank goodness." Aida breathed out loudly. "I am

so sorry, Cat. So, so sorry. I cannot believe I embarrassed myself like that."

"Are you an alcoholic?" Cat asked bluntly. "I'm not judging you. I'd just like to know."

There was a long pause on the other end of the phone. When Aida answered, the frantic edge had gone from her voice. Instead, it was full of melancholy. "I have a problem with alcohol, yes. I had been sober for ten years until…"

"Until you met me?" Cat closed her eyes, remembering their afternoon at the bar with the blue shutters.

Aida hesitated then said, "It is complicated."

"So, tell me." Cat held the phone closer to her ear and repeated herself. "Tell me, Aida. When we met, you promised you'd answer my questions, so tell me what's going on. It's like you're two different people. The woman I met by the fountain was one person and the woman who got drunk on the beach was someone else. Someone who…" Cat sucked in her breath. "Someone who scared me a little bit."

She heard Aida sigh and wondered if she was trying not to cry. "You're right."

Cat waited for her to continue.

Aida made a clicking sound with her tongue. "Catherine, I'm going to be honest with you because you deserve it."

Cat sat up a little straighter and switched the phone to her other ear. "Good. I want you to be honest."

"You were taken away from me because I was an unfit mother. I was fifteen years old when I had you. I was completely incapable of looking after a child. I *was* a child. My parents had thrown me out. I had no home. I was a mess. It was the right thing that they took you. It was better for you. Look at the wonderful life you've had…"

Cat screwed her eyes shut. She felt dizzy.

After a pause, Aida's tone darkened. "Three years after you were taken into care, I fell pregnant again. But I was determined for things to be different this time, so I cleaned myself up. I got a job. A place to live. It wasn't easy, but I proved to the social workers that I had changed."

Cat reached for her bag and opened it. From the inside pocket, she took the picture she'd stolen from Aida's fridge. "They let you keep her," she whispered.

"Yes." Aida sounded as if she was starting to cry. "Her name is–"

"I don't want to know her name." Cat stood up and clenched her fist around the photograph. She watched it crumple at the edges, then dropped it to the floor.

Aida was silent for a moment, then said, "When I wrote to you, for your thirtieth birthday, my daughter – my other daughter – had just told me she was moving away to Greece. With her husband."

Cat blinked hard and shook her head. "Moving away?" She let out a bitter laugh. "So, you were looking for a replacement? Is that it?"

"No," Aida said quickly. "Not at all. It just made me think about you – about the times I'd missed and what a bad mother I was. So, I wrote to you. When you wrote back, I was elated. I had never been so happy. But the day before we met, Sienna–"

Cat sucked in her breath. *Sienna.* She tried to unhear it but the name was imprinted in her mind. *Sienna.*

"Sienna called me and told me she was pregnant."

Head spinning, Cat sat back down – hard – on the bench.

"She and her husband have asked me to move to Greece – to Athens – to live with them permanently when the baby is born." Aida sounded like she was taking a drink of something. Cat didn't allow herself to think about what it was. "I said yes, but as soon as I'd said it I felt horribly guilty. I didn't know whether to cancel our meeting or to go ahead with it. I didn't know what to do. I didn't want to let you down all over again. I thought maybe just one meeting was all you'd want. When we spent the afternoon together, you were so wonderful, and charming, and we laughed like friends. I felt even *more* guilty. I drank a lot when I got home. I spent the days after in a haze. I–"

"Stop." Cat sucked in her cheeks and bit her lower lip. "Stop, Aida. Just stop."

"Catherine?"

"I can't listen to this." Taking a deep breath, Cat bit back tears as she tried to keep her voice steady. "I am sorry you're having a hard time. I'm sorry our being in contact has brought up issues for you, but it's *my* life too. I thought we were starting something – a relationship. I thought we were going to have some kind of future. One where we were a part of each other's lives."

"That's what I want," Aida said quickly.

"But you don't have space for me right now, do you?" Cat didn't allow Aida to answer the question. "I'm not saying never but, right now, this has to stop."

When Cat looked up, she saw that Amelie had followed her outside and was walking slowly toward her.

Closing her eyes, she forced herself to say the words she'd been rehearsing since last night. Since the moment it had dawned on her that now was not the right time for Aida Borrelli to come into her life.

"I have a family who loves me. I have a mother, a father, a sister, and two irritating younger brothers. They have time for me. They love me."

As Amelie reached her, she instinctively sat down, reached for Cat's hand and squeezed it so tightly it hurt.

"I'm going to save my energy for them, Aida." Cat's voice started to crumble. "Take care of yourself and write to me again one day."

Then she ended the call.

CHAPTER FORTY-FOUR

AMELIE

AMELIE WANTED to pull Cat into the biggest hug in the world and hold her, but Cat put her hands up and said, "No, Am, not now. I'll start crying and I won't be able to stop, and I can't do that tonight. Not tonight."

"Okay," Amelie said, nodding. "Okay."

Cat breathed in deeply and rubbed her hands on her thighs. "Go back inside. I'll be there in a minute. We'll do the toast."

"Are you sure?" Amelie didn't want to go, could barely stand the idea of leaving Cat alone in the dark after what had clearly been the most difficult phone call she'd ever had to make.

"I'm sure," she said, forcing a smile to her lips. "Go. Really."

Amelie stood up then leaned forward and squeezed her

sister quickly but tightly. "I love you," she said, "and I'm truly sorry if I wasn't supportive enough before."

"Stop it." Cat wafted her away, shaking her head. "Honestly. I'm fine. We're fine. I love you. Go."

As Amelie walked away, she crossed her arms over her stomach and bit her lower lip. Ever since they were children, when Cat was sad, it was like she could feel it in her own chest. Tonight was no different.

Just inside the barn doors, she stopped and surveyed the party. Stefan Hurst was in the corner of the room looking lost. Amelie glanced back in the direction of her sister, then hurried over to him. "Stefan, if you're looking for Cat, she's outside and I think she could do with a friendly face."

Stefan studied Amelie's face for a moment, then nodded quickly. "Of course. Thank you."

As he walked away, Skye appeared at Amelie's side and nudged her. "Are you matchmaking, Amelie Goodwin?"

She smiled at him. "Something like that." Looking down at her phone, she said, "I'm going to try and get Ethan so he's on video for the toast..." She hesitated, unsure how to ask Skye whether he could put off talking to Ethan about Dallas until later.

"Don't worry," he said, understanding what she meant without her actually having to say it. "I won't dampen the mood." He smiled and took hold of her hand.

Amelie smiled back, although she wasn't sure it reached her eyes; she was picturing Skye's suitcase, sitting in the middle of his cabin, ready to be loaded into a cab and taken to the airport.

Pushing the thought from her mind, she pressed the video call button next to Ethan's name and waited for him to answer. After just a few rings, his face appeared on screen.

"Hey, guys, how's the party?" It was daylight in New York. Ethan was wearing a white doctor's coat and was standing outside in bright sunshine.

"You're working?" Amelie said, "Sorry, Eth."

"It's okay. I'm on a break." He checked his watch. "A quick break."

"We're just waiting for Cat, then we'll do the toast." Amelie looked up at where her parents were swaying together on the dance floor and turned the phone so Ethan could see them.

"The surprise went down well, I take it?" he said, grinning.

"Really well."

"Am, if we've got a minute, is Skye there?" Ethan was peering at the camera as if he might be able to will it to turn in Skye's direction.

"He is but–"

"It'll only take a second," Ethan said loudly, then added in a whisper, "I have good news."

Amelie looked at Skye, who'd moved closer to the phone, and angled it so Ethan could see both of them.

"Hey, buddy." Skye waved. "Looks like a nice day over there."

"Yeah, it is. Listen, Skye…" Ethan breathed in deeply. He looked like he was fighting back a smile. "I have news."

"News?" Skye wrapped his arm around Amelie's shoulders and leaned in.

"They said yes." Ethan was grinning.

Skye blinked at the phone.

"Yes?" Amelie's voice came out far louder than she'd expected.

Ethan nodded. "Molly's with Elena and her cousin now finalising the paperwork. She said she'd call you later but I thought you'd want to know ASAP."

Skye looked like he might pass out. He wobbled and Amelie steadied him. "They said yes? They're keeping her alive?"

"You bet," Ethan said, barely able to disguise the note of triumph in his voice. "You're going to see her again, Skye. In a couple of days, she'll be at Nell's house. Safe and sound. Elena's going to move in to help out and, in a couple of months, we'll bring Dallas to Italy. We'll bring her back to you."

"I don't know what to say." Skye looked like he was about to either scream or cry with joy.

Before Ethan could reply, he looked down at something and cursed under his breath. "Sorry, guys. I have to go. Am, I'll try and call again later. Tell Mum and Dad I send love and kisses and all that stuff."

"Okay, Eth. Thank you." Amelie ended the call and hugged the phone to her chest. When she put it into her pocket, she turned to look at Skye. He'd sat down on a nearby hay bale and was resting his head in his hands.

Crouching down in front of him, Amelie pried his fingers away from his face. "Hey, this is good news."

"I know. I just can't quite believe it," he said breathlessly. "She's going to be okay. She's going to *live*, Amelie."

Amelie grinned at him and rubbed his knees. "She's going to live."

"Ha!" Skye released a whoosh of air and rubbed at his forehead. "Ha!"

Amelie bit her lower lip. "Does this mean you're not going to New York?"

"I think I should still… don't you?"

"If you think you should."

"You don't?"

Amelie took a seat next to Skye and tucked her hair behind her ear. "Will it make her stronger if she sees you?"

"It might," Skye said.

"Then, yes, I think you should go."

"You don't sound very sure."

"I am sure. I just…" Amelie nudged him with her shoulder and sighed. "I'm being selfish. I'll just miss you, that's all, and–"

"And?" Skye caught her eyes.

"And I kind of freaked out a bit at the thought of you leaving."

"You did?"

Amelie nodded. "Especially when you said you weren't sure how long you'd be gone."

Skye's mouth twitched. He was smiling.

"Don't laugh at me."

"I'm not laughing. I'm just pleased."

"Pleased I'd be a wreck without you?"

Skye took his phone from his pocket and swiped it open. Putting it into her hand, he said, "No, pleased I took a risk and booked you a ticket."

Amelie blinked at the phone. "You booked me a ticket? Why didn't you say?!"

"Because I only realised this afternoon that I'd been a total idiot to think of taking off without you. Because I wasn't sure I could get a second flight." He rubbed the back of his neck and laughed at himself. "And because I was a little worried you'd say no."

"Skye Anderson," Amelie said, turning so she could fling her arms around his neck. "I would never say no to you."

"Is that a promise?"

"It certainly is."

"Well then," Skye said as he brushed his lips against hers, "you'd better go pack a bag. We're going to New York."

CHAPTER FORTY-FIVE

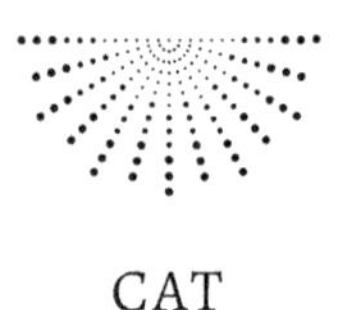

CAT

"YOU DON'T FEEL LIKE DANCING?" Stefan sat down next to her and gestured to the barn.

"Not right now." Cat crossed one leg over the other, smoothing her dress so that it stretched over her knees. After a short silence, she glanced at him. He was watching the barn. "You trimmed your beard again," she said.

Stefan's lips curled into a smile. "Yes. I thought I would smarten up for my last night at the ranch." He chuckled, giving his chin a rub. "I think I prefer it like this."

"It suits you." Cat looked away and wrapped her arms around herself; she should have worn a jacket.

Stefan shrugged his navy coat from his shoulders and handed it to her. "Here, I like the dress, but it's not very seasonal."

"I was planning to warm up on the dance floor," Cat said as she slipped her arms into the warmth of his sleeves.

"But now you don't feel like dancing?"

"No."

"Can I ask why? I've heard dancing is good for the soul."

Stefan was watching her. She could feel his eyes tracing the contours of her face, but didn't look at him. "I'm not sure anything could help my soul this evening, Stefan."

"Aida?"

Cat moistened her lips. "Yes." Cat looked up at the stars and blinked quickly. She'd been determined not to cry.

Silently, Stefan placed his hand over hers. He didn't squeeze her fingers or say anything, just let his palm rest there. It was surprisingly soft, and calmed the trembling in her breath.

"She's moving to Greece."

"Greece?"

"Athens." She pressed her lips together and forced herself to repeat what Aida had said. "Her *other* daughter is about to give birth. She lives there with her husband, and they've asked Aida to move in with them."

"She has another daughter?"

Cat nodded. "She's younger than me but not by much."

"I'm sorry, Catherine."

"Me too." With her spare hand, Cat wiped the tears from her cheeks. "Sorry I let this happen." She tried to laugh. "I mean, I walked right into it, didn't I? Everyone else could see exactly what was happening and, despite everything I promised myself when I contacted her, I ignored them. I was so fixated on the idea of her becoming part of our family that

I didn't actually look at what was in front of me..." She choked on her words, and began to sob.

Slowly, Stefan moved his hand from hers and put his arm around her shoulders instead. As he pulled her close, he whispered, "There, there. It's all right. This wasn't your fault."

"It feels like my fault." Cat moved closer and rested her head on Stefan's chest. In barely a whisper, she finally allowed herself to say what she'd been thinking since she was a little girl – the words that had circulated in her head more times than she could possibly count. "I just don't understand why she doesn't want me." Sitting back, she met Stefan's gaze. "Why doesn't she want me?"

Stefan's steely blue eyes narrowed. Very sternly, as he cupped Cat's face in his hands, he said, "This is *not* about you, Catherine. *You* are wonderful. You are joyful, and fierce, and beautiful, and a little bit funny sometimes." A smile crinkled his lips, and Cat laughed even though she was still crying. "You are everything, and Aida is a fool if she cannot see that."

For a moment, their eyes remained locked together. Beneath Stefan's fingers, Cat's cheeks were warm and flushed.

When he finally peeled his hands away, Stefan blinked at her as if he was surprised by what he'd said. "What I'm trying to say is that people are complicated. Feelings are complicated. You have every right to be upset but, please, don't blame yourself. None of this is your fault. *None* of it."

Cat tucked her hair behind her ear. Her tears had stopped, and her heart felt calmer. "Thank you, Stefan." She gently touched his forearm and let her fingertips linger. "Really. Thank you."

For a long while, they sat together, watching shadows flit across the yard and listening to the hum of people dancing, talking, and laughing inside the barn. Finally, Cat stood up.

"I think I've changed my mind," she said, holding out her hand. "Would you dance with me, Mr Hurst?"

Stefan smiled. Placing his hand in hers, he got to his feet and, in a surprisingly smooth movement, pulled her in closer. With one hand on her waist and the other holding her right arm out to the side, he moved her gently back and forth to the distant beat of the music.

"I'm sorry you're leaving," Cat whispered.

"Me too." Stefan leaned closer and his beard brushed against her cheek. "Perhaps I could book another trip to *Legrezzia* soon?"

Cat felt her lips curl into a smile. "I'd like that," she said. "I'd like that very much."

EPILOGUE

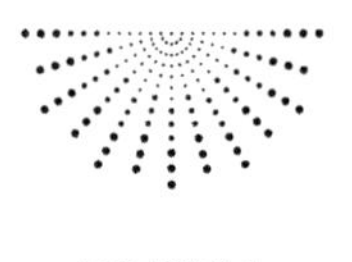

ELENA

SIX MONTHS LATER

"Are you all right? You look a little peaky." Ethan put his hand on Elena's and squeezed her fingers.

Turning away from the window, she gave him a small nod and tried not to let the sloshing sensation in her stomach show on her face. "Fine," she smiled. "Just thinking about Dallas."

"She'll be okay." Ethan took the lid off his thick, dark airline coffee and sniffed it. "She's probably fast asleep. When she sees Skye, it'll all be worth it." Ethan slurped his coffee and winced as the heat stung his tongue. "I can't wait to see Skye's face. I'll bet you five dollars he cries. I mean, I'll probably cry too. The last six months, I've gotten kind of attached to her–"

"Sorry, Eth, I need to use the restroom." Elena unclipped

her seatbelt and squeezed past Ethan's legs. Luckily, the restroom was vacant and she was able to slip inside, lock the door, and splash water on her face before the nausea – which had recently become a daily occurrence – became any worse.

Looking up at her reflection in the slightly grubby mirror, she took a deep breath and counted to ten. Then she peered into her handbag and took out the small paper bag she'd been carrying with her for almost two weeks. She tightened her grip on it, but couldn't bring herself to open it.

"Not here," she muttered, shoving it back where it had come from. "I can't take a pregnancy test thousands of feet above the Atlantic Ocean."

When she returned to her seat, asking the steward for a cup of peppermint tea on her way past, Ethan was nose-deep in a text book.

"We're on vacation," Elena said gently. He'd moved over beside the window, so she took the aisle seat, secretly glad she'd have an easier path to the restroom for the remainder of the flight. "You're supposed to be leaving work in New York and focussing on *relaxing*."

"Technically, we're not on vacation yet," Ethan said sheepishly. "When we get to Italy, I promise you'll have my undivided attention."

Chuckling at him, because she could tell just from the video calls they'd shared with Ethan's family that their visit would be anything but quiet, Elena folded her arms in front of her stomach. "You think your sisters will allow you to give me your undivided attention?"

Shrugging, but grinning, Ethan replied, "Okay, probably not, but I promise I won't think about work."

Elena smiled, but she was flicking her index finger against her thumb – the way she always did when she was preoccupied – and had to stop herself before Ethan noticed; if she was right, he would spend their summer vacation in Tuscany thinking about far more than work. She placed her palm on her stomach and let the warmth of the gesture comfort her a little.

If she was right, this summer could change everything.

Thank you for reading *A Heart Full of Memories*, Book Two in the *Heart of the Hills* series.

Grab Book Three, *A Heart Full of Dreams, now.*

In the meantime, why not travel back to the beginning with Rose and Thomas' love story? The prequel novella to the *Heart of the Hills* series, *Love in Tuscany.* is available now.

THANK YOU!

Thank you so much for reading *A Heart Full of Memories*. It's hard for me to say just how much I appreciate my readers. Especially those who get in touch. Please always feel free to email me at poppy@poppypennington.com.

If you enjoyed this book, please consider taking a moment to leave a review on Amazon.

To stay tuned about future releases, and receive the free short story *Love in the Alps,* sign up for my newsletter at: www.poppypennington.com

You can also follow me at:

amazon.com/author/poppypenningtonsmith
goodreads.com/Poppy_Pennington_Smith
facebook.com/PoppyPennAuthor
instagram.com/poppy_penn
bookbub.com/authors/poppy-pennington-smith

ABOUT POPPY

Poppy Pennington-Smith writes atmospheric, wholesome romance novels and women's fiction.

Poppy has always been a romantic at heart. A sucker for a happy ending, she loves writing books that give you a warm, fuzzy feeling.

When she's not running around after Mr. P and Mini P, Poppy can be found drinking coffee from a Frida Kahlo mug, cuddled up in a mustard yellow blanket, and watching the garden from her writing shed.

Poppy's dream-come-true is talking to readers who enjoy her books. So, please do let her know what you think of them.

You can email poppy@poppypennington.com or join the PoppyPennReaders group on Facebook to get in touch.

You can also visit www.poppypennington.com.

POPPY PENNINGTON-SMITH
Love in the Highlands
The True Love Travels Series

POPPY PENNINGTON-SMITH
Love in the Rockies
The True Love Travels Series

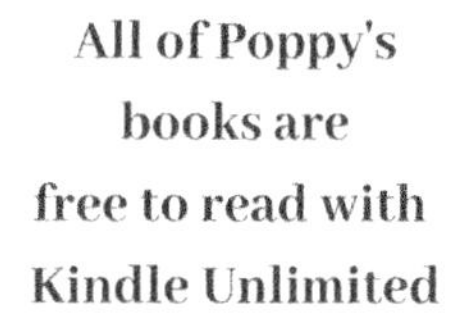
All of Poppy's
books are
free to read with
Kindle Unlimited

POPPY PENNINGTON-SMITH
Love in Provence
The True Love Travels Series

POPPY PENNINGTON-SMITH
Love in Tuscany
The True Love Travels Series

Love at Christmas
A True Love Travels Novella
POPPY PENNINGTON-SMITH

Printed in Great Britain
by Amazon